Old Magic

Old Magic

Marianne Curley

Simon Pulse

NEW YORK   LONDON   TORONTO   SYDNEY

SIMON PULSE

An imprint of Simon & Schuster Children's Publishing Division

1230 Avenue of the Americas, New York, NY 10020

This Simon Pulse paperback edition December 2009

Copyright © 2000 by Marianne Curley

Published by arrangement with Bloomsbury Publishing Plc.

All rights reserved, including the right of reproduction
in whole or in part in any form.

SIMON PULSE and colophon are registered trademarks of Simon & Schuster, Inc.

For information about special discounts for bulk purchases, please contact Simon &
Schuster Special Sales at 1-866-506-1949 or business@simonandschuster.com.

The Simon & Schuster Speakers Bureau can bring authors to your live event. For
more information or to book an event contact the Simon & Schuster Speakers Bureau
at 1-866-248-3049 or visit our website at www.simonspeakers.com.

Designed by Mike Rosamilia

The text of this book was set in Cochin.

Manufactured in the United States of America

6 8 10 9 7 5

Library of Congress Control Number 2009923885

ISBN 978-1-4169-8991-2

ISBN 978-0-7434-5707-1 (eBook)

To everyone who supported me,
especially Amanda, Danielle, Chris,
and John, the eternal optimist.

I would also like to thank my agent,
Anthony A. Williams.

And for their valuable assistance,
Anthony Tonna and Pam Adams.

"Not to know what happened before you were born is always to remain a child. For what is a man's life if it is not linked with the life of future generations by memories of the past?"

—Cicero

Part One

WIND

Kate

His name is Jarrod Thornton. He has blond-red hair to his shoulders, nice clean skin, and green eyes like fiery emeralds; but this is not why I can't drag my eyes off him. There's something else. Something almost . . . disturbing. It's this unearthly element that's got me hooked.

He's standing awkwardly at the front of a class of twenty-seven sophomores, looking as if he doesn't quite know what to do with his hands—or his unusual eyes. As they flick nervously across the back wall of the lab, I glimpse amazing inky blue circles surrounding deep green irises. They've been everywhere without once connecting with anyone else's. He has a black backpack that looks as if it's traveled twice around the world slung across one slightly slanted shoulder, and he keeps shifting his weight from foot to foot. He's in uniform: the usual gray trousers, white shirt, red striped tie. At a guess, it doesn't look new.

Mr. Garret, our science teacher, tells us a little about him. His family shifted from the Riverina only a couple of days ago and he has a younger brother, Casey, who's still in third grade.

Looks like I'm not the only one interested. Tasha Daniels's eyes are on Jarrod too. But hers are fixed in a leering manner, her sultry painted mouth slightly parted, invitation written all over her. God, she's so obvious. Briefly, I glance at Pecs, class loudmouth and Tasha's boyfriend, though there've been rumors lately that not all is well in that camp.

Not that Pecs is his real name. He got it around fourth grade, courtesy of his rugby coach, who'd been impressed by the boy's stocky rugby appearance and muscular arms. It turned out the name suited his personality, which wasn't much even then. I know, I was there. Still, I can't imagine anyone calling him Angus John, named after some long-dead Scottish relative. Not even the teachers dare. Pecs is one of those blatantly rude, in-your-face thugs that can make your life a misery. And does so just for kicks.

He notices Tasha's interest in the new guy, registers the threat instantly, something basic enough for his singularly focused mind to comprehend.

I decide to probe inside Pecs's brain. It's one of the skills Jillian taught me. She says I was born with a natural gift, sensing emotions, *feeling* emotions. Over the years I've polished the skill to a point that now I only have to concentrate for a few seconds and I'm in. Inside his head.

Oh hell! I make a fast withdrawal, my head spinning. He's all burning fuel. Makes me feel as if I stepped too close to a raging fire. Geez.

"Kate? *Kate!*"

Hannah, my best (and only) friend, is staring at me with wide brown eyes. "Yeah?"

"You all right? You went paler than your usual God-awful pale."

I smile, ignoring her God-awful comment. I may look anemic, but I'm not. I am careful, though, to avoid the sun, my skin burns too quickly. Living on Ashpeak Mountain suits me fine. It even snows in winter. I have long, dead-straight black hair, courtesy of a father I've never met. And except for her pale skin, I don't take after my mother at all. She apparently has hair as gold as butternut. At least she did fifteen years ago, which was the last time I saw her. Obviously, I don't remember a thing. My grandmother, Jillian, raised me. People say I have a Hawaiian look. It's my eyes, I think, a kind of gray-blue, and slanting with an upward tilt on the outside. Considering this, I think it's quite odd that some of them still think I'm a witch. They're right, of course, but not in the stereotypical sense of the word.

Hannah's the only one who knows the truth. Sure,

everyone gossips, the community up here is pathetically small. And nosy. But Hannah's seen what I can do, which isn't much, really. Not yet anyway.

And even though Jillian is my grandmother, I don't call her Gran or anything like that. She raised me after my birth mother bailed out when I was a baby. She couldn't hack my crying, apparently—a habit I grew out of. I was only eight months at the time.

As soon as I could understand, Jillian explained about my mother's inadequacies with babies, and told me not to worry though, thankfully, she—Jillian—loved children. At first she didn't know what I should call her. "Mom" just wasn't right. Besides, the whole community knew the truth anyway—that Karen Warren had given birth to a bouncing baby girl at the ripe old age of fifteen years and three months.

And 'cause Jillian didn't like "Nana" words, not, she reckoned, suitable for a thirty-one year old, I grew up calling her by her first name.

One thing Jillian constantly teaches me is to keep certain things a mystery. Like my abilities—to move objects, work spells, sense moods, and, well . . . change things. They're only small tricks compared to what Jillian can do. They never say it to her face, but most everybody around here knows Jillian's a witch. With me they're only guessing. But they've never seen either of us do anything,

Jillian's careful about that. They come to their assumptions mainly because of where we live (buried half into the rain forest), Jillian's New Age shop, and the freelance articles she writes for various witch magazines. Of course they never say anything to her face. They're scared. Scared she'll perform "black magic" on them. They don't know her, of course. If only they'd stop to read one of her articles they'd see what Jillian is: a healer. She doesn't make much money out of the shop, the articles keep us financially afloat. Sure, she's a witch, but most people have stupid preconceived ideas of what a witch is. Jillian's not "typical" in any way. And as for me, I'm still in training.

I hear a noise up front and see Jarrod falling off his stool. Unbelievable. He just reaches across to grab a glass beaker and wham, he's on the floor, a tangle of long arms and legs. The class explodes, laughing their stupid heads off. They're all jerks. I watch as Jarrod tries to compose himself, red-faced, climbing awkwardly back on his stool, his head angling sharply downward so that his eyes don't connect with anybody's. He's good at that. A thick wad of shiny yellow hair crosses his forehead, obscuring his face even more.

I sense his nervousness, and wonder why. Okay, it's his first day at a new school, and Pecs's hostility is tangible; but this is different. So I decide to probe, gently at first, just skirting the edges of his senses. His head suddenly lifts and stills as if . . . Uh-uh, he can't possibly *feel* me. Nobody ever does. Gingerly, I dig a little deeper, feel his hesitation, awkwardness, nerves. I feel his desire, burning away inside, an impassioned need to fit in, as if he's just a small boy lost somewhere in the midst of a great forest, with no sense of direction.

Something hard hits me. It takes a second to realize what it is, as this has never happened before. A wall is between us. He's blocking me out. I'm still staring at the back of his head and notice his shoulders jerk up and stiffen. His head shifts around, slowly at first, like he's searching for something. He sees me and stops. Our eyes collide and lock. He's wearing a frown, which slowly transforms into a look of puzzlement. It's like he wants to ask something but isn't sure what, yet senses its importance.

I know then—he's different too. He *did* feel my probe, even though I gather he doesn't understand what happened. And suddenly Jarrod Thornton becomes much more interesting.

Mr. Garret attempts to regain control of the class, repeatedly tapping the whiteboard with the butt of his blue felt pen. Jarrod swings his gaze back to the front, releasing me, and at last I breathe.

I don't dare probe again. My heart is still pounding from that three-second connection with Jarrod's mind. I try to home in on what knowledge Mr. Garret is attempting to impart; but I'm lost, my concentration shattered. And I can't drag my thoughts away from Jarrod. I'm tempted like crazy to go back in.

At last we get to the practical side of the lesson, and, luckily, the experiment is really basic, mixing an alkali with an acid in the presence of litmus. So there is nothing explosive. Still, it needs my concentration, adding diluted hydrochloric acid drop by drop while continually stirring, then adding sodium hydroxide in the same way, observing the various color changes; but Jarrod has just slipped on a pair of gold-framed glasses and Pecs is keeling over in fits of hysterical laughter. He should be back in kindergarten where his level of intelligence has company.

My experiment turns purple. I glance at Jarrod and notice his shoulders lift and hold for a stretched moment as he fights to control his emotions. Part of me wants to see him lash out as Pecs deserves, but I can tell it's not Jarrod's style. He either lacks the self-confidence necessary to confront a hulking brute like Pecs, or has the patience of a Tibetan monk. I'm going for the lack of confidence. His mannerisms are kind of stilted, awkward, clumsy. It makes me wonder about him, what sort of life he's had. His back remains stiff while he tries to maintain control.

My eyes search for Mr. Garret, though why I'm not sure. The man is a weakling in the face of Pecs and his mates. Especially since his divorce became final last year. Everyone knows about it. He was the talk of Ashpeak for months on end. Without any indication, Rachel Garret, wife of nine years, dropped their two kids off at pre-school and kindergarten, picked up the local pharmacist, and disappeared. No one heard from the pair, not a word, for twelve whole months. Finally she returned, but only to claim custody of the kids, which she got after a nasty court battle. But Mr. G's personal life isn't the only loss, his enthusiasm for life disappeared, as well as any classroom control.

But Pecs, it seems, is searching for trouble. Something he thrives on. We're supposed to be working in pairs, one mixing chemicals, the other taking notes. Mr. Garret, head bent, back to the class, is helping Adam Rendal and Kyle Flint get it right. Pecs leaves his seat, leans down, and whispers something in Tasha's ear that makes her giggle like the brainless airhead she portrays; and in a bare-faced attempt to cause trouble, Pecs walks straight past Jarrod, knocking his glasses off his face in a movement that is so obvious no one could call it an accident. They drop with a clang to the floor.

"Ah, gee, sorry man. Did I do that?" Pretending to pick them up, Pecs then purposefully kicks the gold frames midway across the hard cold floor.

Half the class laughs at Pecs's sick antics, Mr. Garret so far behind it all he may as well have never turned up for class this morning. He makes Pecs pick them up though, which Pecs does, making sure to smudge saliva-slurred fingers across both sides of the lenses. His mouth hangs open, thick tongue lolling heavily to one side of his protruding lower lip. His face betrays a hint of satisfaction. He's really enjoying himself now. Uggh! He needs a mirror.

My mind sifts through the different number of spells I've recently mastered to some degree of success. The eternal body itch could be a possibility. Now, wouldn't that be sweet justice? Giving Pecs irritating rashes on every conceivable part of his body. Of course Jillian would talk me out of it. She lectures incessantly about the dangers of tampering with nature. Right now I can't remember one word she's said.

"What a moron, eh?"

I smile at Hannah's description of Pecs's personality. But the smile doesn't last long. Something sharp hits my senses though I can't place it. Something unnerving. I glance out of the window but see nothing but blue sky on a crisp autumn morning. I home in on Jarrod, careful not to probe past the outer ridges of his mind. It's enough though. I feel his anger, and how he battles to control it. Fleetingly I want him to let loose. I have the feeling if he did these babbling idiots wouldn't know what hit them. But my sensible side urges him to keep it hidden, not to draw more attention to himself. In this way I feel aligned to him on some unnameable scale. It's how I live—skirting the edges.

Things start happening really quickly. Jessica Palmer, Tasha's best friend, and one of the "trendies," all highlighted blondes and sooty lashes, starts screaming hysterically as her half-filled beaker explodes. With the shattering of glass, chemicals spread a sizzling puddle across the bench, quickly slithering to the floor. Luckily for Jessica, her slender fingers, waggling crazily at the side of her head as she continues screaming, miss the scalding mess.

Mr. Garret's voice rises for the first time in a year, yelling at Jessica to calm down and start cleaning up. He has it all wrong, of course. Jessica has nothing to do with that beaker exploding. She didn't drop it or anything. It occurs to me that it's probably better that Mr. Garret thinks Jessica is responsible. I'm not being vindictive, Jessica Palmer has nothing to do with me. God, she probably hasn't spoken more than three words to me in the past two years. But my senses are heightened, alarmed. Something strange is happening, something that borders on unexplainable.

Pecs blames Jarrod. Mr. Garret shrugs it off as ridiculous. "Go back to your seat, Pecs, before I give you a lunchtime detention, and while you're there, help Jessica clean up that mess."

Personally I think Pecs is right, but I'm keeping my

mouth shut. Pecs can fight his own battles, and I secretly hope he loses every one of them.

But, as usual, the jerk can't stop stirring trouble. "He did do it, sir, I saw him," he blatantly lies. "He threw something, sir. Yeah . . . he threw his . . . his . . ." It takes him a minute to think of this. "His lighter!"

Jarrod shifts so that he can see Pecs better. From seemingly nowhere Pecs produces a small, plastic, fluorescent yellow gas lighter. Evidence. I realize by the shared secret smile he exchanges with his friend, Ryan Bartland, how the lighter suddenly appeared.

Unfortunately Mr. Garret misses the smug exchange and starts examining the lighter as if it were Exhibit One in a murder trial.

"Why would I have a lighter, Mr. Garret? I don't smoke."

These are the first words I hear Jarrod say, and though they are uttered softly, calmly, I can tell this seeming serenity is nothing but a screen. Swinging right around, he throws Pecs a hostile glare; and I see his eyes darken eerily, the navy blue circles merging perfectly into those vivid green irises.

The intensity in these eyes intrigues me, so I have to do it. Just once more, I tell myself. Mentally I take a deep breath and start to probe, gently and as deep as I dare, but only for a few seconds. Alarm makes my nerves jump. The air around me suddenly thickens with a bizarre kind of power—restless with an uncontrolled aspect, like a tempest on the verge of breaking across a drought-stricken plain.

But most alarming is my instinct that this power is coming from Jarrod.

Mr. Garret's expression changes from disbelief to accusation, his voice slick with impatience. I've heard it before. It's how he copes when schoolboy pranks continually disrupt his lessons. "Not a good way to start your first day, Mr. Thornton. I hope this behavior is not indicative of things to come." He's trying to assert his authority, but who's he kidding, really?

I lost sympathy for Mr. Garret when he started producing enough self-pity to drown in. And I know he's become gutless lately, but to accuse and convict on the face of one lousy piece of suspect evidence is truly pathetic. Jarrod apparently agrees. His lips snap together as he inhales deeply through suddenly widened nostrils, fingers clenching into tight balls.

He's losing it. Fast now.

The fluorescent lights are the first to go. They flicker uncontrollably, then fizz out with a simultaneous flash and hiss, as if struck by a sudden vicious power surge. No doubt they have been. But not the kind you get from a fault at a power station. The room darkens even though it's still morning. Someone screams and everybody starts murmuring.

Mr. Garret, forgetting the shattered beaker incident, raises his hands. "Calm down, everyone. Remain seated while I go and see what's happened to the power."

Of course nobody pays attention to him, and as soon as he leaves the murmuring becomes frantic. It's really strange how one minute the sky is cloudless on a brisk autumn morning, and now, with the lights off, it has transformed into an eerie twilight. Dark, thunderous-looking clouds roll toward us really fast, like a big hungry mouth gobbling up the soft blue sky and everything in its path.

"Look at the sky!" Dia Petoria yells from near a window.

Some people rush over but then everyone's attention zooms back to Pecs. With Mr. Garret out of the room he's decided to have another shot at Jarrod. "Such lovely hair," he taunts, lifting some of it, letting it drift through his rugby-thick fingers. "Are you sure you're not a girl, pretty boy?"

Jarrod moves once, jerking his head just out of Pecs's reach. I marvel how he takes so much without retaliating. I would have lost my cool ages back, and thought about casting the first spell that flicked through my mind. I've never been able to master the art of shape-changing spells, but a sloth—hairy, slow, and weighing 440 pounds—

would be appropriate right now. Pecs would make a good one. Instantly, visions of him hanging upside down in one of the giant eucalyptus trees that predominate the forest up here saunter through my subconscious, and I can't help but smile. Thinking about changing Pecs into a sloth takes my mind off the encroaching storm. But just as suddenly it zeroes back as windows fling open on their own, vibrating with the force. Papers, pens, test tubes, Bunsen burners, and anything that moves lift off the benches, getting caught in the increasing wind, and start smashing against walls or other moving objects.

"What the hell!" Pecs, momentarily distracted, goes to close windows. So I'm surprised when, considering his size and strength, the windows still don't budge.

Mr. Garret returns looking stunned. "What's going on?" He soon collects himself, remembering, I guess, that he's the teacher in charge, and starts yelling orders at us. "Hurry! Close those windows! This is apparently the only room that's got a power problem. Where did this wind come from?"

He's babbling a bit; I guess it is a little strange. I don't understand it either. It feels *unnatural.*

"They're stuck, sir!" Pecs yells over the gathering wind. I remember then that strange feeling I sensed earlier. This is it—or rather, the result of it—anger, dark and intense.

A couple of girls huddle together in a corner screaming. Others race around stupidly trying to collect their work, which is circling the room. One girl, sitting on the floor, wraps her arms around her knees and cries like a baby. Only Jarrod looks calm. He's still sitting at his bench, and his eyes have gone really weird, like he's staring at a ghost or something. Wind tears at his shirt, thrashing his long hair about his face. He has to notice this as it whips across his nose and eyes, but he remains unmoved.

Lightning flashes and I think everyone except Jarrod screams and buries their heads. It's as if the lightning is right in the room with us. Without even getting our breaths back it flashes again, filling the room with a staggering light and the sound of a horrifying sizzle. Everyone screams as if in unison, clutching at each other and hitting the ground. Hannah grabs my arm just as thunder explodes so loudly it near deafens us all, her fingers digging so deeply her nails are going to leave holes in my skin. "What the . . . ?"

I yank her hand off my arm. "I don't know."

"Then it's not *you* doing this?"

I stare at her, shaking my head. "I can't do this sort of thing." I have to yell over the wind. "I've never been able to manipulate the weather, Han." What I don't add, as Hannah already knows, is that I try, and keep trying, to the point of driving myself mad with frustration. But I just don't have that sort of *power.* My eyes shift to Jarrod and linger. He may not be aware of it, but Jarrod Thornton *does.*

Unfortunately, I don't think he knows it, and certainly he has no control over it. These latter thoughts are scary.

Thunder roars as lightning and thunder follow each other in one continuous dramatic roll. Mr. Garret tries to calm the class. He wants us to leave, but his words are lost in the battle nature is having in his lab. Not knowing where this is going to end, I decide Mr. Garret's idea is best.

"We have to get out of here!"

"What!" Hannah's mouth moves but her words disappear, ravaged by the wind that has now accelerated into cyclonic mode.

I see other students at the door, seniors, being pushed back against the far wall. They look stunned and race off to get help.

Empty stools suddenly become dangerous projectiles. I duck out of one's way and glance at Jarrod. He's still sitting on his stool, staring into the face of the wind. He must be catatonic to do this without flinching. A window shatters, and, as if in slow motion, I watch as everyone hits the floor in self-protection. Everyone, that is, except Jarrod. He remains rigid in his seat, completely mesmerized, his eyes wide and vacant.

Inevitably, something hits him. A piece of jagged glass rips into the skin of his inside lower arm, then continues wind-driven across the room. Strangely enough it's the catalyst that breaks the spell, or whatever it is. Suddenly the wind drops as if it never was, quietly disappearing, its work apparently done. The remaining jammed windows slide down and those threatening clouds roll briskly away.

For a whole thirty seconds there is complete stillness. I think the entire class is in shock. Slowly Mr. Garret comes round, organizing groups of students to attend to different tasks in a cleanup campaign. Jarrod still hasn't moved, and I'm worried about this. He's unbelievably pale, like you could only imagine someone might be if they were dead. Of course half the class doesn't look much different, except Jarrod's skin looks completely drained of blood. But it isn't. Where the glass slashed his arm, rich red blobs have dripped onto the bench top.

Mr. Garret seems oblivious, apparently unaware of Jarrod's injury. I push through the wrecked furniture and equipment to stand beside him. "Jarrod's been hurt." I sound defensive without meaning to and glance around for something to use on the bleeding arm. I spot a box of old rags, mostly just discarded clothing that's been cut up to use in the lab to clean up spills and things. The wind has knocked it about, but after a quick hunt through the few remaining items, I find a clean-looking piece.

Mr. Garret's eyes bulge at the sight of Jarrod's blood. "Oh dear." He sounds more like a blubbering idiot than a man of thirty-nine. "You'd better get to the nurse's office, boy, right away."

I get the feeling the sooner Jarrod's out of his class-room, the better Mr. Garret will feel. What a jerk. Look-ing around I guess he has his hands full putting the lab back together, but the condition of his students should come first. He looks so unsure of himself. It's a relief, I think, when several other teaching and office staff arrive, shocked and outraged. As Mr. Garret calls them over and starts attempting to explain, I wrap the white cotton mate-rial tightly around Jarrod's lower arm. I take his other hand and put it on top to keep the makeshift bandage from slipping and to stem the blood flow. "Keep it there until it stops bleeding," I say.

His eyes look odd as they shift to mine, like he's been off with the fairies. I try not to probe, it comes too natu-rally sometimes. Jillian's always warning me to be careful. With Jarrod I'll have to be even more so.

Mr. Garret shifts his gaze back to the one problem he knows he can get rid of quickly—Jarrod. "Off you go, boy. To the nurse's office. Someone will look after you there."

Jarrod slides off the stool. "I don't know where it is," he mutters, still holding the bandage.

"Er, um, oh dear," Mr. Garret stammers, flicking his gaze around the room, looking for someone to take Jarrod to the nurse's office. Meanwhile, I'm standing directly in front of him. "Yes, well, okay, I'll just find someone . . ."

"I'll take him."

Mr. Garret's eyes zoom back as if seeing me standing here for the first time, which doesn't really surprise me. Teachers are used to seeing through me. I like it like that, so I don't go out of my way to be noticed. But Mr. Garret was my form teacher last year, and came to Jillian's shop to see for himself what all the rumors were about. Of course he found nothing suspicious or even remotely sinister. All the same, Jillian didn't want him misconstruing her personal stuff. She didn't show him inside her private rooms. No one goes there except me. Not even Hannah. "Of course, Kate. Good idea." Mr. Garret glances at the white bandage, seeing it for the first time, and looks relieved. "Did you do that?"

I nod.

"Good girl. Now, off you go. And be careful where you walk."

Jarrod follows me to the door, and as we step through it I hear Pecs's sarcastic voice trail behind, "Be careful, pretty boy. Watch out for *Scary Face*. Don't follow her into any broom closets! *Oooh, I'm scared, I'm scared.*"

Ha ha. Gee, I'm laughing.

Typically, the class roars with laughter. They have no thoughts of their own. He leads them like a pack of brainless sheep. An embarrassing chorus of wolf whistles follows us down the corridor.

Jarrod

I think I've been hit by a truck. My head is throbbing and my arm is aching with a sharp sting. I'm supposed to follow this girl to the nurse's office, but that's not where she's taking me.

And what was that comment Pecs made about a broom closet? I shrug it off, the guy's a half-wit.

I want to ask where this girl is heading, but can't remember her name. Mr. Garret called her something, but at the time I felt as if I was living in dreamland. Well, not exactly in it, but like I was watching the whole thing from the outside. Strange, yet not really surprising. I'm kind of used to weird things happening to me. And to my family, come to think of it. That's how we ended up here, in this godforsaken isolated mountain community in the middle of nowhere. They call it Ashpeak. I don't want to ask why. Fires probably once devastated the rain forests. I've had my gutful of fires, and floods too, actually.

A new start, Dad had said. That's what he says every time we move. I've grown to hate my life. I just want to stay put for a change. Making new friends has never been easy. I used to think, what was the point? But it gets lonely hanging around by myself, being labeled a loser. By the time I finally get settled into a new school, manage to make some all right friends, we're moving again. Dad hasn't had a steady job for sixteen years. Two years is the longest we ever stayed anywhere. That time I even made a couple of good friends. But we moved eventually, a freak flood washed away the house we were renting, even took the business that had drained our savings. The following year we went bankrupt. Sometimes it seems our problems never end. And now, after the accident that damaged Dad's leg, he'll be incapacitated for the rest of his life. He's dosed up most days on morphine for chronic pain, has to use crutches when he walks, and will end up losing his leg, the doctors tell us.

It's up to Mom now, but what can she do? She had a lot of ill health the first ten years of their married life and never developed any work-related skills. They don't often talk about it, but I know it took ten years of trying before I was born. She's good with her hands though, and has an artistic flair. She makes these clothes, girls'

things, with hand-stitched beads and colored stones—
jewelry too. Cowboy stuff, I call it. It'll never sell.

My head starts clearing just as we leave the school
building. I'm still following the girl and can't help noticing
things. Like how she walks, casual yet determined. She
knows exactly where we're going. She's wearing a gray
school skirt midway down her thighs. Not short but high
enough to see she has brilliant legs. Her skin is pasty white,
like she's anemic or something. It's odd because her hair is
completely black. Long too, all the way to her waist. It's
attractive though, quite unique. I noticed her eyes earlier
in the classroom—blue, yet so incredibly light they were
almost see-through, like crystal gray. That was a strange
thing, come to think of it. The hairs on the back of my neck
had stood on end as an eerie feeling of invasion throbbed
inside my head.

Kate. Finally it comes to me. *"Of course, Kate. Good idea,"*
Mr. Garret had said. We start heading into the scrub. At
this rate, we won't even get close enough to the nurse's
office to smell the antiseptic. "Hey," I call.

She stops a few paces in front of me and swings around.
"Yeah?"

This whole scene is getting weirder by the second. I
shrug a little, my bleeding arm bent at the elbow, the makeshift bandage stained red with blood. I tip my head toward
it. "You're supposed to be taking me to the nurse's office."

She scoffs. "Why? They don't know anything about healing there."

As if that's enough explanation she spins around again, giving me her back.

I lunge forward and with my good hand grab her arm, losing the makeshift bandage in the process. Her eyes look really strange for a second, the blue-gray almost disappearing into black, their unusual almond shape rounding out to that of an egg. "Are you kidnapping me?"

She glares for a second, and I think she's taking me seriously. Then her eyes drift to the bandage at my feet. She picks it up, gives it a little shake, and wraps it around my arm again. While she does this she starts laughing, and her face transforms. I stare at her sudden beauty. I swear it, the girl is truly unique. And her laugh is like music, an enthralling melody. She stops laughing and I shake my head, amazed at what I've been thinking. It has to be stress. Either that, or I'm losing my sanity. No girl has ever affected me this way.

"I'm taking you to see my grandmother," she says.

"Is she a nurse?"

Her mouth twitches a little, just in one corner, as if she's holding back a cynical laugh. Slowly an incredible smile forms. "Not exactly, but she's a whole lot better than the office staff playing with first aid."

For some reason I suddenly trust her. Okay, maybe

I really do know the reason—it's all because of that smile. I'm a sucker for smiles. Having changed schools so many times, a smile has often been a lifeline. But this one is something special. It changes her whole face. Makes her look . . . *ethereal*. Now, where did that word come from?

We shove our way through the scrub to the main road and follow this for a while until we reach a fork in the road. I think for a minute she's taking me home as the road to the left leads directly to the property my parents are renting, but then she turns right, taking the narrow dirt and gravel road into the rain forest. It looks fairly steep from here, winding upward. I lose sight of the main road after the first hairpin bend. I realize now how Kate gets her fantastic legs; climbing this road every day would shape the legs of a rhinoceros.

The farther we climb though, doubts set in. It looks lonely and secluded. "Where does your grandmother live? You know, at this rate I could bleed to death before we make it to her front door."

She spins around, giving me an incredulous stare that makes me feel like a real wimp. So, Mr. Garret's not the only one who doesn't like the sight of blood. I feel my face fire up in embarrassment.

"If you're still bleeding, apply some pressure to that bandage. That's the idea." She looks at my wound, winces when she realizes it's probably deeper than she first thought, then rewinds the bandage, making it tighter.

Her fingers dealing with my wound are steady and warm. I glance into her face when she finishes "Thanks, Kate."

My words stun her for some reason. Her head shoots up and our eyes lock. The moment is intense. We could be lovers on a secret rendezvous. At least this is what my vivid imagination comes up with. Sure. As if.

Then somehow the sensation intensifies, as if her eyes and her mind have found a secret passage inside my head. I recognize the buzz. I felt this same sensation in the classroom, when my head had felt invaded. I swear loudly, giving myself a good shake. "Hell, what was that?"

She breaks away and starts climbing the lonely road again, ignoring me.

"Hey!" I catch up with her, needing an answer. "Do you know what happened just then?"

She doesn't stop walking, just looks straight ahead. "Yeah, of course."

So casual, when my head is still spinning. "So, what was it?"

"You don't know?"

"If I knew," I practically yell, "would I be asking?"

She smiles as if she's playing a game. "What do you think it was?"

She's testing me. It's in her voice, challenging. I don't like challenges. I have a golden set of rules I try to live by. Challenges sometimes force me through my self-imposed limits. "I have no idea. Only that it doesn't follow any of the rules."

She slows a little but keeps walking. I'm grateful but don't say anything. My legs are tiring from the climb.

"What rules?" she asks.

"I don't know . . . normal, everyday life rules."

"Does everything in your life follow the rules, Jarrod?"

I don't have to think long about that. Of course they don't. Maybe that's why I dream of an ordered lifestyle. I've never had it.

When I don't answer she says, "It's funny, you know."

Though I try, I can't see the humor. That intrusive feeling in my head was unreal. Actually I'm starting to think Kate is bad news, a little crazy even. "What's funny?"

"You're completely oblivious of yourself."

"Interesting observation. Don't stop there."

She does stop, walking that is. She looks me straight in the face, unflinching. I want to look away but can't. Both her hands lift, palms up. "Your *power*. You have so much of it."

I stare, not understanding a word she's talking about.

"Inside you." She taps a long finger at my chest. "I sense it. No, I *feel* it. And I'm good at that sort of thing."

"You're a little funny, aren't you?" I point to my head and rotate a finger in little circles.

She snorts and grunts. The only thing she hasn't done is stomp her feet. She takes off and I catch up with her, trying to ignore the throb of my arm. "Sorry," I mumble.

She shrugs. "It's okay. You're not the first one to say something like that."

"Really?"

Her head swivels sideways with a smile. "You're a jerk."

"You know, that's not the first time someone said something like that to me."

Her smile deepens, reaching her eyes, and I feel instantly better. I want her to keep talking. I like the sound of her voice, the way her mouth moves. I try to find something safe to talk about. "So, what does your grandmother do for a living?"

I'm so not prepared for her answer. "She's a witch."

My first thought is that she is obviously joking. I mean, I *really* believe she's joking, except something isn't right. For starters, she isn't laughing, or even smiling, not a crinkle around her unusual eyes. "I see," I say as I try to understand.

"Please don't tell anyone I said that. I shouldn't have told you, but . . . well, I know that you're different too."

I decide she *definitely* must be joking, pulling my

leg. Her sense of humor is really warped, but, well, I guess I can handle that. "Ah, black magic and all that stuff."

I hear her suck in a deep sharp breath. Great. Now she's mad at me. "Never black, Jarrod," she says in all seriousness. "At least not black in the traditional sense of the word when referring to witch practices."

I stare at her and she says, "Jillian would never do anything to hurt anyone. She's adamant about that. All her magic is pure. She's a healer."

I realize she is 100 percent dead serious. She notices my stunned-mullet look and spins around. "Look," she starts explaining, fast realizing she's losing me. "I wouldn't be telling you any of this, believe me, I don't usually *encourage* gossip, except I believe you have the *gift* too. I'm guessing you don't know it, let alone understand it," she continues in one long rapid burst. "I can see all that, and I'm sorry if I've shocked you or anything, but you have to understand, the gift as strong as yours could be dangerous. Manipulating the weather is something . . ." She hesitates, searching for the right words. I get the feeling it isn't so much searching for an explanation as trying to find words that won't incriminate her sanity even more.

"Look," she tries again, and I'm surprised to see her actually blushing. Her cheeks turn the color of tomato sauce. "Usually only *sorcerers* can do this sort of thing, enchanted sorcerers, not ordinary people like us. D'you know what I mean?"

I stare at her even harder, my mouth hanging open. Is she really saying this stuff? I decide to see just how much she'll admit. "So, both you and your grandmother are witches?"

She takes her time answering like she's choosing her words extra carefully. "I guess you could say that."

"*Jillian* and *Kate*. They don't sound much like names of witches."

"Well, what did you expect?"

"I don't know . . . Laeticia, maybe."

She frowns at me, but a smile is pulling at her mouth. "*Laeticia?* Where did you dig that up? A grave or something?"

"It was my grandmother's name."

"Oh."

"Yeah, and she even looked like a witch."

"Maybe she was."

"I don't believe that for one second. Besides, witchcraft doesn't exist."

She says softly, "It exists."

"No way. You would never convince me. It just . . ."

"Doesn't follow the rules?"

"Not mine, that's for sure."

"Look, Jarrod, I've seen your gift in action. And if

you're not trained to handle your skills, anything could happen. People could get hurt. Just look at your arm. What if it'd been your throat that glass had slashed?"

I stare at my arm. The white bandage has slipped again but it's stopped bleeding now. I take this to mean I'm not about to drop dead at this strange girl's feet, nor am I in desperate need of a transfusion. All the same, her fun with me has gone far enough. "What are you saying? That *I* caused that storm today?"

She nods and smiles and looks genuinely relieved.

I know for sure then. It hits deep in my gut. And it's such a shame because I find myself attracted to her in a way I've never felt with a girl before. But this one is bad news. She's crazy—in the head. There's no other explanation. I start walking backward, down the deserted mountain road, picking up speed with each step, calling back briefly, "I think I'll take my chances with the nurse's office."

"Geez!" she hisses between clenched teeth. "I've frightened you."

I keep moving and hear her mutter something under her breath. I can't be sure but I think she says, *"Not that it would take much."*

She runs over, takes my elbow, crooning softly and patting my arm. I suddenly feel like an abandoned puppy she's found on the side of the road. "It's okay. Don't worry," she says. "I shouldn't have gone off like that. Jillian is always better with words than me. C'mon, Jarrod, come back with me. It's not far now."

Eventually I let her lead me. It's easier to give in. My policy is to avoid scenes wherever possible. And I guess my curiosity has kicked in. Surely she can't be too sick, at least not dangerously. She has to be about sixteen, like me. She's in my class. And I imagine they don't let delusional teenagers into schools nowadays. They have special homes for that sort of thing.

Don't they?

Kate

I found out heaps about Jarrod Thornton really quickly. The scariest part is the fact that he has absolutely no idea of his talents. His *gift*, I mean. And he lacks confidence in himself, badly. I wonder why? What sort of life could have reduced his self-confidence to zilch? Especially in the face of all that power he's sheltering. I wonder what Jillian will think.

There's only ever been Jillian and me. We keep mostly to ourselves, except for Hannah. And even though Hannah has no natural talent, it doesn't make any difference to her enjoyment of the magical arts. I've only heard from my mother once, a brief note explaining she's found happiness at last, living in Brisbane with a man with three grown-up children. That was a few years ago and the note was addressed to Jillian, as if she can't acknowledge that I was actually born. I reckon the man she's with has no idea I even exist. I should feel relief at this really 'cause I don't ever want to leave Jillian, or Ashpeak, but sometimes I can't stop thinking: What on earth is wrong with me that my own mother doesn't want to know me?

Jillian too was a single mom, but she rarely talks about it. All I know is that her old folks turfed her out as soon as they found out about the pregnancy. She hooked up with an artist for a while, but he was so moody she had to move out. She moved in with a couple of witch wannabees, both into fortune-telling, seances, materialistic spells for cash, and other stuff like that. They weren't very good either, made their money from ripping off gullible members of the public. Once they distressed an elderly widow trying to contact her deceased husband, telling her his spirit was lost, that he was miserable without her and couldn't settle. A couple of days later Jillian found out the woman had swallowed a whole packet of sleeping pills, putting herself into a coma from which the doctors couldn't revive her. This tragedy pushed Jillian to move out on her own. It ended up the best thing she ever did. She started her own business, selling her craft, herbs, incense, crystals, and stuff like that, at a local market. She worked hard, saved her money, and now she has her shop—the Crystal Forest.

I never ask Jillian to tell me more than she wants to. Privacy I respect. It works both ways.

I lead Jarrod through the last of the three hairpin

bends, the road ending in a private cul-de-sac. My house is now the only building in sight. There are other properties lower down the mountain, but mostly Jillian and I live by ourselves. Jillian likes it this way, and well, it suits me too.

The cottage is small, A-frame, mostly timber and a little brick around the foundations with an old detached garage on the side. The lower front half forms the shop. Standing here you can see straight through the full front glass windows where Jillian's trinkets blink back the mid-morning sunlight. At the rear are Jillian's rooms, and a kitchen–living room and bathroom. My bedroom is the entire top floor. It's small but I love it there, even though I can only stand full height in the center where the sharply angled roof is tallest. But it has privacy, and the sounds of the forest inhabit my room at night comfortingly.

I suddenly wonder what Jarrod thinks of my home. Strange, I'll bet. I won't dare probe his mind again, it only alarms him when I do. He's not very receptive to new ideas. What he doesn't understand straight off, what doesn't follow his "rules of life," scares the hell out of him. I'll have to tell Jillian to take it slowly.

The door chimes ring as I lead Jarrod through the front glass door. Jillian is out back, but comes through the timber-framed arch at the sound of impending customers. I smile at her. Even though it's unusual to see me here at this time of day when I should be at school, I know she won't be angry. That's the way she is—nonjudgmental.

My smile shrivels on my face. The second Jillian sees Jarrod her mouth drops open and her eyes squint like she's trying to figure something out. We step closer and her eyes suddenly spring wide open in startled shock. She looks comical, but I'm not laughing. Something is wrong. She fumbles in her jeans pocket for her glasses in a mad kind of panic. She puts them on and starts screaming.

Her terrified screams hit a high pitch. I sense wildlife scattering at the sound. I can't understand her reaction. She's mumbling something about evil this or that, but it's hard to distinguish any actual words.

Finally she stops but is still breathing hard, a hand splayed across her heaving chest. Of all the unexpected things to happen, today is definitely the day for it. First that bizarre storm in the lab, and now Jillian losing control. And it's so out of character, I can do nothing but stand here stunned. Slowly, I slide a sideways look at Jarrod. This is all he needs. He'll think we're both crazy now. Predictably, it's written all over his face, skepticism, shock, and fear of being in bodily danger. His pathetic spirit makes me mad. Where is his backbone? Can't he see the woman is upset?

"What happened, Jillian?"

She points to Jarrod with a trembling hand. "Snakes. I saw snakes."

Jarrod's eyebrows lift.

"On *him*?"

She nods, sucking in a deep gulping breath. "A vision. It must have been a vision. They're gone now." Reluctantly she draws her gaze away from Jarrod, locking her blue eyes to mine. "There were at least twenty, Kate. Covering the top half of his body, green slimy things that weaved all around him, over his shoulders, his head, into his hair."

I don't doubt her for a second. "God, what does this mean?"

She shudders and slips her glasses back into her pocket. "I don't know, darling. Snakes are vile creatures, indicating the presence of evil."

"We've only just met, but I don't sense evil on him." I think about this and shake my head. "Nah, not evil, Jillian. No way. He's more . . ."—I shrug as images waft across my subconscious—"kind of puppy-doggish."

"If you'll excuse me," Jarrod's placid voice unfolds between us. "This is all very amusing. If I ever get my sense of humor back, I'm sure I'll laugh—in about twenty years. Right now though, I gotta go, get that Band-Aid, y'know?"

Wonderful. Of course I know what he's doing. Ignoring his obvious urge to get the hell out of here, I try pushing past his skepticism and mounting fear. "Wait, Jarrod. Let me explain."

He adjusts his glasses, then points a finger with a negative shake of his head. "I don't think I want to hear it. No offense, but . . . this isn't my scene. You wanna know the truth? I hate snakes. I had an incident with snakes in my bed once." His whole body shivers. "Never ever again."

He turns, but I beat him to the door. "While you're here let's just fix your arm. It's the least we can do, really."

"I think the least you can do has already been done — to my sanity. Now, don't bar that door, or I'll take you through it with me, Kate."

A strange breeze starts to blow, trinkets and wind chimes start dancing erratically. It hits my face and swirls my hair around and it feels sensational. It isn't angry, like before in the lab. This wind is mystical yet tame, and it sings to me. I wish I could share it with Jarrod, 'cause he created it. I'm sure of this. And it's such a beautiful wind, swirling around my feet, pushing gently upward to the ceiling. I get so caught up in it I start to move, with it, through it, into it.

I almost forget about Jarrod and his urge to flee. But he's noticed the wind too. He's looking at me oddly, his head tilted, a peculiar expression on his face, like he's intrigued against his will.

"Ooh, how delightful." Jillian comes back in, her hands full of bandages and herbal antiseptics. "If you'll just sit down for a minute . . . Jarrod, isn't it?"

He nods, his mind momentarily distracted from running, and sits on the stool Jillian points to. I watch him peer through the glass windows at the stillness of the trees in the forest. He's wondering how there could be such a breeze in here when outside is calm, almost still. It's good that he's wondering. I allow him to do this without jumping on his thoughts. I have just learned not to go too fast with him.

The breeze disappears the instant the first drops of antiseptic sting Jarrod's open wound. "Hey! What the hell is that stuff?"

"A tincture of Saint-John's-wort. A very good antiseptic, anti-inflammatory, and sedative," Jillian explains. At least she seems composed now, that frightening vision hopefully gone.

"Can't you use normal antiseptic?" he asks sarcastically. "Nothing on a supermarket shelf would sting half as much."

Jillian keeps working gently. Her fingers, I notice, are still trembling a bit. A hangover from the vision. "There now, not too deep." She pushes his skin together where the wound is deepest, and sticks three adhesive strips over the top. "At least I don't think it needs stitches," she says soothingly, in complete control now. "Are you up-to-date with tetanus?"

He nods. "Oh yeah, I would be. I'm always . . ." He

glances up quickly, his cheeks filling with bright color. "Never mind," he mumbles.

"Good," Jillian replies absently as she finishes working a sterile bandage over the wounded area. "It should be fine, but do see a doctor if it becomes angry."

"Angry?" Jarrod asks, bemused.

Jillian starts putting away the bandages and bits and pieces.

"Hot, red, or swollen," I explain, having seen Jillian's handiwork hundreds of times. The neighbors know her skills with cuts and stuff. And since it's a good twenty-minute drive to the local hospital, and sometimes takes days just to get an appointment at the only medical center in Ashpeak, she often has neighbors dropping by for little incidents. Not just human incidents either. Jillian takes care of injured forest creatures too, nursing them back to health then setting them free again. It's not unusual for someone to call in during the night with a possum or koala they've found injured by the road.

Apparently satisfied with my explanation, and content with the first-aid job on his arm, Jarrod's curiosity overtakes his fears. He starts browsing the various bits and pieces of oddities Jillian keeps in her shop, mostly for tourists—crystals, oils, charms, New Age books. Jillian pulls me aside. I give her a brief rundown on what happened in the lab this morning. She listens intently, sometimes nodding.

"He appears so gentle, yet . . . ," Jillian whispers, her voice trailing off. "I sense more. His aura is really quite spectacular."

"He's filled with power, Jillian. I saw it. I felt it."

"It's strange that he's so unaware of it, Kate. Those that are born with supernatural talents either realize it early, or never at all. And so it can thrive — as in your case — or lie dormant. Those unfortunate ones who remain oblivious usually do so their entire lives. I've seen it happen so many times. Years ago, Denise Hiller's baby used to pick the phone up every time someone was dialing their number. It used to annoy Denise when people would complain her line was always busy. She scolded her daughter continuously until the child learned it was bad behavior. Now the child is grown, and there's no way she will ever harness that strength of power again. She can do little things with a remarkable sixth sense. But that's all. We've been trying to regain more, but most of it is lost."

"Jarrod's power is immense, yet he's completely unaware of it."

"That's strange, like something's triggered it."

I try to follow her line of thinking. "Do you think there's a reason his power is emerging now?"

She shrugs. "I don't know, Kate. Just guessing."

I think about this for a minute, but something else is wrong too. "If Jarrod's power is so strong that he can manipulate the weather, and he doesn't learn how to control it, anything could happen. The science lab was nearly destroyed today. Sheer luck no one else was hurt."

"You need to hunt around in his past, see what turns up. Unleashed power can cause mass destruction, Kate. But go slow. He seems somewhat frail."

She's being subtle. He comes across as spineless.

We stop whispering as Jarrod comes back. He thanks Jillian and we go outside. But even the brilliance of the bright blue sky can't stop Jillian's warning ringing in my ears.

Jarrod

Not much point going back to school now."

I look at her; she has to be kidding. We're standing in the quiet cul-de-sac outside her grandmother's wacky shop. I glance at my watch: 11:00 a.m. "That's fine for you, but I don't want to face a suspension on my first day."

"I want to show you something."

"Sorry, I don't think so." I start down the road, and can't seem to get away quick enough. Kate is definitely weird, her grandmother, too. Now I know where she gets it from. Poor kid, she hasn't got a chance. It's in her genes. "Another time, maybe." *Like never!*

"It's not far." Her persistence is manipulative. "C'mon, Jarrod. Give me a break. I want to make up for what happened this morning, with Jillian and the . . . you know." She shrugs. *"Snakes."*

The incident with her grandmother shook me up more than that unusual storm in the lab. That at least is a foggy memory. I try to look unfazed. "Forget it."

"You'll love this place. It's enchanted."

Enchanted! That does it. "Uh-uh."

She realizes instantly her mistake and scrunches up her nose. "No, I don't mean . . . You know, in a magical sense," she corrects quickly. "Just pleasant, endearing."

"Hmm." I'm being obstinate, but I've had a gutful of this magic nonsense.

"Look," she persists annoyingly. "This place is really special to me. And I bet you haven't seen much of the mountain yet."

She has me there as we only arrived a couple of days ago, and I've spent most of that time fixing the old place up to make it comfortable for Dad, easy for him to get around with his crutches. "So what?"

She takes my arm by the elbow. Her fingers are firm and warm. I look down into her face. She's a fair bit shorter than me, at least a head length. Her blue-gray eyes reflect the sunlight as her face expands into that smile again. She tugs my arm, and without giving it any more thought, I follow her into the forest. "You're dangerous."

She laughs but doesn't answer. And for the next twenty minutes neither of us says anything as we fight our way through a maze of thick hanging vines and half-rotted fallen trees that are now probably residences for goodness knows what forest animals. My mind flips through a mental list of the many different creatures that are probably right now hanging on to my shoes, inching their way up toward the first sign of exposed flesh—ticks, leeches, *snakes*!

Finally we get there, and I have to admit the serenity of the place is really breathtaking. There's a shallow stream tumbling down a collection of haphazard boulders, the water so clear I can see every smoothly shaped pebble beneath the surface. On the other side of the stream stretches a field of deep green bracken ferns, thousands of them, about knee-high to thigh, dancing to the musical notes of a very light breeze.

"Well, what do you think?" She's standing beside me, gazing proudly across the crystalline stream as if this picturesque scene was all her own doing.

I pick up a small pebble and attempt to skip it. It sinks on the first hit. "Nice."

She frowns, disappointed, but I'm fed up with being agreeable. She says, "Is that all you can say, just 'nice'?"

I sit on a spilled log, start checking my shoes for leeches. "Okay, very nice."

She sits beside me and groans, apparently conceding this is the most she'll get. "Sorry about Jillian going off like that. You probably won't believe this, but she's known around here for her extreme tolerance and calm under duress. Sometimes she might appear a little abstracted, but that's just her way. She's intelligent, loves nature, is a wonderful magi—"

Wisely, she doesn't finish. "She raised me from a baby when my mother ran away."

She shrugs her shoulders as if her mother's rejection doesn't concern her anymore. I don't need to be psychic to see that it does. Jillian's hysteria gradually begins easing into a distant part of my memory. "Hey, look, forget it. It was no big deal."

We're quiet for a minute, taking in the pleasant surroundings—water spilling over rocks, a gentle breeze playing tag with the ferns and vines and millions of eucalyptus leaves, an earthy smell of damp soil and moss. Kate is sitting beside me, her head angled, eyes gently closed, totally involved, relaxed with herself. Suddenly I envy her. This mountain is her home, has been probably all her life. This forest is her roots, and it's obvious she loves it. It's something I've never had the pleasure of enjoying—a place to call home, a group of friends. "Is it just you and your grandmother then?" I wonder fleetingly if she will think I'm intruding.

She just shrugs. "Yeah, I don't know who my father is. There was never a name."

"Hey, that's rough. He could be anybody. Do you have anything to go on?"

She gets defensive. "Who says I wanna know?"

She glances away, but I can see her eyes are troubled. When she finally speaks again her voice is soft. "I know he was a camper, here in the forest. That's how he met my mother. She used to come here, sit by the river and dream about living in a big city one day. She never liked the mountain."

"What happened?"

"He had just finished his final exams and had come up the mountain for a bit of relaxation. He ran into trouble with some poisonous nettle and my mother looked after it. Apparently she looked after a lot more."

"D'you think they loved each other?"

Her eyes change, like she's slipped into the past, visualizing her parents as they would have been so long ago, young lovers, meeting in the forest. "How would I know? Can two people fall in love so quickly? They only had a couple of days."

Like an exploding bomb, it hits me. The reason Kate feels this place is special. "It was here, wasn't it?"

Her shoulders lift just a little.

"This is where your father camped, where your parents . . ."

She takes the defensive quickly again. "Yeah, so what?"

"Nothing. Look, I didn't mean . . ." She's glaring at

me with daggers for eyes. My words dry up.

"So why did your family move up here?" she asks, switching subjects. "Even though *I* love it, it's not the most pleasant place at times. Especially in winter. It snows, you know, and some days the wind has ice in it, rips through everything you're wearing. The mornings are already chilly. Winter's coming fast this year."

I decide she has a right to her privacy—the past obviously hurts. Well, so does mine. We have at least that much in common. "Dad had an accident that injured his leg pretty badly. He got so depressed that Mom thought he needed the serenity a place like this could offer."

She nods, accepting that it would. "How did it happen? The accident?"

"He washed his hands in the garage where he'd been working on an old tractor, and dropped the soap. A few minutes later he slipped on it, falling against some steel shelving, which came down on top of him."

"Ouch."

"Smashed his leg, causing permanent tendon and muscle damage."

Her almond-shaped eyes grow roundish, her mouth opens just a little. "Freaky."

"That's what they called it—a freak accident."

She's probably remembering now how I fell off my

stool this morning in the lab. "You don't have to say it. I know, clumsiness is inherited."

"I wasn't going to say that."

"Yeah, sure," I say softly.

"It must happen often then."

"What?"

"Accidents in your family."

Bad luck follows us like a plague, but I don't say this. Instead I shrug. "We've had a few broken bones."

She looks surprised. "Yeah? How many?"

"Oh, I don't know. Seven, eight, ten."

"What?"

"There was the car accident. Mom broke two ribs, an arm, and chipped her collarbone. Casey, my little brother, he broke his elbow falling off a swing set a couple of years ago. When I was four, I fell out of my bunk bed and broke a leg in two places. When I was seven, I broke my hip jumping over a bench at the local park. There's Dad's leg—though that's not technically broken."

She's staring at me with disbelief. "I've never broken anything."

"You're just lucky."

"Any other incidents worth relating?"

My fingers run through my hair. It's a habit. I do it a lot when I'm pushed. I'm reluctant to tell Kate about the family business going broke, or the fire at our last school that demolished the entire art department. I had nothing to do with it—I just happened to be the only student working late on my major art work when a gas leak exploded, taking with it three classrooms. I was lucky, I'd just stepped outside to go to the bathroom only seconds earlier.

She's perceptive though. I think she can see straight through me. "C'mon, let it out." She pushes my shoulder with her palm.

"All right, all right." I grab her wrist to stop her doing it again, but don't let go of her hand. I like the feel of it. "There was a flood that wiped away the house we were renting."

"Really? Was anyone hurt?"

"No, but it was close. The State Emergency Service helped us evacuate. But Mom stubbornly insisted on rescuing a box of photos and nearly got swept away."

"A lot of people say they'd do that—rescue photos. Not me. I'd go straight for . . ." Her eyes flick briefly to mine, then back to the creek again. "Never mind. Were you near a river or something?"

"Sure, but it was only a stream. It had never flooded before. Took the whole town by surprise."

She's shaking her head sympathetically. I'm amazed at the ease with which I've been spilling my guts. I've never been so open with anyone about my family's continual run of bad luck. But with Kate it's just slipping out. No, more like *pouring* out.

"So you lost everything?" she asks. "Except for the photos?"

"And Dad's precious family heritage book," I explain. "He guards it with his life. It was the first thing he saved. He's been working on it for more than twenty years. Traced the Thornton line right back to the Middle Ages, 1200s I think. To the borderlands that fell between England and Scotland then—the Disputed Land. The Thorntons had one of the very first stone-built castles. It's still there apparently, though Thorntons don't own it anymore. They lost it somewhere along the way. But it doesn't look the same now, it's been rebuilt with bricks and proper rooms and everything."

She looks really impressed, her eyes growing huge again. "You're kidding? Have you seen it?"

"Nah, but I've seen pictures."

"God, Jarrod, that's unreal. I'd love to see your father's book. My family is so small. All I know is that Mom took off to Brisbane, and Jillian was a single mother. End of story."

This blows me out. I feel her tug her hand out from mine. Reluctantly I let it go. Here I am thinking how lucky she is, having an established home, living in one town all her life, when she's not much different from me, really. I may not have her connections with this mountain, but she doesn't know her ancestry. She doesn't even know her parents. I have a sudden urge to share my family history with her. "If you like I could bring the book round one day."

"I'd love it."

I can't believe how different—normal—she is when she's not talking about magic and stuff like that. Somehow I know it's too good to last. I stand, deciding I can make it back to school for afternoon classes, when she does it again. "I think your family might be jinxed, cursed, you know?"

My eyes roll at the absurd thought. "I don't think so."

Her enthusiasm incites her imagination. She climbs onto the spilled log as if her sudden height will make her wacky theory somehow more credible. Her hands weave an invisible pattern in the air as she tries to make her point. "Think about it. All those accidents. And . . . and your *powers* . . . the curse must have something to do with them." She clicks her fingers as a sudden thought hits her. "The curse could have triggered them free from your subconscious."

I decide to give up, and start walking in the direction we'd come. "Don't start again, Kate. You'll spoil the morning."

She jumps down and catches up with me, totally immersed in her crazy theories. "I think your powers are growing for some reason. Maybe this curse is getting stronger."

"I don't recall establishing there is a curse."

"Look," she goes on, "your father's condition is serious, not just a repairable broken bone." She grabs my good arm and yanks me back, hard. Her strength surprises me. "Can't you see?"

Strong or not, I've had a gutful of this rubbish. I shake off her hand. "Will you quit it? Bad luck is just that, bad luck. It doesn't mean anything. I don't have any so-called 'powers.' That's absurd. Just leave me alone. I want to be normal like everyone else in this world."

She stands very still. "Do you think I don't want to be normal like everyone else? Do you think I like living with this?"

I peer at her. What is she saying? "You?"

"I have powers too," she replies, her voice so low I can barely hear it. "Not strong ones, really. Not as strong as I'd like. But I can do a few spells and stuff. You know, turn on the radio from another room, make the digits on the clock change faster, tricks like that. But most of my talent is getting inside people's heads."

This last part is too much. "Are you saying you can read minds?"

"No, nothing that grand. Although I have tried, with Jillian and Hannah. But I can sense emotions. I can tell if a person is angry, or sad, or frightened, even if they're not revealing a thing on the outside."

"Very interesting," I reply sarcastically, a desperate urge to run pelting down on me. I realize I have to get away, from the forest, from Kate, and everything she's saying. I start running and leaping, shoving foliage out of my way, hoping I'm heading in the general direction of the road.

"I was in your head this morning, Jarrod Thornton!"

I don't slow down until I finally break through to the road. It's not the same place we went into the forest, but, hey, who cares, as long as I'm outta here. Unfortunately, Kate is right behind me. I spin around, determined to get her off my back. "You're one crazy chick, Kate . . . whatever your last name is."

"It's Warren. And damn you, you felt me!"

Still breathing heavily I try to catch my breath. She can't know what she's talking about. She's fast freaking me out. And I know my words are going to hurt, but I have to do it. "Listen, Kate Warren, you're delusional. You're insane. They gotta lock you up before you hurt someone."

I start running again, along the winding road to the first hairpin bend, the going much easier now, downhill all the way. Yet I can't make my legs run fast enough, away from Kate, away from her psychotic accusations.

I hear the softly spoken words in my head as if she were standing right beside me, whispering in my ear. *"With your powers unleashed, you're the one who could hurt someone."*

I shake my head and look around. No one. Yet I swear it's Kate's voice. Goose bumps crack the surface of my skin. I must be losing it. It can't have been her. It has to be my subconscious. That's all.

"Anything could happen!"

Her madness is rubbing off on me. I promise myself that I will do anything, *everything!* to stay away from her. I'll find out who she hangs around with at school and make sure I get in with a different group. Even if that group is Pecs's. It will be way safer than hanging around with Kate.

Kate

Friday morning we're all grouped in the quadrangle outside the cafeteria before school. Hannah and I usually don't hang around this area. It doesn't have a sign anywhere that says "Trendies Only," it's left unsaid; but everyone knows these tables are the popular group's hangout. But today it's raining, a chilling wind is blowing right through our uniforms. I wish I'd worn my blazer as well as my maroon wool sweater. The quadrangle area is the only part of school that offers moderate shelter from bitter weather. It's supposed to be large enough to house the entire school population under cover, but really only if we were sheep.

I've had almost a week to think about Jarrod. Not necessarily by choice, my brain just refuses to think about anything else. I've had nothing to do with him since that first day, or I should say, *he's* had nothing to do with me.

He's keeping his distance, and well, I just have to accept that's how he wants it. And I know exactly what he's on about, hanging around with that other lot. Not only does he think I'm crazy, he's also running scared. Scared of my "bad luck" theories.

"Looks like he's settled in nicely," Hannah says between sips of hot chocolate. "And why not," she goes on. "Looks count for a lot with that group. He's pretty hot. Whatd'ya reckon?"

In my direct span of vision, I see Jarrod's arm casually slung around Jessica Palmer's back. I try to drag my eyes away from his fingers sliding rhythmically up and down her left arm. Unfortunately I can't stop the sounds of her twittering voice chirping on and on about how cold she is even though she's wearing a sweater, blazer, and long pants. I try to concentrate on what Hannah is saying. *Jarrod hot?* I guess I agree with that, but wording my thoughts out loud? I don't think so. If Hannah catches on to my feelings for Jarrod, she'll stir the hell outta me for the next ten centuries.

He glances my way and our eyes meet and hold for an undefinable fragment of time. I swallow hard, the buzzer sounds, and we start moving to class.

I haven't answered Hannah, but it seems she's taken my silence as general agreement anyway. "I mean," she rambles on, "he's clumsy and all, can't seem to stop dropping things—like those raw eggs in Food Tech yesterday, what a mess, and the chickens got out when he was supposed to have locked the cages in Agriculture; but somehow with him, it just makes him cuter, if that's possible. Even the glasses look great on him."

Her analysis grates on my nerves. "Oh shut up, Han."

She tosses her empty cup into a bin. "What's with you?"

I throw her a look that should have her breaking out in big blistery facial acne if I add the accompanying chant. It's a mistake. Straight away it clicks.

"Oh no," she groans with a half-laugh. "You've got it bad, haven't you?"

"I don't know what you're talking about," I lie. I do have it bad, bordering on obsession. And I don't like feeling this way—vulnerable. Geez, I'm conscious of everything about him: where he is any minute of the day, what he's doing, who he's talking to, what he's possibly thinking. It's driving me crazy.

There's a bunch of us now, making our way inside the corridors. At least it will be warmer in class today. The only attraction.

Hannah laughs loudly, amused by the thought of me hung up on Jarrod. If I'm being honest I can see her point. The guy is way out of my league now. Apparently accepted by the elite group, what would he want with me? He would be shunned if he got caught fraternizing with the *weirdos*. Unless they have to, nobody talks to Hannah and me. We're different, we don't conform to strict society rules. Hannah is simply too poor, the holes in her shoes and dilapidated backpack, her second-hand uniform, and charity shop clothes adequate testimony to that. She could never keep up with the latest trends, and, of course, she hangs around with me—*Scary Face,* as Pecs likes to call me. Hannah's been my friend since kindergarten, when I was the only one who didn't laugh at her borrowed and old-fashioned clothes or make nasty snide remarks about her family's poverty status. Everyone knows the Brelsfords live on handouts. Five children, a father who walked away when the youngest was just three weeks old, it has to be hard.

"Sucked in!" Hannah exclaims, still laughing.

In my present mood this just makes me volatile.

"Gotta do something to cheer you up," she says, spinning around and causing a hassle as others have to move around her to get past, and everyone's in a rush to get out of the cold. "Let's go to the movies tonight. It's Friday."

The theater up here, a refurbished old Anglican church, holds showings only three days a week—Friday nights, Saturday, and Sunday afternoons.

We discuss what's showing, something about a witch on trial in the sixteenth century. We both burst out laughing at this.

"Forget it," we say simultaneously, bursting into more fits of giggles. We decide to go to the Icehouse instead. The local cafe. At least my mood begins to improve. It will help me get through the day. Ashpeak High is such a small school, the whole of the sophomore class—twenty-seven students—fits into one classroom. The only time we ever split up is for optional subjects. The social scene is a bit like that too. The only place in town worth a look is the Icehouse. Run by an Italian family that's lived on the mountain longer than I've lived on earth, the cafe has a distinct Italian flavor. The cappuccinos are great. Ashpeak's only claim to culture.

We agree to meet at eight. I spend the rest of the day wondering whether Jarrod will be there, and if so, will he be taking Jessica Palmer? This thought grates on my nerves—Jarrod and Jessica. I can't concentrate and eventually my mood takes another dive. Of course he'll be there, and of course he'll take Jessica. That group always hangs out at the Icehouse. Where else is there?

By the end of the day I've convinced myself the only reason I'm interested in Jarrod is because I'm concerned for his well-being. At least, other than his clumsiness, nothing else extraordinary or odd has happened. Either he's keeping a firm hold on his emotions, or I made a huge mistake last Monday, and he really didn't cause that storm in the lab. It all seems like a dream now, even though a temporary lab has been set up in the Admin block until the repairs are complete. But what about that enchanted wind in Jillian's shop? Was that simply my imagination?

If Jarrod doesn't have the gift then I've made an earth-shattering fool of myself and given a complete stranger enough ammunition to have the whole town laughing in my face, snickering behind my back even more than before. These thoughts are disturbing. My face goes hot like I've just stuck it inside Jillian's kiln.

I'm relieved when school is finally over for the day. The chilling wind is actually quite refreshing, cooling me off. I start reliving the things I told Jarrod—every stupid word.

As I make my way home I realize, either way, I've blown it.

Kate

The Icehouse is crowded. Everyone's here, everyone, it seems, except Jarrod. Jessica Palmer's here though, hanging out with a loud group of boys mostly—Pecs, Ryan, Pete O'Donnell—her usual crowd. I wonder what's happened to Tasha? Pecs has an arm thrown over the back of Jessica's seat. Occasionally his hand slides down and grips Jessica's shoulder, giving it a revolting squeeze.

Hannah notices this little play. "Look at that." With disgust in her voice she indicates with a flick of her head the rowdy group consisting of Pecs and his mates. They have the center two tables drawn together, so they're hard to miss. Their desired effect. "Did you hear? Tasha's given Pecs the shove."

I stare at her. This is big news.

She's rapt she has my whole attention. "Apparently she gave him an ultimatum: accept Jarrod into their group, or get lost. Can you believe it? Underneath that macho exterior Pecs is a kitten licking Her Highness's feet. And," she continues without even taking a breath, "rumor has it, Tasha's got Jarrod dangling off her royal hook."

I try to remember to breathe.

"Of course, Jessica Palmer didn't get a say. She knows her place."

I try to absorb it all; the image of Pecs in the form of a thickset furry animal on all fours at Tasha's feet almost makes me laugh. It goes to show who really rules around here. The feminists would be pleased. I guess Jarrod is too. The part about him and Tasha, though not surprising, devastates me anyway. It's something he's longed for—to be accepted. I sensed it on his first day, the need burning deeply inside him to be part of a group. He sure hit the jackpot with this lot, they are *the* most popular group in school. He's really winning.

We sit in a distant corner, farthest booth from the door. We don't come here a lot, but when we do, this booth is my favorite, semi-concealed behind the jutting corner of the cafe counter, nearest the kitchen—out of eyeshot unless you're looking.

I guess I know where Jarrod is now—out with Tasha Daniels. They're probably taking in a movie first. I cringe at the thought of him watching that witch-burning rubbish they're showing this weekend.

They walk in about half an hour later, Tasha swaying her skinny hips as she dances around the tables. She looks stylish and leggy, her long blond hair bouncing around her slender shoulders as she flicks a look back occasionally, making sure Jarrod is right behind her. He may as well be wearing a collar and chain.

I try not to stare at Tasha's short, tight, bright red skirt. She's wearing black tights underneath that give the illusion of eternal length. Her ice-blue midriff top reveals a perfectly rounded navel pierced with an expensive gold ring. She has to be freezing in this getup. I snort loudly, seething with jealousy. The malignant thought hits me as I reach into my jeans pocket for a tissue: She has Jarrod to keep her warm. God, it's so unfair!

"What a turn," Hannah remarks, shaking her head. "You never told me, whatd'ya think?"

She means Pecs getting dumped for Jarrod. I can't help remembering only this morning when it appeared Jessica Palmer was with Jarrod. I bet she's not pleased with the switch. But of course, what Tasha wants, Tasha always gets. It's her upbringing. Ultra rich. Unbelievably spoiled. Her parents own a Hereford stud farm, but they don't work it themselves. It's *Doctor* Daniels, and his wife's a lawyer and president of the local Country Women's Association—Ashpeak's most prominent professionals.

I blow my nose, hating these pre-winter sniffles, and

think about it all. We should have seen this coming. Tasha's been drooling over Jarrod ever since that first memorable morning in the science lab. Even Pecs saw her interest. But Tasha is one hell of a manipulator. I mean, who am I kidding? She has more social pull at this school than Pecs would in a lifetime. He's just a brute, while Tasha is *it*. The one with whom everyone wants to be seen. Pecs adores her. Pecs ogles her. Tasha is queen of Ashpeak High. There is no other on this mountain who can match her on all three counts: looks, arrogance, and social standing.

It occurs to me, now that Jarrod is so obviously an accepted member of their group, Pecs will have to find someone else to get stuck into. Pecs is like that, has to have his kicking bag.

Hannah's looking at me strangely, as if she's waiting for a reply from someone who's just left for another planet. I try to recall what she said, something about Tasha being involved with Jarrod and not Pecs. "Who cares?"

"Ahh, you don't, of course," she returns with sarcastic sweetness.

I roll my eyes and decide to get another cappuccino. No way can I get a waitress's attention in this crowd so I go straight up to the counter. Bad move. Two people see me. The first is Jarrod with a weird expression on his face, like I've caught him off guard. I pay for my coffee, keeping my eyes lowered, but sense he's still staring. I can't stop myself from stealing one quick glance. But when my eyes catch his they don't budge. Moisture dries in my mouth.

Pecs looks up to see what Jarrod is looking at, and when he sees me, he scoffs loudly. "Can't blame you staring, man." He slaps Jarrod on the back in an all-male, best-buddies gesture. "Don't worry, you'll get used to it. We call her the *Freak Show*." His hands fly up, one on either side of his thick face, fingers splayed, exaggeratedly trembling.

Some of my coffee spills as I hurry back to my booth. It isn't Pecs's sick remark that has me worried. I can take plenty of them. It's the look on Jarrod's face—bitten with sudden hardness. I've seen it before—in Mr. Garret's science lab moments before that bizarre storm. His green eyes are blazing at Pecs, who's so oblivious he's still snickering under his breath.

"Don't mind her." This from Tasha, her hands all over Jarrod now, tugging him back down, claiming his attention. She's sitting so close, if she moves one more centimeter she'll be in his lap. "Sure, she's good entertainment value, but her grandmother's the wild card. And even though her shop's interesting enough—I go there myself sometimes—the real stuff is hidden in the back rooms. Jillian's into live sacrifices, you know. They drink blood and hold black masses." He stares at her incredulously, eyebrows raised. Immediately she pouts. "It's the truth, Jarrod. Every word." Her eyes widen while her gleaming pink mouth trembles affectedly. "I've seen drops of blood on the carpet myself." Her head swings momentarily to the side. "Something red, anyway. And," she adds in a husky whisper, close to his ear now, "they've been seen dancing naked in the rain forest. It's disgusting—pure devil worship."

Her head swings away so that the others at her table (and the surrounding half-dozen tables) hear her distinctly. "There's only the two of them, but, well, who would have them?"

The glass shatters just as the waitress lowers Pete O'Donnell's drink. "What the . . . !"

"Sorry. Oh my goodness. Sorry, Pete." Dia Petoria, the girl from my science class, is the waitress. She's a nice girl, studies a lot even though it doesn't show up in her marks. But she's a trier all right. Instantly I feel sorry for her. This incident isn't her fault. She doesn't need Pete O'Donnell's anger on top of her confusion. "I don't know what happened. It just exploded!"

Bella Spagnolo, one of the owners, comes rushing over, whipping past where Hannah and I are quickly making up our minds to leave. She looks so angry I think she's going to get stuck into Dia. She must be having a bad night 'cause she's not usually like this. She comes to Jillian's shop sometimes, looking for decorative pieces to dress up her cafe, trying to make it more appealing to a younger age group. I met her a couple of times. She even asked me what I thought young people liked. She seems nice.

I glance out of the corner of my eye as I wait for Hannah to organize herself. Her jacket has slipped to the floor so she has to climb down between the bench and table to retrieve it. Bella is listening intently to Dia's explanation. Thankfully, she can tell Dia is innocent—no one is that good an actor. Bella helps her clean up the mess, promising the entire table a free cappuccino or soft drink.

At this stage leaving is our best option. I mean, I'm no coward. I can do damage to the lot of them if I want. But what would be the point? If I did hurt them, I'll just be sorry later—not for them, for Jillian. Her shop is her livelihood, and even though she doesn't make a lot of money out of it, she enjoys it, collecting things, experimenting with what sells, what doesn't, and especially talking to the many tourists that come through.

I guess if I'm honest, I have to admit I'd be worried about what would happen to me as well. They think I'm weird now, and they don't know the half of it. If they discover the truth, my life would be hell in this small community. And I like it here too much to jeopardize anything seriously. It's quiet, and most people leave me alone.

One look at Jarrod and leaving becomes an urgent priority. He looks livid, and if he really does have the gift and loses his temper, things could start heating up.

I almost make it to the door, except Pecs is up to his tricks again, and I apparently am making a return appearance in the form of his momentary kicking bag. The wording of several malicious spells flicks through my mind like electricity. I have an inner battle to stop myself from going through with some of them.

"Hey there, *Scary Face*," he croons, his fingers tightening around my elbow so that it actually hurts. "Leaving so soon? We haven't had any fun yet."

"Push off, Pecs. Your breath smells like frog dung."

I stun him, but only for a second. It isn't enough to break free. I send out a silent plea to Jarrod to remain calm. He doesn't get it. This time glass shatters everywhere. No table or shelf or window is spared. Drinks spill onto tables, floors, customers. People scream, and Bella loses it completely, reverting to yelling out phrases in rapid Italian. Kitchen staff come tearing out in white aprons and funny little white caps.

For a second I think Pecs is going to release my arm, his concentration easily distracted by the surrounding chaos. I move a bit, try to yank my arm out of his grasp, but he just digs his fingers in deeper. I swear there'll be bruises tomorrow. "Not so quick, *Witchy One*." His head flicks about. "This is your handiwork, isn't it?"

He means the shattered glass everywhere. I scoff and say, "I didn't realize you were ugly *and* stupid."

He doesn't take this well. He snorts and grunts like a pig that's been caged too long. "I know what you need, something to help you learn the art of socializing."

Before I even get a chance to move my head, his mouth comes down on my throat. I feel his hot, moist lips slither across my shoulder. I could vomit. Instead I opt to get physical. As he comes up for air I aim a punch right into his ugly face. It doesn't connect though. I have to give him one thing, for such a big slobbering brute, his reflexes are quick. He covers my balled fist with the palm of his hand, closing his fat fingers easily around it. "Feisty," he mouths, licking his lips with his thick tongue. "And freaky. I like it. Take me home on your broomstick."

Hannah's teeth grind together at that comment. She tries to yank Pecs's hand off my arm, letting fly with a couple of choice words, but he just brushes her aside, and with one hard shove, she finds herself on the cafe floor, sprawled on her rear.

Two things happen. Jarrod jumps up, tipping his chair over with rage, and a thundering vibration reverberates under our feet.

It has the incredible effect of bringing a sudden stillness into the chaos. Everyone goes quiet, listening, looking at each other, asking questions with their eyes.

The vibrations spread to the walls, tables, curtains, light fittings. Soon everything is in motion.

Pecs drops my arm as fear descends. The thunderous rumble grows louder and everyone panics. They start screaming, thinking it's an earthquake. There's a mad rush for the door, which causes a jam. Hannah grabs my arm and starts yanking me after her. I can't move, though, 'cause I have to find Jarrod. "You go, I'll catch up. I have to see if Jarrod's okay."

"He can look after himself, Kate. We gotta get out before the whole place collapses. This is an *earthquake*!" Her big brown eyes grow unbelievably huge.

A large group of people shove us aside in their rush to the door, knocking us into a corner. The rumble grows more intense, making it difficult to stay standing. Everything appears to be moving. The floor especially is going up and down like ocean waves. And where the floor rises up, tables and chairs follow, and more crockery crashes to the ground.

"Thank goodness, at last. There he is!" Hannah points toward the center of the room, yelling over the growing hysteria. Jarrod's standing still, a vacant expression on his face, his eyes glassy. "Hurry up, Kate. Go get him!"

"I will, Han. But you go home and I'll call you later." I take off, losing her, before she has a chance to follow. For some reason I don't want Hannah suspecting Jarrod of anything paranormal. She can handle it, of course, she's used to Jillian and me. It's just that Jarrod himself is oblivious. This whole situation needs careful handling.

When I get to him he's alone, his friends long since deserting him. Well, what does he expect, they're all dogs.

It's like he's in a trance. He doesn't even move when I talk to him. Nothing I say has any effect. For a moment I don't know what to do. A massive crystal chandelier comes crashing down where a great crack has opened in the ceiling. I shove Jarrod hard out of the way, landing on top of him. It does little to break the trance. But at least he's moving now, slowly pulling himself upright.

Leading him, I find the back way out through the kitchen.

At last we're into a back alley that's amazingly still and quiet. Looking around I see nothing unusual in any of the other buildings, no vibrations, no cracking walls, no hysterically screaming people. I shake my head, promising to think about it all later, at home. Now I have to get Jarrod to safety. If the others see him in this semicatatonic state someone might just remember how he was in the science lab during the storm and start asking questions. Questions Jarrod can't answer.

It might be the effect of the chilly air; whatever it is, Jarrod starts coming around. He's still vague though, and exhausted. He can hardly walk. We have to keep stopping so he can refocus and catch his breath. I slide my shoulder under his arm most of the way, especially the last uphill half a kilometer.

Eventually we arrive, out of breath but in one piece. Jillian helps me put Jarrod down on my bed upstairs. She has questions but she's holding back until we get him settled. I appreciate this, as I'm too tired to think. He looks completely out of it, his eyes, like magnetized weights, close immediately. His breath is unusually slow. I glance worriedly at Jillian and flop on my dresser stool.

"I'll brew something to revitalize his senses. And while it's working, you can explain what happened."

Jillian returns about ten minutes later with a steaming, strong-smelling drink. It's a mix of herbs mostly: basil for mental fatigue, bergamot for stress, clary sage for muscle strength, lavender for anxiety and head pain. There's something else but I can't distinguish the aroma. Between the two of us we get most of the stuff down his throat. He falls back to the bed, and while he rests I explain about the cafe, Pecs's sick display, Jarrod's trance, and the violent earth tremor.

Jillian listens intently, sometimes shaking her head like she can't believe it. "He doesn't know how to handle the *gift*," she explains. "His brain is triggering the trance as a coping mechanism. He has a lot to learn before he can control it."

"That's the problem, Jillian. He won't learn while he's

in denial. And there's another thing, I think he's *cursed*, or his family at least."

I explain about the accidents and bad luck that Jarrod's family has had over the years, right down to the clumsy things Jarrod can't seem to help doing.

Jillian looks thoughtful. "It could explain the reason his gift has been released. Perhaps it's meant for him to use as a tool—a subconscious attempt to counter the curse. But, of course, there's no way of figuring it out without Jarrod's help. His acceptance is vital. And by the sounds of things, Kate, time is essential. As Jarrod's powers grow, so could the powers of the curse. These things are probably linked."

Jarrod

I feel so strange. There's a heat inside my body, a burning sensation. It's as if I can actually feel every muscle, every tendon, every nerve cell.

"He's waking."

Kate! Please don't tell me she's in my head again. I open my eyes and she's standing in front of me, her head and shoulders slightly stooped. I'm lying on a firm but comfortable bed. Looking about, other than Kate and her grandmother, I can't recognize anything. There's a softly glowing amber light beside the bed, an antique-looking dresser and stool, crystal wind chimes hanging in front of a closed lead-light window. There's a wooden bowl on the dresser, and Kate is running a finger around its rim. It appears to be filled with water and fresh flower petals. Beside this is a ceramic oil burner that isn't being used. The room smells clean and woody, like the forest.

"How are you feeling, Jarrod?"

I lift myself up on one elbow to answer Kate's grandmother and wonder how to address her. "Better, thank you . . . ?"

"Just call me Jillian," she suggests. Her smile is warm. At least this time she isn't screaming and ranting about snakes.

"Is this your room?" I ask Kate. She nods and helps me sit up. I swing my legs to the floor, resting my elbows on my knees. That inner burning, that strange awareness of my insides, is easing. My head starts clearing. "What happened? How did I get here?"

"What do you remember?"

I have to think. "I was at the Icehouse. You were there with Hannah. The waitress broke a glass, it spilled all over Pete." I also recall Pecs's slack comments. I look up to see if she's remembering too. But her eyes, and Jillian's, are busy elsewhere. The crystal chimes have started spinning, filling the room with flickering pastel colors and little tinkling noises.

When they stop, Kate glances at Jillian; a knowing look passes between them. "Is that all?"

What does she want? An instant replay? My thoughts spin back to the moment. When Pecs grabbed Kate's elbow and started mauling her throat I wanted to do damage. And I've never been a violent person. If anything,

I usually run at the first sign of trouble. I haven't got the stomach for blood, let alone spilled blood, especially mine. But Kate is waiting for my answer as if she wants to hear all the gory details. "Pecs spewed some very descriptive stuff about you, then slobbered all over your neck."

There's an awkward silence. I've probably hurt her feelings. Whatever Kate is—strange, weird, wacky, even psychotic—at this moment I don't care. Her unusual blue-gray eyes lock with mine and I can't look away. I take in everything about her. Long, silky black hair, pale—almost translucent—skin, the exotic shape of her eyes, and I know no girl could look more . . . I dunno. Striking.

"Thank you, Jarrod," she says softly, and I wonder about this.

"Why are you thanking me?"

"For what you did tonight. In your own way, even though it ended disastrously, you did what you did because . . . Well, at least at the time, you cared. Pecs insulted me, and you got angry."

I try hard to follow. Sure, I remember getting angry. "What did I do?"

"You caused an earthquake."

Okay, I hear what she's saying. *I caused an earthquake.* I stare at her. "I caused an earthquake!"

A smile forms, but there's no humor in her voice.

"I can't be sure exactly what it was. Let's put it this way, there's not much left of the Icehouse Cafe."

"I remember something now. Breaking glass, screaming." I shake my head, trying to clear it. There's more I'm sure, but the memory of it is fuzzy. "Maybe I got hit on the head. If it's as bad as you say, something must be responsible for my hazy memories. I don't remember an earthquake."

Kate is shaking her head in frustration. "You almost *were* hit on the head, by a collapsing ceiling and crashing chandelier. But I pushed you out of the way."

"Are you saying you saved my life?"

Suddenly the frustrated look mutates into something definitely hostile. "Oh, for goodness' sake, Jarrod, you're missing the point."

Jillian touches her arm, an attempt, I realize, to calm her. "A little slower I think, my dear."

Kate tosses her head aggressively, spinning around and muttering under her breath. She moves to the center of the room where she can stand without stooping, her hands on her hips.

Jillian is still hovering by the door. I realize these are the only two places a person can stand without hitting their head on the ceiling. "I met your mother this afternoon, and your little brother, Casey, isn't it?"

"Yeah," I reply. Jillian is trying to lighten the atmosphere.

I'm glad of the reprieve. Things have a way of growing eerie very quickly with Kate.

"They had a browse in my shop."

I drag my eyes from Kate's stiff back. "Did they? Mom would like that. She's into all this weird stuff."

Jillian's eyebrows lift. Oh no, I've probably offended her, too. "I didn't mean . . ." I stumble to find the right words. As usual they never come when I want them.

She smiles reassuringly, and I see a resemblance to Kate. Not in appearances; they're different there. Jillian's hair is wavy, kept short, especially at the back, and light brown. Kate doesn't look anything like Jillian except in the eyes. It makes me wonder about Kate's father's origins—Asian probably, or some Hawaiian island perhaps. I bet she wonders too.

"She told me about the clothes and jewelry she makes," Jillian says. "They sound interesting. She's going to drop in with a sample next week. We're going to hang them in the shop, see if we can generate some movement. Tourists like that sort of thing. You know, *weird stuff.*"

I can't help but laugh. Jillian is all right. She has a sense of humor. I wish she could've passed some on through her genes to Kate.

"I'm going to make you two a couple of sandwiches." And to Kate, Jillian says, "Remember, Kate, you've had sixteen years to adjust to your talents, but can you tell me you're totally at ease with yourself, with your abilities, even now, after this length of time?"

Kate nods without replying. It seems Jillian doesn't require any other confirmation anyway. I'm glad. The thought of them discussing powers and talents and abilities gives me the shivers. Jillian leaves and I decide to set this discussion straight before it gets out of hand. "Look," I begin and Kate spins around with an aggro look on her face. "I know you're into magic and stuff." She glares at me, her incredible almond-shaped eyes narrowing defensively. I put my hand up to stop whatever she's going to say. "That's okay with me. I can handle that, I think. At least, I will, as long you don't involve me in it. I mean, you can involve me but not *include* me. The point I'm pathetically trying to make is that I don't have any magical powers, or mystical talents, or anything like that, unless of course you count *clumsiness* in your list of paranormal qualities."

She actually smiles, then lowers herself to the floor so that her back rests against the edge of the bed. My knees are level with her shoulders. My hand is so close to her head I have a sudden urge to touch her, feel for myself if that hair is as soft and silky as it looks. I don't though. As much as part of me wants to, I'm just not sure. She's beautiful. In a really exotic sort of way. But looks aren't everything. Kate is different from other girls. Maybe that's the attraction. Those other girls at school, Jessica Palmer,

Tasha Daniels, they're really shallow. I guess their only appeal over Kate is that they're "safe." They don't scare me, like Kate does. And that makes me comfortable in their company.

"Snakes are an ancient symbol of evil."

I hang my head in my hands. "Oh, God."

"I looked it up. Here, I'll show you." She scrambles to her knees and carefully lifts a thick ancient-looking book off the dresser, holding it like she's afraid her fingerprints will make the soft leather cover disintegrate. She sits back on the floor cross-legged, the book in her lap. It has to be a thousand years old, with thousand-years-old yellowed and tattered pages. The soft black cover is bare except for a twisting pattern of gold vines like a border. "This is the oldest book Jillian has. It's unique, you know. Handwritten and filled with *Old Magic*."

"Oh, right," I mutter, not knowing what she expects.

Her head lowers as she finds the page she's marked and starts reading. "'Snakes are an ancient symbol of evil. Many snakes, especially around the head, indicate that evil surrounds the figure and all those to which the bearer has alliance.'"

I yank out my glasses from my jeans pocket and scan the script. It's handwritten, all right, articulately in black ink, but the letters are completely indecipherable. I wonder what language it is. "How can you read that?"

She spins her head around and looks up. "It's an early form of English, dating back almost a thousand years. Jillian taught me how to speak and read the ancient tongue."

I'm going to be sorry I ask, but I just have to. "Why? It seems like a lot of work for something you're never going to use. I mean, if you learned French, or Japanese, sure, you could travel there one day."

Kate's eyes widen as if she can't believe anyone can be so stupid. "So I can read the ancient scripts, of course. I'm fascinated with this era, Jarrod. Magic was alive then. There were some really powerful sorcerers around."

I decide to go along with her. Even though I don't believe in this stuff, I can see it means a lot to her. She must spend half her life on the subject. It's all she thinks about. I guess she doesn't get to talk about supernatural stuff with friends very often, except perhaps for Hannah. Most people already believe Jillian is a witch. How would they treat Kate if they knew just how deep she is into this stuff herself?

"And you think," I begin, leaning forward with what I hope is a mild amount of interest in my voice, "this snake stuff relates to a curse or something."

Her smile transforms her face into a picture of relief and excitement. It very nearly blows me away. I experience a moment of instant regret, and hope my humoring hasn't accidentally misled her. Her eyes sparkle. "Look here," she says, holding the heavy book up high for me. Why? I wonder. I can't read this ancient script anyway. So I focus on the diagram, sketchy but still clear, a bit like a 3-D drawing. I peer closer and see that it has incredible detail—a half-man, half-bird creature. I think it's a crow. The half that is human grips a smoothly polished wooden staff with a serpent's head. His—its—eyes are eerie, crow-like and tilting sharply upward at the outer ends, yet oddly human. I swear the creature is looking straight at me.

"A shapeshifter," Kate explains with a shiver. "Only the most powerful sorcerers can do this. They're rare, and even reading about them gives me the creeps."

It's an admission I'm relieved to hear. At least something gives her the creeps. Just looking at the figure on paper is enough for me. I take the book she's got practically in my face, and find my hands shaking. This doesn't surprise me as I hate the unknown, things beyond my control or understanding, especially the paranormal. I like the simple things that follow the rules, like the sun rising every morning from the east, and that annoying family of kookaburras that insist on cracking their jokes outside my window every dawn, or the way I can look in the mirror and know my own reflection will be looking back, whether I like it or not.

My life is complicated enough; this book I simply don't need. It even has a smell about it, musty, old, remarkably authentic. I want to hurl it back to her and get the hell out of her bedroom. That sudden urge to run returns, hitting me hard in the stomach, making my adrenalin surge. But Kate is smiling excitedly, pointing to the undecipherable words, quoting bits here and there.

"'Once a curse is placed it can take several forms. The most powerful can linger through generations to eternity. . . .'"

Her finger trails the words across the page. My head tilts to the same slight angle the book is held, and I can't stop my eyes from following. They're foreign words. I try to relax, try to make my mind wander, but nothing's working.

Suddenly I find myself gulping for air. I feel nauseous and need this extra oxygen. I wonder fleetingly if I'm about to pass out. My vision blurs and a sinking feeling kicks into my stomach. My eyes are still riveted to the page where Kate's finger is passing across the foreign words. I jerk with a start as the ancient script disappears. But it's only for an instant, and I relax a little when my vision clears and I see the fancy writing again. Yet somehow I sense it is different now. I adjust my glasses in a gesture that is more habitual than necessary. It's really strange, but suddenly I find I can read the ancient script too, as if the words are present-day English. "'. . . legend has it that the most powerful sorcerers can enfold a curse that spontaneously recurs through future true-born inheritors of such curse . . . True-born inheritors in the form of the magical number seven. Every seventh-born son of succeeding generations shall carry the curse in its entirety, and for as long as the curse is left to fester unborn, it shall grow in strength and enormity until it is released. . . .'"

A sudden crash breaks my concentration and the words become undecipherable again. It's Jillian at the door. I peer up at her through my glasses. She's dropped a tray that was carrying orange juice and sandwiches. Bits of grain bread, tomato, salad stuff, and juice are spread out over the shiny timber floor.

"Jillian!" Kate calls out, the book slamming shut in my hands as she goes to help Jillian clean up the mess.

"I'm sorry," Jillian apologizes, her eyes wide and wary, remaining on me. "I've never heard the script read with such perfect enunciation," she says softly.

My eyes jump to the book in my hands, which suddenly seems to burn my fingers. Did I really *read* those words?

I must look confused. Jillian leaves the mess on the floor to Kate to tidy, her voice gentle and sincere. "Who taught you to read the ancient tongue, Jarrod?"

I shake my head, unable to accept that I *was* reading from that book. "I don't know what you're talking about. Those words were in perfect English."

Kate lifts the tray now, carrying a load of broken china

and bits of soggy sandwiches to her dresser. "Old English, quite undecipherable today."

"That's not true," I counter, even though they were my own words. I recall something from last year's history lessons. "English today has retained many of the ancient words. In fact it's just an expanded and revised form."

Kate accepts none of this. "Wake up, Jarrod. You said yourself it *wasn't* English."

I stand a little unsteadily, aware that I need to get out of this house really quickly. "Look, I don't know what happened just then, my imagination ran away with me, that's all."

Kate groans. "Sit down, Jarrod, and listen. There's only one way I can make you believe this stuff."

I stare at her, wondering what she has in mind. The hairs at the back of my neck bristle. She raises one arched brow, challenging me to sit and watch and obey. I open my mouth to say I have decided to stand and run, but she has her hands on my shoulders, shoving, firmly, until I sit again on the bed.

Kate exchanges a quick glance with Jillian, who moves to the dresser and lifts the tray. "Nothing too startling now, Kate. I'll just be downstairs if you need me."

I have a sudden urge to grab Jillian and drag her, albeit probably screaming, back into the room. I don't want to be alone with Kate while she's in this mood. Anything could happen. My heart starts pounding so fast I think it's going to catapult up my throat and hurtle across the room.

Kate's voice is soft as she pressures me to stay calm. I think this is a joke, or a dream. I feel disoriented, and fight the need to move. She sits down again by my feet, and I'm trapped. Kate's back leans against the bed frame and she twists her body so she can look up at me. "I'm not going to hurt you, Jarrod. I just want to show you a little magic."

I nod, words do not form in the arid desert my mouth has become.

"Relax," she murmurs soothingly. Her fingers start spinning around a ball or something in her hands. I missed seeing where she got it from, but then I'm not exactly in the most alert state of mind. It's a glass ball, I realize, as I catch glimpses of it through her twirling fingers. She notices where my eyes have focused. "It's a clear crystal Jillian gave me when I was three. It's a training tool. I don't need it anymore, but sometimes, especially when it's late and I can't sleep, I play games with it. Simple tricks really. Like this one."

She holds the crystal up to my face. I'm not exactly sure what I'm supposed to be looking for and don't see anything unusual. All the same, it might be my agitated senses, but I find it impossible to drag my eyes away. It seems to loom closer, grow larger even, but this perhaps is an illusion. I'm concentrating hard now. Vivid, shifting colors, like fancy silk scarves, move inside it for a minute, then nothing. I start wondering, is that it? And I'm glad in a way that nothing too amazing or outlandish happened. I mean, shifting colors of reds, oranges, and blues. A good trick, sure. I wonder how she did it. As I'm about to ask something else happens, drawing my focus right into the center of the ball. Something is moving inside and it's more than colors. There are shapes. Odd gray shapes that shift and change. I adjust my glasses. Everything has a slight blur without them. I use them for reading mostly. Now I see people. Three of them. The first I make out is a man, his face filled with pain; then a woman with brown hair and mousy eyes, weary-looking; the last a child, about eight or nine, with hair like mine. It takes a full minute before it hits me. I'm looking at a miniature visual image of my parents and little brother, Casey.

It blows me out. For more than one reason. As far as I know Kate has never seen my family. How would she know what they look like? My chest struggles for air; this is all too unreal. I physically pull back, and lift off my glasses.

Kate gently slips the globe under her bed. "What did you see?"

I stare at her, words stuck dry in my throat.

"What did you see, Jarrod?" she repeats insistently.

"Don't you know?"

"I only saw the colors," she shocks me further by saying. "But you saw more."

"My family."

"Oh," she groans softly as if this explains everything. I wish she'd tell *me*. "Now I understand completely."

Her comment makes me want to scream. "So what do you mean by that?"

"I suggested to the crystal it reveal to you your most worrying thoughts."

I feel my mouth sag open as I suck in a couple of good breaths. What happened just now? Did I really see my family in that glass ball? Did Kate somehow manipulate my thoughts to *think* that I saw them? She says she's good at sensing moods and that sort of thing. I guess she is gifted in some ways. There are people who can sense things sometimes even before they happen. That's not unusual. So what if Kate is capable of a little ESP? A little thought projection? Maybe she really was in my head the other day. I can handle that. With this thought in mind I calm a little. "Very interesting."

"That's all?" Disbelief.

I shrug my shoulders. "What did you expect?"

She shakes her head and drops it into her hands. Her words are muffled. "I thought that you would believe in the world of magic. That by showing you it exists, you would believe you have the gift."

I scoff really loudly. Her eyes peek out from her hands. "It was a great exhibition, Kate. I'm really impressed. Believe me, you blew my mind. But how is a little thought projection going to make me believe *I* can do magic? We're talking about me here. You know, the idea alone is absurd. Don't you pay attention at school? I do something stupid every day. I'm clumsy, okay? I'm a nobody. I don't belong anywhere."

Her hands fly into the air. "Jarrod, you're so wrong about yourself, it makes me cringe."

"I'm sorry I do that to you."

"You idiot." She strikes my knee with her knuckles. I grab her hand to stop her from doing it again. I don't let go straightaway. "I mean," she begins, and I swear her voice has become a little unsteady, "you say you don't belong anywhere, yet you told me how your father has traced your ancestors back almost a thousand years. Now, that's really *something*."

I think about this. She's right, of course. It makes me feel better, like maybe I do belong. At least this conversation feels safer. I like where it's going. I decide to try and keep it there, leave the supernatural stuff behind. "I could bring Dad's book around tomorrow, if you like."

Her eyes light up with excitement. "Could you? That'd be great."

It's a timeless moment. I lace my fingers through hers

91

and feel my pulse accelerate like crazy. "I want to thank you for getting me out of that cafe tonight, and for saving my life."

"I don't think that old chandelier would have killed you, but that's okay all the same."

"I, ah, really should go. Mom'll be worried by now."

"Hmm, if you have to."

She says the words so softly I have to lean forward to hear them. At least that's my excuse. Honestly, the room is dead quiet except for the hammer pounding away in my chest. I lean down even farther, our faces mere centimeters apart. My eyes drop to her mouth. The timing is perfect. If I don't do it now, I doubt I'll ever have the guts again. If anything, other than clumsy, I'm also a coward. I don't know what's come over me. I just know I have to give it one shot. So I lean into her face before my nerve deserts me completely. I can almost taste her lips, they're so close.

Maybe I really am cursed. I feel myself falling, and instead of the sensual kiss I imagined, I land, long bony limbs and all, directly in her lap! "God, Kate," I mutter, my face heating up like a Bunsen burner on full flame. "Sorry. What a mess. I hope I didn't hurt you." Being careful where I put my hands, I climb awkwardly out of her lap, catch my foot on the corner of a rug I never even noticed before, eventually stumbling to my knees somewhere near the door. "Damn."

"Are you all right?"

She isn't laughing but it can't be far. I decide I don't want to hang around when it happens. So I nod, not trusting myself to make intelligent conversation, and mumble, "Yeah . . . Fine . . . Gotta go . . . See myself out . . ."

She escorts me to the front door anyway, probably just to make sure I don't crash into anything on the way through the shop. But I don't hang around. I tear down the road as if I truly am cursed. By the devil himself.

A shiver rips up my spine causing every fine body hair to stand on end. Okay, it's cold and eerie considering it's late and dark and isolated around here, but somehow I know it has nothing to do with all this. It has to do with Kate. Just how, and in what way, I have no idea. I just know it.

Kate

We make the city papers and the national news. Unbelievable. The earthquake at the Icehouse Cafe apparently didn't register on any Richter scale, and this is causing a huge amount of confusion; but the destruction is real, as are the many eyewitnesses. The whole town is crawling with official-looking people and news crews. It's Saturday morning and through the night the newshounds have been coming in from all over the country. Several theories have been put forward by scientific professionals but witnesses disagree. It was no bomb, or freak storm, like the one that hit the local high school a week earlier. Most swear it was an earthquake.

It's Sunday before two investigating police officers make their way to the Crystal Forest. They introduce themselves, briefly flashing ID. It's just routine by now. I'm probably last on their interview list. Their faces tell me they're not expecting I have anything new to tell them. I don't disappoint, describing the tremor as it swept through the place with just the right amount of anxious excitement. I wonder how Jarrod handled the questioning. His recollections, though vague, are probably enough to satisfy the investigators. Any lack of memory could surely be excused as trauma, I assume, without suspicion.

The police leave, apparently satisfied, though no wiser, and I decide I'd better do a little homework. But my mind isn't on it. I'm expecting Jarrod, who doesn't show. He mentioned coming over with his father's heritage book but I guess he's changed his mind, probably deciding to stay well away from all the officials, police, and investigative scientists lurking around.

I see him at school on Monday, but he ignores me. He's sitting at a table in the quadrangle outside the cafeteria with his usual crowd—Pecs and Jessica, and of course Her Highness, Tasha Daniels. It hurts, but I'm not about to let him know this. Realization hits me and makes me want to cringe. Jarrod may be incredibly gifted, but inside his soul, where it really matters, he's nothing but a coward—pathetic and spineless. He would sooner hide than confront anything he doesn't understand, or makes him uneasy, or doesn't conform to his stupid set of rules.

He continues to avoid me all week. At least nothing else crazy happens. I cop some cheap remarks from Pecs, who reckons it was witchcraft that caused the destruction at the Icehouse, but after a few days of this most people get bored with the idea and leave me alone. So I'm surprised to see Jarrod in the Crystal Forest the following Saturday. As usual, on the weekends I help Jillian out, giving her time to do other things. Jarrod's mother is with him. I watch quietly from my spot on the floor where I'm restocking a bottom shelf, as she lays a handful of unusually beaded and decorated skirts and jackets over the counter. There's some jewelry too—dangly earrings, colorful matching necklaces and bracelets. Jillian examines them with genuine interest. Some of the garments are denim, some linen or silk, but all have distinctive decorative trims of beads, rhinestones, or simply colored gems and fringes. They're not bad if you're into country and western stuff, or just looking for something different. They've got style, but I don't think they suit Jillian's New Age line. She caters to the tourists with mostly novelty items. But she decides to give the trinkets and clothes a go, saying she will display samples on a rack near the front window.

Jarrod's mind is elsewhere, so I watch him for a few moments before he notices me. He seems particularly fascinated by the miniature pewter wizards. His fingers linger on one when he becomes aware I'm watching from across the room. His hand goes still as his eyes lower to mine. He smiles, an innocent boyish grin, and points to the book wedged in the crook of his arm. It's his family heritage book. I have to stop myself from looking too keen. Sure, I want to see that book, it might be able to fill in a lot of blanks about Jarrod, but it isn't just that.

I try not to let it show how totally hung up I am on him. After all, he ignored me all week. Trying to look casual I get up and stroll across to where he's standing. "So, you brought the book."

With his elbow he points at the counter where his mother and Jillian are trying to work out where best exactly to hang the garments and stuff. "Yeah, and Mom."

I look at Mrs. Thornton and try not to probe. She would be an easy subject, her face is well-worn but trusting. She has light brown hair, with a fair bit of gray she apparently doesn't try to cover as other women her age might. She's wearing dark blue trousers that make her legs look really skinny and a pale yellow smock top that exaggerates a small roundish belly. "You didn't bring your little brother?"

"Nah, Dad promised he would take him fly-fishing in the creek that runs along the back of the farm."

Their business done, Mrs. Thornton follows Jillian to where Jarrod and I are standing. Jillian introduces us as if the two of them are old friends. I smile and shake Mrs. Thornton's hand. It's small and cold, yet surprisingly strong. She tells me to call her Ellen, which is nice and casual and explains a lot about the woman. I like her instantly, even as she passes an uneasy glance at Jarrod. They've been talking about me. The thought irritates. So I have to do it. Just once, I promise myself. One brief probe.

She's wary, a little fearful even, her senses sharply alert, which means Jarrod has told her I'm strange, or crazy, or something similar. It disappoints me, but doesn't change my opinion of the woman. After all, her wariness is based on the advice of her son. It's Jarrod's opinions that suck. How am I going to get through to him when he thinks I'm a head case?

Jillian invites Ellen to a cup of tea, but she declines. "Next time perhaps," Ellen explains. "I have to check on my husband, Ian, and our other son, Casey. I dropped them off at the river that borders the back of our farm this morning, but Ian's leg isn't the best. His medication sees him dozing often."

She leaves and Jarrod follows me upstairs. We sit on the floor together with soya munchies for morning tea, the book sprawled between us. It's thick and rich with history, beginning with the most recent families up front. Apparently Jarrod's father, Ian Thornton, is an only child, whose father died several years ago at the age of sixty-six from a major stroke. His mother, who is still living, is in a suburban nursing home in Sydney with an older sister.

Immersed in history, our time soon disappears. We

break for lunch, and go downstairs where I heat up some vegetarian sausage rolls. We finish these and talk for a while, sticking to *safe* subjects like teachers and homework and Jarrod's little brother's antics.

We take our drinks up to my room but soon forget them as we sink back into the heritage book. It turns out Jarrod's favorite subject is history, just like mine. We laugh about this and the feeling in the room is warm and relaxed.

I'm not sure what I'm looking for. I guess it's a sign that proves there is a curse on the Thornton family. It turns out to be quite an informative book, giving interesting tidbits on heaps of families from way into the past. There are the usual family skeletons in the closet, some more so than others. Eventually a trend starts to take shape. Accidents, tragedies, appear more prevalent in certain families, I realize, the really large ones, where there are heaps of births. It keeps me riveted.

It turns out Jarrod's descendants go far back into English history to the Middle Ages, long before proper records were officially kept, so the early information is stuff that's probably been handed down from parent to child. In that respect it's hard to decide what's fact and what's elaborated fiction, exaggerated for entertainment value, perhaps retold around a hungry fire on a cold winter's night.

I try to keep this in mind, especially when reading in the back of the book about the oldest family, which is steeped in controversy. There's a kidnapping of a newly married bride by the bridegroom's illegitimate half-brother on their wedding night, followed by the disappearance of the newly married couple a while after. It was rumored that the young bride carried the illegitimate half-brother's child in her womb, and that he used some form of sorcery on her, but as the young married couple was never seen again, it couldn't be proved. Yet the controversy continued when their eldest child, a son, returned to the family home on his twenty-eighth birthday to claim his inheritance. His identity was rejected, and a bloody battle followed. I wonder how much of this is true? No matter what I read after this my mind keeps zeroing back to this memorable family.

And though it's all fascinating, especially the mention of magic, I force myself not to dwell too long in one place. By late afternoon I recognize a definite pattern, adding credence to the story of the oldest recorded family. "It has to be it," I announce, sitting back on my heels, folding my arms, quietly satisfied. "I think I know who the sorcerer is."

Jarrod's head swings up. "What did you say?"

I flick the pages back to the first family. "The illegitimate half-brother used sorcery. It must've been something extraordinary to have passed down through those early generations. I'm guessing—"

"Yeah, right," Jarrod scoffs, interrupting me.

"It's all there, Jarrod. All you have to do is look."

"Sounds like a matter of interpretation. Didn't you say the information in those early registers could be suspect?"

I groan. He's impossible. Totally negative. "I admit the information's a little scattered, and sure, some of it could be exaggerated, but you have to look at the book as a whole. There's a definite trend of bad luck, disasters, and deaths in the larger families. This is evidence, Jarrod. It stands for itself. All these things happened mostly to families with at least seven male births. And that first family was shrouded in sorcery. Don't you see? This is when it must have started."

"So there's been a lot of bad luck," Jarrod concedes. "But sorcery? You're kidding, right?" He still can't see the reality, and goes on to add, "The fact that all these families are unfortunate has nothing to do with how many births are in their families, and especially doesn't mean they're cursed." He's trying to rationalize my theory. In fact, he's trying to rationalize everything. An annoying habit.

"How can you say that?" I argue. "Every family with seven or more male births is jinxed."

"That's ridiculous. Besides, most people experience difficulties at some time or other. Especially, I would imagine, in those medieval days. Even more so the families with seven or more kids. Your family's just so small you haven't had the benefit of experience."

I stare at him and even though it hurts, I try to ignore his last comment. My main concern is Jarrod's lack of faith. Why can't he just let himself believe? Why does he hold himself back from the obvious? "What would *you* call hard times, Jarrod? Bankruptcy? Lost limbs? Unexplained deaths? Kidnapping? Murder? It's all there, in every family that gave birth to seven or more sons."

Frowning, he glances across the top of my head to the window. When his eyes come back he looks uncertain. I have an inner battle to stop myself from probing his mind. Finally he shrugs and stands, apparently deciding it's time to leave. "Look," he begins, "it's an interesting theory, but it has no substance with me. My only brother is Casey. I'm the *first*-born, not the seventh. So try explaining that."

Of course he's right, and suddenly I feel so stupid. All this talk of ancient evil curses and sorcery. It's ludicrous. At least that's how Jarrod must see it. How he must see *me*. I shake my head, stand, and hand him the heritage book. But I can't meet his eyes.

"Keep the book if you like, Dad won't miss it for a few days. But I'd better go. Mom should have been here hours ago. She must have forgotten she said she'd pick me up. I'll start walking."

"Jillian could drive you home," I mumble.

"No!" His reply is too quick. He's obviously had enough of this insanity and can't get away fast enough. "I mean," he mutters, "I don't mind the walk. It's not that far. Really. Downhill all the way."

The phone rings downstairs. I'm so embarrassed I leave it to Jillian. We're quiet for a minute, facing each other, neither knowing what to say. Downstairs I hear Jillian talking but I can't quite make out her words. Finally I say, "I'll see you out, then."

"Nah, don't bother." He moves toward the door really quickly and bumps into Jillian.

"That was your father, Jarrod," she says gently, and instantly I know something is wrong. "There's been some sort of accident. . . ."

Both our heads shoot up, Jarrod's hits the ceiling with a bang. He rubs it unconsciously. "What's happened?" His voice is unsteady. "Is Dad still on the phone?"

"Sorry, no," Jillian replies. "He was in a hurry, said for you to meet him at the hospital, where he'll explain everything. I'll get the car out and run you in."

"Oh no, what now?" he groans, murmuring to himself. Then to Jillian, "How did he sound? Did he say who was hurt?" We're already halfway down the stairs.

"I don't want to alarm you, Jarrod, but he did sound terribly distraught."

It takes about twenty minutes to reach the hospital.

Jarrod sits in front with Jillian. There is nothing any of us can say. We don't know enough to even speculate, except that Jarrod's father is the one who called, so he must be all right. That leaves Ellen, Jarrod's mother, or his nine-year-old brother, Casey.

Ashpeak Mountain Hospital looks more like a retirement village than a hospital, but it has an emergency section that remains open twenty-four hours a day. Up here we have our occasional tourist injury. A lot of backpackers do the trails in the forests; some get into difficulty not knowing the terrain well enough before starting out. And then there are the car accidents. It's a twisting mountain road that leads up from the valley. Of course I can't forget the locals, mostly farmers, a notorious occupation. Today there's an obviously distressed baby with rosy cheeks being nursed by his mother while the father looks on. The man glances up as we hurry past, probably wondering why the rush on such a pleasant Saturday evening.

A nurse behind the counter leads us to a small room off to one side. Ellen is there, sitting half curled up in a ball, her fingers tightly clenching a white linen handkerchief in her lap. She looks incredibly small and when she glances up as we enter, I see she is an emotional mess. Her eyes are red-streaked and swollen from a lot of crying, her complexion colorless, if anything, a sullen gray. "My nightmares have come back," she murmurs.

I glance briefly at Jillian, whose eyebrows and shoulders lift just a little. She moves to sit beside her.

Jarrod is embraced by a man who has to be his father. The resemblance is striking, except this man has stooped shoulders and uses a pair of crutches to support himself. His hair is a pale replica of Jarrod's, thinner and sprinkled with gray. His eyes are vivid green, yet weary-looking, and he wears a face hardened by too much sun or hard knocks, making him look far older than he should.

Jarrod introduces us. "Jillian, Kate, this is my father."

He forgets to give us a name, but I remember it from this morning when Ellen mentioned it in Jillian's shop—Ian.

Jillian and I are invited to stay. I'm glad, because I can't leave yet. It's obviously Casey that's hurt. And even though I've never met him, I feel as if I know him already. Jarrod mentioned him a lot today, and always with affection. Which is odd for siblings. They move around heaps, and I think this is why Jarrod gets along well with his brother. I can tell he's protective.

"What happened?" Jarrod asks his father, flicking his mother a brief glance.

"We were fishing," Ian begins. "Goin' at it all day. He was having so much fun. God knows there hasn't been much of that lately." He stops as words choke up inside. He swallows and closes his eyes for a long moment, then continues, "Mom watched him for a bit while I had a nap in the car. Then she went home to prepare dinner, said she would come back in an hour to take us home. You know your brother, all boundless energy, can't drag him away until the last minute." He pauses again and his eyes glaze over.

After a moment he finds the courage to continue. "He caught sight of a whopper trout, tried to cast his fly directly over the top of it, but his hook got caught on a drifting log. I waded in a bit to help tug it free. Damn leg," he curses. "But the log jerked forward with the current. That's all it took."

"What happened then, Dad?"

"Casey held on to that rod so hard, fearful of losing it and getting an earful from me." He almost cries as moisture floods his eyes, but he sniffs and keeps going. "He fell into that river, swollen a bit from recent rain. I couldn't hold him. I yelled at him to let go. He did eventually, but by then he'd drifted into choppy water where the current claimed him. He went down over a small waterfall into much faster running water. I couldn't do anything. *Damn leg!*" He thumps it with the palm of his hand, then winces with the sudden pain. "I watched him go, sure that I would never see him again."

Jarrod slides his arm around his father's stooped shoulders and they embrace. "It's okay, Dad. I know you would've done everything you could."

"Your mother, God bless her, was already on her way back by then to collect us. We got in the car and followed the river. But it was useless. We'd lost him, couldn't see him anywhere. People from the other side heard us yelling and screaming, and came to see what all the ruckus was about. Thank goodness they had a mobile phone. They called an ambulance and helped us search."

"Tell me you found him," Jarrod's voice drops to almost a whisper, his face bloodless white.

Ian Thornton nods to reassure his son. "About a kilometer south of where he went down, he was floating in a pool. He wasn't breathing though. By then the police and ambulance arrived. They revived him, but it took so long, son. So long, we don't know . . . the effects. You know what I mean?"

"Yeah, I understand, Dad. What have the doctors said?"

It's Ellen who answers, her voice high and edgy. "They said they won't know till they've run some tests. He was breathing when they brought him in, but unconscious. He could be in a coma, Jarrod." And adds with a hint of hysteria, "I mustn't lose him."

Jillian's arms tighten around Ellen's shoulders as the woman's whole body begins to tremble. She's losing control and I feel helpless. "He'll be fine," Jillian soothes. "He's in expert hands now."

"You don't understand," Ellen mumbles, losing control

again. Her head is shaking, eyes enormous jittery balls. She looks wild. "I can't lose *another* son!"

It is this agonized statement that makes everybody go dead still. Both Jarrod's parents look straight at him, guiltily. Jarrod's voice is deep, his eyes narrow and intense. "Mom?" It's only one word, but the tone demands an explanation.

His father replies, "I'm sorry, son. It's not something we talk about anymore."

Jarrod goes deathly pale. "What don't you talk about, Dad?"

Ian sighs loudly. "The others. The babies. Nobody knows the hard time your mother had. We swore after you were born, so strong and healthy, we'd start afresh and never mention the pain of the past."

"You have to tell me now."

They look at each other like they're trying to stare each other out. Ian is first to look away. "We were both so young when the first came early. He was ten weeks premature and only lived twenty minutes. Doctors said it was best that way and we hoped for another child real soon. A year exactly later the twins were born. But they were premature too, their tiny lungs hadn't stood a chance. Both picked up infections and died within their first week."

He pauses, his eyes pleading with his son not to make

him continue. But Jarrod's need to know is stronger. "Go on," he urges through grinding teeth.

"We waited three years to help your mother build her strength, and we hoped this time it would be different. Alex, we called him. He was beautiful, but tragically frail, born with only half a heart. He lived three weeks, but every day was a miracle."

Ellen whimpers into her handkerchief. The woman is distraught. She doesn't need to hash this out now, recalling the painful past, but Jarrod is driven. "Was that it, then?"

"No," his father replies in a whisper-soft voice. "You may as well know the whole truth, now that it's come out. Your mother had some surgery to clean and strengthen her womb. We had already decided to stop after that last one, but the doctors were sure this time she had a good chance. . . . Technically, they couldn't find anything wrong." He paused, the past coming back to haunt him. I sense he knew some day it would. "There were two more, both boys, both stillborn."

Tears flood my eyes, and when I look at Jillian, I see her eyes are teary too. There is so much feeling in the room, it is literally an energy that pulses like a heart beating on its own. It startles me to realize the strength of it is coming from Jarrod. It isn't anger, but an interesting mix of wonder and shock and alarm.

"When you came along," Ian continues a little more

brightly. "You were so strong and healthy—a true miracle. Your mother and I swore to put the past behind us. To move forward we had to forget the pain that went before. You see, if we didn't, we may have raised you as if you were made of fragile glass. You would have suffocated in our fears."

"So you never told me," Jarrod replies softly.

"When you were seven, and still strong and lively, even if a little clumsy, you gave us courage to try again."

"Casey."

"Your little br-brother." Ian attempts a smile, but his voice breaks on the last word.

I watch Jarrod as he takes this all in. I want to probe, but don't dare, not when his feelings are so obviously intense. It would be insulting and intrusive. But his emotions are clearly displayed anyway. He shifts from open shock to a kind of stunned awareness. After a long few moments, Jarrod's deep green eyes narrow and shift sideways, catching mine. Even though his words are meant for his father, he never stops looking at me. "What does that make me?"

"You?" Ian replies. "You're our seventh son. Our lucky seventh."

Jarrod

Dad's revelation shocks me. This is the moment I start to believe in the curse. Actually it's quite an enlightening moment in many ways. I have a clear picture of the struggle my parents endured in the years before I was born. The pain of it goes straight through my chest, like a dagger to my heart. How much pressure can one family take before it collapses? I feel a sudden swelling of pride for both of them. They're strong. Stronger than I could ever be.

So now I have to look at things differently. The vision of my world has radically changed. My family is cursed. Whether I want to admit it or not, the evidence is there. What family these days has six births and six deaths and continues to try for more? It's as if I *had* to be born—so the curse can live. Have my parents been manipulated by some force greater than life itself?

What am I thinking? Can I hear myself? Cursed, as in jinxed? Cursed, as in ancient sorcerers wielding magic from centuries past? I don't believe in this stuff. It's not possible. It's pure fantasy! There has to be an explanation for everything. I live by this rule.

What is happening to me?

I try to pull myself together and put reason to this sudden madness. I'm just distraught, that's all. I'm in shock from Casey's accident. My little brother could yet die, or be brain-damaged for the rest of his life. On top of this I just found out I had other brothers—six of them, all dead before I was even born. I wonder where they are all buried. It's a thought that hits me unprepared. My eyes fill with moisture.

Kate is staring at me, wondering I guess what I'm thinking. It's a wonder she's not in my head right now, trying to figure me out. In some ways I wish she was, then maybe she could tell me what's going on in there. I have to sit down, get a grip. My head drops into my hands, it feels good there, not so heavy.

A warm gentle hand touches my shoulder and I look up. It's Kate. "Are you okay?"

I nod, not trusting words. Something might come out that sounds like an admission, and I'm not ready to hear my doubts verbalized. It will make it all too real.

The doctor appears. I only notice when Dad's crutches

strike the tiled floor with a hurried sort of tap. All of us stand and form a half-circle around her, eager for news of Casey. Her name is Dr. Reed, and she was on duty when Casey came in. "He's a strong young man," she begins, letting us know right away he's okay. "We've had to drain a lot of water from his lungs, but fortunately the rivers and creeks up here are pretty clean. They bottle it, you know. So I don't expect problems with infection. All the same, I want to keep him in overnight just to be sure."

Even though we all have them, Mom is first with her question. "Do you know if there's any . . . ?" but she can't finish. *Brain damage.*

Dr. Reed's smile is reassuring. "There's no permanent damage, Mrs. Thornton. He was apparently resuscitated within a safe margin of only minutes. He's a very lucky boy. It could have been a lot worse."

We sigh collectively, and there's plenty of tears, this time with intense relief.

"Would you like to see him?" Dr. Reed asks with a kind of chuckle, like she's cracked a personal joke. "He's keeping our nurses on their toes. He's wide awake, hungry, and full of energy, which is amazing considering the ordeal he's just been through."

We all laugh at this. Not because it's particularly funny, it just helps release a potent amount of stored tension. Casey is small but incredibly active. He can eat like a starved pig. It would be nothing for him to go all day without food, too busy racing and tearing around, only to find when he finally does stop, all the food in the house isn't enough to satisfy him.

Jillian turns to Mom with a warm embrace, then Dad and me. Kate stands back quietly, her eyes dewy and understanding. I'm glad for her silence, right now nothing makes sense in my head except the relief sweeping through me at Casey's good news. She knows, and I know, that soon we will talk. About the curse. Yet, I'm not looking forward to it. Maybe, just maybe, she might be right.

They leave and we go to see Casey. He's sitting up on a clinical-looking hospital bed in a room on his own. No wonder he's giving the nurses a hard time, he hates being alone. He looks in pretty good shape, considering. He's eating vanilla ice cream and when he sees us, he chucks the spoon down and starts grinning his head off.

Mom and Dad start crying again, and when they finally finish smothering him with hugs and kisses, I get my turn. I hug him and hold him tight. It's the strangest experience. Not that hugging Casey is strange. Growing up I always helped Mom look after him. I'd push his pram, rock his cradle, pick him up when he fell, and sometimes I'd just sit and watch him sleep, like I couldn't believe so much energy could look so peaceful. It always made Mom happy when I did this, like nothing could possibly happen as long as someone was watching him. And when he was older, I kept an eye out for him at school. But this feeling I've got churning inside right now is something more than just the usual protective older brother stuff. Reluctantly I pull back, and to cover my erratic emotions I smile and mess his hair.

A distinct and unshakeable feeling hits me hard in my stomach — Casey's near death is somehow my fault.

Kate

The whole town hears of Casey's accident and by sunrise, Sunday morning, a community team has been put together. Hannah arrives for breakfast, filling Jillian and me in on the details. They're not a bad lot when something's wrong, or someone's hurt. Mrs. Daniels had the Country Women's Association members baking early so the Thorntons had three hot meals delivered by 8:00 a.m. Ken Derby, who owns the local hardware store, took over a new fishing rod for Casey, to replace the one he lost in the river.

"There have been offers to clean their house and do gardening around the yard," Hannah explains. "Someone even offered to fence off the river from the back of the house."

We're sitting around the kitchen table while Jillian loads our plates with pancakes and Hannah piles on heaps of butter, maple syrup, powdered sugar, and maple syrup all over again. I smile at this, wondering where she's going to put it all as she has no stomach, and think about these people who have shown real kindness. It's one of the reasons I love living here, even though I doubt their kindness would extend as far as Jillian and me. Most people, while often browsing through the Crystal Forest, never include us in their social calendar. I'm glad for Jarrod though, it will make him feel *accepted*. It's something he deeply desires, to the point where he loses objectivity.

The front door jingles and Jillian swears under her breath. She's a mess and customers are in the room next door. "I'll go," I tell her. She turns to me with a relieved smile. I leave Hannah happily finishing off a second and third helping of pancakes, licking the maple syrup off her dripping fingers. I smile and shake my head. I know she never gets to indulge in little luxuries like pancakes and syrup at home. Food is scarcer there, has to go round more mouths, including an elderly grandparent who recently joined them. And it's not as if she's going to put on weight. Hannah is as thin as a sheet of paper.

On Sundays Jillian opens at nine. I tell her to wait another hour, but it's her busiest day. A lot of people come up from the cities for the weekends, the tourist park is full almost every weekend, except through the winter. She's making the most of it while the weather's still okay.

But it isn't a customer that's in the shop browsing. It's Jarrod. I see his bike out front.

I wait at the back of the counter and he walks toward me. "Can we talk?"

His tone is deadly serious, his eyes understandably red-streaked. He obviously hasn't slept much, yet I have this feeling it's more than Casey's accident that is giving him insomnia. "Sure, come upstairs."

We almost make it too, but the front door jingles this time with real customers, and when we turn at the sound and recognize who they are, both of us, for our own reasons, freeze.

"Jarrod!" Tasha Daniels purrs. She's followed by her favorite lap dog, Jessica Palmer. "Fancy seeing you here. I heard about your brother. I hope he's all right. Mom's been cooking since the crack of dawn. Did you get the food?"

He doesn't reply to the verbal onslaught, just gives a kind of nod and angles his body subtly so that now I have his profile and Tasha his full attention.

Jessica Palmer moves in closer, edging her "best friend" slightly behind. I think the action quite brave, especially for Jessica. Generally, she knows her place — well and truly in Tasha's shadow. Apparently she's decided Jarrod is worth the risk of upsetting Her Highness. "Ryan's throwing a fancy dress party on Saturday night, the official first day of winter. D'ya wanna come?"

So, both of them are after Jarrod. This, I decide as I grate my teeth, could prove interesting. Their jealousy could very well erupt into the catfight of the century. I hope I'm there to see it.

Tasha pouts sulkily. The image sparks a vicious thought. One thing that really annoys me is Tasha's portrayal of a blond airhead. She's not dumb. In fact, she's the most intelligent girl in the whole grade. But she acts like a bimbo, pumping out feminine charm by the bucket load. And the guys love it. I think of a spell that will make her body create a flush of testosterone. I colorfully visualize her delicate flawless cheeks disappearing beneath a layer of bristly dark facial hair. The thought makes me dizzy.

Jessica's words reluctantly return my focus and I file the idea for later experimentation. "Ryan's been throwing fancy dress parties on the first day of winter ever since I can remember."

What she doesn't say is that Ryan's annual fancy dress party has become Ashpeak's event to die for. It's a tradition his older brother started years ago, before he went off to university. Ryan invites almost everyone, including the senior grades. Nobody ever turns down an invitation. As for me, I never get one, and I've never been asked by someone who has. So, what else is new? They're always leaving me out of their parties. So what? They're just a bunch of pathetic snobs. Still, just once, I wouldn't mind going. Especially if Jarrod asked.

"Er, well, I haven't given it much thought," he says.

Tasha, completely put out by Jessica getting her invitation in first, pouts again, this time seductively, and somehow manages to step around her lap dog and still look graceful doing it. Now there is practically nothing between her own and Jarrod's body. Jarrod inches backward as Tasha forces herself forward, but his back hits the counter, where he stops. "I'm looking for something really different," she explains, giving their reason for being in the "Witch's Hut," as the Crystal Forest is generally referred to by her lot.

"Great," he says, "don't let me hold you up."

The guy is absolutely spineless. He has a natural gift, and this could strengthen his character, but because he won't acknowledge it, it lies dormant, useless to him. Only when he experiences strong emotions, does it make itself known, and from what I've seen, with catastrophic results. He's quite an anomaly—a coward, and a walking time bomb.

"So," Tasha whispers huskily, spreading bright red manicured talons across the front of Jarrod's T-shirt. "What are *you* doing here?"

It's a moment of truth. His eyes flicker to mine and back again really quickly. I can actually *feel* his inner battle. To tell Tasha the whole truth is impossible, but I guess I do hope he tells her he has come to see a friend — me. It's a hope I don't put much faith in. Why should Jarrod turn out any different from the rest of them? Be seen with *Scary Face*? That would take a lot of courage.

Still, a part of me, a *huge* part of me, really wants him to acknowledge that I'm his friend. That I'm worthy of friendship.

"Er, um, yeah well," he hesitates, stalling. "Mom's got some clothes and stuff hanging in the window. I, ah, thought I'd check out the display," he lies.

My eyes close as I bite back any sign of disappointment. The jerk. Stupid tears well up but I force them back. I'm not going to cry, especially not in front of this lot. I open my eyes and Jarrod's looking straight at me, apology written in his too wide eyes. Well, tough. Too late.

"Can I help you, girls?" Jillian suddenly appears, all cleaned up. "Are you looking for anything in particular?"

Slowly, her eyes lingering on Jarrod's reddening face, Tasha moves toward Jillian, eventually giving the woman all her attention. "I'm going to be wearing white, a full length fairy dress. I have these gorgeous silver shoes and I'm looking for a wand, and a silver mask to match, shaped like a butterfly. I'd really like some glitter but that's not a big problem, I can add that myself. . . ." She keeps going but I quickly tune out.

Turning my back on them I run out of the room. I tell myself I don't care what Jarrod thinks. Humiliating tears well up again, which I viciously fight back. I sprint past Hannah gulping orange juice at the kitchen table and go straight up to my room. She follows, wondering I guess, what's the rush. She's shaking recently washed fingers when she reaches my room. It's probably the mood I'm in 'cause I really need a friend right now. If I don't talk to someone I'll explode, or worse, cast a spell. Something I haven't tried before—changing skin color to fluorescent green.

I tell Hannah everything about Jarrod: the curse, how he has the gift with a lot of power, and my stupid, but definitely-in-the-past, fatal attraction.

"Yeah, sure," she mutters when I finish.

"Sure what?" She's lying across my bed, her head resting in her hands, her shoeless feet across my pillow, while I sit cross-legged on the floor.

"Sure you're over him," she replies sarcastically.

Stubbornly, I insist, "You bet I am!"

"So you're not going to help him get rid of this curse?"

I have to think, there's only one way I can be sure I'm over my unrealized obsession with this guy. "I don't care if his curse was brewed by the devil," I announce dramatically. "Jarrod can beg and plead and crawl on his hands and knees, clean my feet with his tongue, shake the grit from the bottom of my muddy boots, scrape the bird droppings off my windowsill, and I still won't lift a finger to help."

Stupidly, I don't realize that Hannah has left the door open. Jarrod's voice has me jumping. "What if I say I'm sorry?"

My head jerks up, going red really, really fast.

How long has he been standing there?

It doesn't help that Hannah bursts out laughing, thoroughly amused.

"Shut up, Hannah." My mood is black.

Eventually she does. "Sorry," she mumbles, but I know she isn't really. She does sit up though, and Jarrod sits beside her on my bed.

"You told Hannah everything," he says miserably, and I have the answer to my question—he'd obviously been standing there a long time.

"Do you always eavesdrop at people's bedroom doors?"

"If the conversation is interesting enough."

Hannah remains amused, trying to contain an occasional cackle, even though it's apparent the tension in the room is so thick you could grab great heaving chunks of it by the handfuls. "She's right, you know."

Jarrod glances at Hannah. "About what?"

"Everything," she replies casually. "You don't know

her, *I* do. Listen, if Kate says you're cursed, believe it. She knows about these things. If she says you're gifted, you gotta believe that, too. Accept and don't knock it. Wow, what I'd do to have the gift."

"I don't have your same faith, Hannah."

"Pity," she mumbles, stretching and rubbing her non-existent stomach. "Anyway, I gotta go now that I'm full and I've had a good laugh." She turns around at the door. "Seeing you've got company I'll see myself out. Gotta thank Jillian for the pancakes anyway. See ya."

Jarrod shakes his head as her footsteps tread lightly down the stairs. "Why did you tell Hannah everything?"

I'm not in the mood to be nice. "Why didn't you tell Tasha and Jessica you came to see *me*?"

He accepts defeat better than I would have. "I'm sorry about that. It kind of just slipped out."

"You're a jerk."

"I'll make it up to you."

His eyes are pleading. I like it so much I almost smile. "Yeah? How?"

"Anything you say. I promise."

Impulsively, for I would never do this otherwise, I say, "Take me to Ryan's party."

He doesn't say a thing, just stares with those vivid green eyes. The silence grows suffocating. For a second I almost feel sorry for him. I know I'm asking a lot. But I've said it now and refuse to take it back. Not that I would really make him go through with it. I guess I just need to test his friendship. All I want is to hear him say something like, "Yeah, sure, no problem." And mean it.

Instead, he says, "You don't really want to go, do you?"

It's hard to decide whether he just doesn't want to take me, or in some absurd way is attempting to protect me. I guess he knows that if I turn up at Ryan's party I'd find myself the center of attention, the kind of attention nobody wants. And Pecs will be there.

I shrug and look away. At least no one can call me a coward.

"If it's what you really want, I promise to take you."

I glare at him. He obviously feels indebted. Well, sucked in. Maybe I should go through with it. It would teach him a lesson—in loyalty. Instead, I mumble, "I wasn't serious, you know."

He leans forward, his voice softly menacing. "I don't like being tested, Kate." The chimes start moving, pastel colors flicker across my bedroom walls as they catch the sun through the window. His temper is simmering and I get the feeling I'm playing with explosives.

Then again, I don't scare easily. "You're just relieved you're off the hook. Of course I wouldn't dare ruin your chances with Tasha or Jessica. They'd be so disgusted, they might even kick you out of their elite little group."

"I don't care about them," he stuns me by saying.

"You lie badly."

He shrugs as if the subject actually bores him. As quickly as they started the chimes stop spinning. At least my house is safe for now. "I thought being accepted was your major goal in life."

His forehead wrinkles with worry lines. "My priorities are changing."

His dead serious tone scares me. Surely nothing else could have happened? When would it all end? I search his face and say quickly, "Has some other horror happened to your family?"

He sits thinking for a quiet moment, and my pulse leaps. When he looks up there's just weary sadness. "That's the thing, Kate. I'm afraid of what might happen next. My family's been through so much already, how much more can they take before they self-destruct?" He looks at me then with an intensity that would frighten a hardened criminal. "I never thought I'd believe in curses, but right now my head's in such a spin, I think I could believe anything."

His acknowledgment takes me so much by surprise I instantly forget about Ryan's party. I bring my knees up to my chin, wrapping my arms around them. "Are you saying you actually believe it now?"

He heaves, pushing out a long deep breath. "I don't

know what to believe. This is hard for me, Kate. I haven't had your upbringing—magic, enchantment, sorcery, they've never been topics of conversation at the dinner table."

I nod, understanding. "But you accept there might be some truth in the curse."

"At least it's an explanation. It gives a reason for all the things that have gone wrong over the years. And the strangest thing happened last night when I held Casey in my arms." He throws his head back, his eyes examining the sharply angled ceiling for a timeless few seconds. I've seen him do this before when he's trying to work something difficult out, or is deeply worried. It makes him appear vulnerable.

Finally his head lowers and he looks at me. "God, Kate, I feel responsible for what happened to Casey. Everything that's happened to my family could be *my* fault."

I consider this for a moment. "You feeling responsible could be a kind of acceptance, an inner awareness of the truth. But don't be so hard on yourself. You didn't put this curse on your family."

"But if all this curse stuff is true, Kate, what can be done about it?"

"I've been talking to Jillian. She says the ancient texts reveal there are two ways to end a sorcerer's curse."

He leans forward, his attention thoroughly focused, waiting.

"Death," I explain.

"What? Whose? *Mine?*"

"No. Apparently this type of curse will end when the instigator is put to death by the bearer."

He stares at me incredulously. "I have to kill the sorcerer?"

I nod.

We're quiet for a few moments, but Jarrod's thoughts are spinning. "You believe the purported sorcerer is an illegitimate Thornton who lived about eight hundred years ago," he says in all seriousness. "Which means he's already dead. Maybe the curse will end if *I* die."

I don't like where this conversation has detoured. I try explaining more. From Jillian's ancient witchcraft manual I start reading, "'To end the curse the bearer, or one of the descendants'"—here I glance at Jarrod—"'would have to destroy the sorcerer, if not by his own hands, by contrived means.'"

His frown increases. "That's impossible, Kate. This man's already dead."

I sigh, this is getting us nowhere. "Yeah, I know."

"Besides, I couldn't do it anyway. You know . . . kill someone. Sorry, it's just not in me. Murder." And then he adds very softly, "It'd be easier to kill myself."

I look into his face to make sure he's joking. But he's so serious I can't be sure. "Don't even think about it," I try to joke. "Your death wouldn't stop the curse appearing again in your descendants."

"But if I die before I leave descendants . . ."

I jump in quickly, "The curse would find a way."

He nods and grunts a kind of sarcastic agreement. "Like it did with me. My parents would never have had seven babies if they'd all survived. Only by their deaths did they continue to have more."

He has a point. His parents would have stopped making babies after the third or fourth and probably decided to adopt. But seventh and eighth? No way. So the curse found a way to be reignited. It actually caused all those babies' deaths. My skin tingles all over. Whoever created this curse has to have been one hell of a powerful magician. A wizard, no less, and evil at that. My mind ticks over. There has to be something we can do. I soon forget my decision not to help. "We could try a spell."

This has Jarrod's full attention, and I'm pleased. At least he isn't thinking dark thoughts now. "Yeah? You reckon?"

"It was magic that put you in this situation, maybe all we need is a little magic to get you out. Besides, you've got nothing to lose."

"What sort of spell?"

I have to think. Something effective enough to override powerful alchemy. Not an easy task centuries after the initial curse. "We'd have to go to the creek at midnight on a full moon. Luckily, that's tonight. Oh yeah, we'll need some goat's blood. Can you manage that? I'll get the fish heart. I think Jillian's still got some fresh toads."

He has a funny look on his face that spells disbelief in big bold letters.

"Humor me," I plead softly with a smile. "All you have to do is meet me by the creek in the forest, you know the place. I took you there once. A little before midnight. Oh yeah, and wear black."

"I'm afraid to ask why."

I smile. "To merge with the dark and not frighten the animals, so the forest will remain calm and in harmony with the moon. Oh, and the four essential elements. We're going to need them."

One eye narrows more so than the other, his head tilts in a disbelieving, are-you-all-there kind of look. "What about the other way?"

"What?"

"You said Jillian found two ways to end the curse. One is death to the sorcerer. What's the other? Maybe we could try that."

I bite my lower lip. It's just a childish nervous gesture. I rarely do it anymore. How do I explain the other way? Jarrod would run a thousand kilometers if I told him, laughing all the way. "Um, well," I begin tentatively, searching for the right words. Ultimately I decide against it altogether. There is just no way we could do it anyway. "It's a stupid idea. It would never work."

His shoulders lift, his mouth turns down at the edges, apparently accepting my explanation.

"It has to be the spell, Jarrod."

"I don't know, Kate. It's so . . . ridiculous."

"No, it's just a matter of courage." Testing him could become an interesting pastime. It gets to him where nothing else does. "Well, do you have the courage?"

"I know what you're doing, Kate." His tone is sour, but I can see his curiosity is starting to kick in.

"Are you in?" I goad further.

"Just tell me where to get the goat's blood, without having to kill a goat."

Jarrod

I can't believe I agreed to do this. Goat's blood, for goodness' sake. What on earth am I thinking? I've lost it.
I've completely lost it.

Well, seeing how I've already lost it, I guess there's nothing left to risk. Except perhaps the remnants of my sanity.

The house is sleeping; it's almost time to leave. But it's
so quiet, I have to climb out my window if I'm going to
sneak out without waking Mom or Dad. With a bit of luck
they might be sleeping deeply. They haven't had much of
that in the last couple of days.

I tumble bum-first out of the window, scraping my arm
against a cracked timber frame, landing with a loud thump and
whack in a pile of dry, crackly leaf residue. I glance up, glad it's
a single-story house, and rub my sore elbow. No lights go on so
at least I didn't wake anyone, or break another bone.

Outside it's already freezing, and it's only around 11:20

p.m. Just enough time I reckon to cycle to Kate's and tread through the scrub to the place by the creek where I have to meet her. She told me not to use a flashlight unless I really have to. The full moon tonight is supposed to be enough. And my senses. Rely on them, she said.

She has to be kidding. My senses are on red alert, nothing is working except fear and adrenalin. And that predicted full moon has decided it's not coming out. Who could blame it? It's not stupid.

I shouldn't be doing this.

I feel for the jar of goat's blood, tucked neatly into my shirt pocket beneath my black ribbed sweater. I groan, but only in relief, the jar is still intact. It should be after all I went through this afternoon to find some. The town vet gave me a list of farms with goats, but assured me *milk* would be easier to obtain than *blood*, then looked at me as if I weren't all there. He wasn't far wrong. Striking out on the farms, whose owners had at least enjoyed a good belly laugh at my expense, I ended up at the slaughterhouse where I had a nightmare of a time convincing the attendant it was goat's *blood* I needed for my biology assignment, and not the usual animal organs such as pig's brains, or livers or eyes. He assured me I was making a mistake, had some-how got my instructions muddled, but seeing how my little brother came so close to death recently, made an exception in the case of my sanity.

I cycle harder at the memory: At least this is something I can do without falling over. And I need to get some speed up to tackle the hills leading up to Kate's. The streets are quiet. In fact, there isn't a car or anything in sight. Which is good for me. No one will see me in this ludicrous getup—all black from my toes to my head, just as Kate ordered, except for the small red insignia of the NBA Chicago Bulls on the front of Casey's beanie. But the air is so icy, this close to winter, I decide to risk the slight oversight on Kate's instructions.

By the time I make it to Jillian's shop I'm exhausted, having walked my bike up the last steep incline. I leave it out the front and head for the rain forest track that Kate once showed me. Of course in the dark I can't find it easily and have to use my flashlight. It's hardly a track at all, and after a few minutes my heart starts thundering. If the noise my feet are making crunching the millions of dry fallen leaves doesn't alarm the forest animals, surely the sound of my thumping heart will throw out the harmony between the forest and the moon. Or whatever it was Kate said.

It turns out newly formed spiderwebs with fat juicy spiders in their centers, just waiting for easy prey like me, are my worst enemy. I keep my head buried, hands spread wide in front of me as I knock down one web after another. With every step adrenalin pumps harder, making my pulse go berserk. Sweat forms everywhere even though the temperature keeps dropping. I suddenly wonder if I'm even heading in the right direction. A seasoned bush-walker wouldn't attempt a forest walk in these conditions, at this time of night, without a compass.

These particular thoughts make me even more edgy. My breathing starts coming in rapid short bursts, exhaling smoky puffs into the chilling air. What if I end up way off course and miss the creek altogether? What if I find a gully or ravine instead? Hypothermia will set in. I could freeze to death before anyone finds me, probably in two or three days' time.

Panic sets in, destroying my nerves like acid on sugar. I'm drawn into making a decision. I can't continue. I spin around in a mad swirl, too fast. Which way is which? I become disoriented. It's at this moment I see a faint glimmer in the distance. At first I think it's a fire, but it lacks a familiar orange glow. Whatever it is, my breathing instantly slows. It has to be Kate. No one else would be out here in the middle of the night, except perhaps an axe-wielding murderer.

I grope my way toward the light, calming with every step, so that by the time I reach the spot, I have taken on a transient image of physical control.

"You made it," she says, as if she entertained some pretty realistic doubts.

I shrug, attempting to look unconcerned. If there's

one thing that hits deep, it's Kate's lack of faith in me. She thinks I'm a spineless wimp. I don't mean the accidents, she's not shallow, she's looking deeper than that—right into my soul. "Sure. Whatd'ya think? I said I'd come."

She has a wand in her hand that she points in a wide arch. "I've already cast the circle. The candles are its perimeter. You can only enter at the place directly behind me."

I go along with her, even though her words send an icy chill along my spine, and do exactly as she says. I end up sitting cross-legged opposite her. It's then I start to absorb everything around me. The creek is here, familiar and very close. I can touch the crystal water if I stretch my fingers far enough to the right. A steamy mist hovers low over its surface. It looks spooky and surreal like a scene from a fantasy movie. There are very small flames coming from heaps of white candles burning smoke-free in an odd-shaped circle surrounding us. Strangely, they don't appear to be burning down, either. On Kate's right side sits a gold box, shaped like a small treasure chest. The lid is open and inside I see a perfectly smooth pink crystal, a silver goblet, a pair of scissors, a length of blue cord, and a few other oddities. My eyes feel huge in my head and I decide not to investigate anymore. There is a putrid smell coming from somewhere. I really don't want to ask about it. Yet, it is the light that is strangest of all. Other than the small flames burning around us there seems to be no other light source, but the entire area, like a dome, is filled with a strange white light, as if the very air is glowing.

She sees the wonder on my face. "It's just a bit of magic Jillian taught me," she says softly, her voice smooth and melodious. I envy her calmness. It makes me feel more gutless than ever.

"Do you like it?"

What does she want me to say? "Er, yeah," I stumble. "How . . . ?"

She merely smiles. "It's complicated, and I'm not sure you're ready to hear it. Einstein would love it though."

I have to be content with that, though I want to ask more. I start relaxing a little at the evidence of her magic, and start to hope. If Kate can do this thing with the light, and there truly is a curse on my family, perhaps she can solve my problems after all.

"Are you ready, Jarrod? It's almost midnight."

I nod slightly. "Yeah, I guess."

She smiles again, and I start to unwind, my pulse finally slowing down to something resembling normal. She's in her element, totally in control. Some of it brushes off on me. "You will have to remove the beanie, and strip down to your jeans."

My head shoots forward, eyes the size of eggs. *"Strip?"*

"Not everything!" She laughs. "Just the top part."

My face forms a smirk. "I didn't mean that. It's just, well . . . it's like two degrees out here."

She frowns and looks puzzled. "Are you cold?"

Her question, issued as a challenge, has me reassessing the situation quickly. I realize our breath isn't steaming anymore, and my fingers aren't numb. Even my toes are comfortable now. I touch the skin on my face. Amazingly, it's not icy cold as it was only moments earlier, but warm. I look at her, intently. "How did you do this?"

"I didn't really. I have no effect on the weather, though I've tried lots of times. It's the light that's generating a little heat, enough at least to take the chill out of the air."

"Wow," is all I can say. My mouth is a desert.

"Did you bring the blood?"

This brings back my attention quickly. I reach into my shirt pocket with a bit of a smirk, remembering the embarrassing afternoon chase, and withdraw the half-filled jar, all the attendant would give me. I hope it's enough.

"Excellent," she says, relieving my fears.

"What are you going to do with it?"

She reaches behind herself and drags round the source of the putrid smell—a small bowl with something squishy and brown and slimy inside. Carefully, she pours the goat's blood over the top of the foul-smelling mixture and stirs it with a plastic spoon. "Jillian's vision of snakes circling your body means that evil spirits surround you. You know," she remarks in an offhand manner, "you probably carry them with you all the time. Snakes are just their mortal form."

Exactly what I want to hear.

"The odor produced by the goat's blood mixed with fish heart, liver, and toad's entrails is supposed to," she adds softly, leaning forward, "*hopefully,* get rid of them. At least long enough for our magic to work. It's a temporary tactic, but if the spell works tonight, it might help get rid of the snakes on a more permanent basis."

"Really?" is all I can manage. Vivid images of snakes circling my body suddenly make my skin crawl as if these fictitious snakes are real. I lived on this farm about six years ago that used to be a horse stud before Dad decided to try his hand at growing turf. It was twenty-two hectares of prime river flats. We saw the first snake the day we moved in. By the end of the week, we were ready to move out. They came up from the river as if they were drawn to us. Must've been the dry spell, the neighbors told us, that lured them to the farmhouse. We took a huge loss on that place, couldn't sell it fast enough, especially after I woke up with three snakes in my bed, and had threatened to never sleep again. Just thinking about the memory can still spook me. That impulse to run starts thumping away inside again.

Kate finishes stirring and lays the stick down beside

the bowl, which she pushes just a little out of reach, but still within the circle of flames. At least now it's a little easier to live with. "Relax," she says softly. "I won't hurt you, Jarrod." Her eyes, now brilliant sapphires, hold mine in a kind of promise. "Ever."

I'm glad to hear it. "What now?"

"I'm going to cleanse you." Her words stun me.

One eye narrows as I try to absorb this bit of information, recalling her request that I strip down to my jeans. "Excuse me?"

"Of all evil."

The curse, of course. Was I really thinking she meant a sponge bath? As entertaining as that would probably be in a cozy environment, the thought of it out here in the middle of the night is somehow a lot less exciting. "How?" I ask quickly to hide my embarrassment.

"With the help of the elements—earth, air, water, and fire."

Is she serious? The words sound like dialogue from a cheap-thrills horror movie. "You've been watching too much television."

Her reply is straight to the point. "We don't own one."

"Okay, then tell me this. How are you going to get these four elements to help you? Ask them nicely?"

She stares at me with slits for eyes. She's mad

as hell and I can't hold her stare. "Sorry," I mutter.

"This isn't going to work without some cooperation from you, Jarrod. Sarcasm won't do anything except cause a block. A cleansing spell is far from easy."

"I said I was sorry."

"All right then." She's still angry and I really am sorry now. I remember she's doing this thing for me. "Try not to question everything, just flow with me. Okay?"

I nod, contrite.

And then she says, "Now take off your beanie, sweater, and anything else under there."

My nerves are jumping but I do what I'm told, laying the clothes down in a small pile by my side. Heat floods my face as I feel her gaze on me. Though far from naked, I may as well be, the way I'm feeling right now. I feel like a scrawny bag of bones. I try to look anywhere but at Kate. She's doing something with her hands, and I recognize with an odd sensation in my gut that they're raised in prayer. She's speaking too, but it's not to me. Her head is tilted backward, and I can't distinguish her words. After a few seconds of this she shifts into a kneeling position and grabs her scissors, taking them toward my head.

"Hey, wait a minute. What are you planning with those?"

Her voice is amazingly calm, if anything, kind of flat, as if she's entered a trance. "I need your hair."

"Hair!" I lift up on my haunches, ready to run somewhere, anywhere, quickly. This little charade is going too far.

But she's smiling at me gently. "Not all your hair, just a few strands, that's all."

She snips quickly, in case I change my mind, then wraps a length of blue cord around the little bundle. "This might smell a bit." She holds the bundle over a candle on her left and starts reciting again, this time a rhyming chant.

Personally I don't think anything can smell worse than the goat's blood concoction. The wrapped hair sizzles as it curls up and disintegrates in the yellow flame. When it's all gone I look up at Kate. She seems ethereal in the way her still vivid blue eyes reflect the candle flames, a soft breeze gently tugging and playing with wisps of her long black hair. Right now Kate actually does look like a witch even with those light, unusually shaped eyes; all that is missing is the legendary broomstick.

Her eyes lift to mine. "You're not going to like this next part," she says softly.

My pulse takes a flying leap.

With the goblet she scoops up some moist dark earth. "Breathe slowly and deeply from way down in here." Her hand touches my stomach just above my navel. It's firm, yet soft and comfortably warm, and it takes all my concentration to do what she asks this time. Her hand, her eerily flat voice and glazed eyes, are doing strange things to my level of concentration. I try hard not to let my emotions show as Kate is good at sensing moods and feelings. Eventually I got the hang of breathing deeply from my abdomen. She allows her hand to move up and down with my breaths a few times before she raises it and slowly tips the cup of moist earth over my head. Using a circular motion she then starts rubbing the dirt into my scalp, forehead, and chest with her fingers. As she does this she repeats that same rhyming chant.

My eyes close in a feeble attempt at self-protection as dust and tiny gravelly bits of rotted leaves and stuff try forcing their way into my eyes and mouth. I wish now I'd remembered my glasses.

When I open my eyes Kate is smiling. "You're doing really well."

I nod but the motion causes more dirt and grit to fall out of my hair. "You're really enjoying this, aren't you?"

She laughs a little, and I'm glad to see the glaze that shrouded her eyes a few minutes ago has disappeared. She looks normal again. Well, as normal as Kate is going to get, I guess. "There's just one thing left," she says, and reaches out to the creek, giving her fingers a quick clean. Then, with both hands cupped, she scoops up a handful of water and holds it dripping a bit toward my face.

She doesn't need to say anything, I know she means

for me to drink, but the thought alone of sipping water out of her cupped hands does strange things to my anatomy. The gesture crosses some sort of invisible line. That line known as intimacy.

She nods at the water trapped in her hands. "C'mon, what are you waiting for?"

I watch as drips seep through tiny wedges of space between her fingers. Trying hard not to let any of my feelings show, I lean forward and start drinking. I don't dare look at her as she would know instantly how she has affected me. When there is none left I drag in a long hard breath and sit back on my heels. I glance up and see Kate's mouth moving with whisper-soft words, her body gently swaying backward and forward. Shivers ride over me in waves as a strange heat suddenly fills me from feet to head. In an instant it passes, leaving me breathless.

Kate sighs softly, then smiles. "Feel all right?"

"A little strange, but it's passing."

"Good. We're done." Briskly, she starts tidying up, collecting her scissors and other bits and pieces into her treasure chest. "We have to leave the circle as we entered," she says. We do this and Kate puts out the candles. With the plastic cup, she makes a shallow grave, burying the stinking concoction of goat's blood, fish heart, liver, and toad's entrails. "You can get dressed now, it'll quickly turn cold."

As she says this the glow surrounding us becomes less

and less until it disappears completely. The cowardly moon finally makes an appearance now that it's all over. I catch a glimpse of it through the forest canopy, the little light it's giving helps me locate exactly where I put my clothes. The air becomes chillier, and after giving my head a quick shake and brushing dirt off my face and chest, I throw on my clothes, beanie included. "So that's it?" I ask, climbing to my feet, still wiping dirt off my forehead.

"That's it," she repeats.

I rummage in my jeans pocket for my flashlight. It's a relief when I find it and switch it on. "So what happens now?"

We start walking toward the road. At least I assume we're heading in the right direction. Personally I have no idea, but Kate seems sure of herself, so I follow close behind. "Wait and see, I guess," she says.

She doesn't sound too confident. "How long will it take, you reckon?"

"*If* the spell worked, then the curse should lift pretty much straightaway."

"All right then!" I allow a little excitement. Maybe this whole crazy night will have been worth the adrenalin rush, among other things. "But how will I know if the curse has been lifted?"

"That's pretty obvious," she replies. "You won't be so clumsy anymore and your family will have a break from their endless list of disasters."

We come to the road and Kate walks me to my bike. There's a lot more light now as clouds roll off, exposing a brilliant full moon. I switch off the flashlight. The miniature treasure chest is under her arm, and it reminds me of what we've just done. I suddenly feel awkward. How do I thank a witch for casting a spell that might lift a timeless family curse?

"Look," I begin tentatively. "What happened tonight, I, er, well . . . Thanks, for your help."

She smiles and looks brilliant. "It mightn't work, you know. I'm only a novice, and the sorcerer who created this curse must've been a powerful alchemist." She briefly looks away. Then adds softly, "You have to remember it wasn't *Old Magic*, Jarrod."

"So?"

"We're dealing with a curse generated by magic that lived almost a thousand years ago. There was a sense of things, then, an intensity. It's different today, far too commercialized. It's caused a . . . well, kind of weakness. Jillian can work *Old Magic*, but there aren't many like her. It's a rare few that can handle it."

"Well anyway, you tried and went to a lot of trouble for my sake."

She shrugs. "That's okay. I don't get to practice powerful spells very often. There aren't enough volunteers around here. Except for Hannah, and well, some spells are too dangerous to try on your best friend."

She's joking, and I know this because her eyes are laughing as she speaks, but it makes me realize just how seriously Kate is into this stuff. Magic, sorcery, witchcraft. I still have my doubts, but have to admit, Kate does have some eerie talents, like making the light out of the darkness, and the candles with flames that never burn down. Now that my brain is functioning normally again, I wonder how she managed these tricks.

I shine the flashlight at my watch but can't read the digits.

"It's four a.m.," she says.

This leaves me stunned. Have we really been in the forest four hours? "I gotta go," I say. "It's late."

"Yeah, I guess you'd better go."

She sounds reluctant, mirroring my feelings exactly. Even though the temperature out here has to have fallen to minus five by now, I'm in no hurry to leave. I could stand here for the rest of the night as long as I'm with Kate. This realization hits me like a sledgehammer. I make myself move and get on my bike before I make a fool of myself. "See ya, and thanks again."

She nods but her smile is slow. Her face is momentarily like an open book. She's wondering if I'm going to pretend she doesn't exist in class on Monday. I give a quick wave and start cycling, visualizing Tasha and Jessica, Pecs, Ryan, and Pete. There's a comfort in the vision, knowing they've accepted me into their group. The pull is strong.

I wish I wasn't such a coward. I hate myself. The thought occurs to me that Kate deserves better. She's strong, stronger than me. She's talented and beautiful, both in utterly unique ways. It makes her different and for that she is crucified mercilessly by the inner, elite crowd, ignored by others.

And me?

Well . . . I can't say I'm any better.

Kate

It doesn't work. The spell meant to lift that blasted curse. I realize first thing Monday morning when Jarrod turns up late for class, explaining to Mr. Dyson in History that he ran over an empty beer bottle, puncturing his bike tire. He backtracked home so his mother could drive him in, but the car wouldn't start for seemingly no reason.

"This morning was the heaviest frost so far," Mr. Dyson explains. He's not angry or anything, which is good for Jarrod, who looks flustered enough already. "Tell your parents to put an antifreeze in your car's radiator, it was probably just cold. All indications point to this year being a record cold winter."

I don't think Jarrod realizes the spell has failed until much later in the day during a practical PE lesson. We're doing gymnastics and the boys have to form a pyramid with their bodies. Jarrod, not largely built like Pecs or some of the others, misses out on the ground level. After a lot of huffing and macho snorts Pecs settles down, and the bottom row is ready. Callum and Todd climb on next, leaving the inside position for Jarrod. As he starts to climb I hear a few snickers. It's not nasty stuff, just Jarrod's reputation preceding him. He's clumsy, and everyone knows it. He's continually misplacing things and tripping himself up. He's not wearing his glasses now, but it would make no difference even if he was.

He's on top of Pecs's and Ryan's backs and he's looking good so far. The class starts cheering and whistling. He buries his head with an embarrassed smile. Ms. Milan tells everyone to quiet down, but she's laughing a little herself. It's good-natured and the atmosphere in the gym is relaxed.

Ben Moffat is the smallest sixteen-year-old boy I'll probably ever meet. He had leukemia when he was a kid in second grade, and the chemo and radiation treatment slowed his growth. For all that he's small, he's physically fit, and it's no effort for him to climb up to the first level. It's only when he tries to balance on top of Jarrod and Todd that Jarrod somehow loses his balance. One knee drops, which causes him to tilt sharply sideways. Ben Moffat hurtles backward, the pyramid collapsing in a domino effect, and Ben nearly drowns under a mass of human flesh. Ms. Milan is quick to pull and push until she gets to him. She's pretty sure his ankle is only sprained, but she wants an X ray just in case. Her main concern is the possibility of a cracked rib.

She lays blame nowhere, but Jarrod's apologizing anyway. Ms. Milan sends someone to the office for help, dismissing the rest of us to the changing rooms.

Jarrod's still sprawled on the heavy blue mats, his head buried in his hands. He looks up slowly and catches my eye. There's recognition in his look and bitter disappointment. I smile and shrug. At least we tried. But he looks so depressed I feel like saying something comforting. Of course I don't. Goodness knows how he might react with the others looking on. Until just then, he hadn't acknowledged me in any way.

Tasha doesn't hesitate though. She rushes to him and helps him up. He smiles and thanks her. My teeth gnash together. The whole sickening scene spoils the rest of the day.

Later, Jarrod catches up with me just outside the school grounds. We walk in silence for a while, heading home, but there isn't a second I'm not aware of him. He makes me tense, and even though I promised myself I wouldn't do it again, I just have to know what he's feeling inside. So I probe, very carefully, into his mind.

Surprisingly there's no resistance this time, and stranger still, I sense the walls aren't there because that's how he wants it. There's disappointment I realize, deep concern, and confusion too. There's a lot of doubt and I gather from this his belief in magic has shrunk even further. The spell has only made things worse.

He knows I'm in there yet he doesn't stop me. It's as if he wants me to sense his mood, understand what he's feeling. It's easier for him this way, rather than have to find words to explain himself. And this makes me angry. I can't believe he lacks the courage to air his own feelings. What's the matter with him?

The tension grows so thick I just have to say something or explode. "I'm sorry," I mutter grumpily. "About the curse, and the spell that didn't work." He shrugs as if he doesn't care, which is a cover-up for his real feelings, and this makes me angrier still. "It's not the end of the world, for heaven's sake!"

He shifts his backpack, reaching in for a bottle of water. "What do you suggest now?" He takes a long guzzle. "Should we sacrifice a virgin? What if you make me *bathe* in the water and *eat* the dirt? Or should we shave off my hair and feed it to a goat?"

"You don't have to be a complete idiot."

He groans loudly in self-disgust, snatching his drink bottle with his other hand. "I know, Kate. I'm sorry. None of this is your fault."

His switch to self-pity is absolutely sickening. I hate

this part of him. I have to snap him out of it somehow. "Wake up, Jarrod, it's not your fault either!"

He doesn't believe me. Since acknowledging the possibility of a curse he's planted the entire worry of his family's troubles on his own shoulders, taken responsibility personally for all that afflicts them, past and present.

"Jarrod, listen to me." We reach the fork in the road. From here Jarrod takes the asphalt track west to his place about a kilometer away. I know where he's staying—the old Wilson homestead. Vic Wilson died about five months back, leaving his estate to his solicitor son, Stephen, who lives in Sydney. Stephen never intended returning to Ashpeak, so decided to lease the place. It's rundown, but not uninhabitable. "There's a couple more things we can try."

"Another magic spell, Kate?"

I wish he would kill his black, self-absorbed mood. "No, you idiot. Jillian's got an idea, but it's a bit farfetched even for me. So we won't consider that an option at this stage." With a bit of manipulating, hopefully, we would *never* need to consider it.

"So what's the other idea?"

"You."

He gives me this disbelieving look again. I'll never get used to it. Why can't he just accept? "Like how?"

"Your *powers* of course. When are you going to admit that I may be right about this?"

He grunts and spins toward the road that leads to his place. "Kate, for God's sake, leave it alone."

I grab his arm and yank hard. "No, I won't. Look, not everything fits neatly into your simple book of rules. There are things in life that cannot be explained. The paranormal is only one example. With the help of your gift, Jarrod, we might just be able to fight this thing."

"You're confused, Kate. I don't have any "gift." The things that happen to me, if anything—and I can't believe I'm actually saying this—are caused by that stupid curse, not from any unrealized supernatural powers."

"No, Jarrod, you're wrong. Sure, the accidents and misfortune, broken bones, clumsiness, they're from the curse, I'm almost certain. But the storms, sudden winds, *earthquake*! *You* are the one causing those."

He's quiet and hopefully thinking about what I said. Using his powers is our only way really. Jillian's idea won't work. It *can't* work. Besides, the mere concept is outrageous, and would only make Jarrod positive we're both ready for a spell in a psychiatric center.

But he only shrugs and slips his empty water bottle into his backpack's side pocket. "What's the other way? Jillian's idea? The one she read about in that ancient manual."

I stare at him but can't find the words.

"What is it, Kate?"

Frustration has me seething. I spin away, toward home. "Forget it. You don't want to know."

"I asked, didn't I?" he calls into the distance I place between us.

My wave is half-hearted. "Go home, Jarrod."

He doesn't. Instead he jogs up beside me. I glare at him. "What do you think you're doing?"

"Well, if you won't tell me the other way, I'll ask Jillian myself."

I groan, instantly regretting opening my big mouth. Ever since Jillian read the ancient texts, she's been in a spin putting her idea into practice. Other than essentials, she's been doing little else except running around in a mad frenzy making preparations, even to the extent of whipping up handmade original clothing right down to authentic leather boots. I shudder just at the thought. If Jarrod discovers what Jillian's plan is he'd only laugh, and I'm not confident he would keep it to himself. I can't trust him. The way gossip spreads up here, the whole town could be laughing by midnight. If he asks Jillian, she'll tell him. It's as simple as that.

I have a lot of faith in Jillian. I've seen what she can do. As a healer, especially of animals, she's brilliant. She knows her herbs, but it's much more than that. There's power in her body. There's power in her mind. She draws deeply from her ancestral heritage. She can transcend to a different level, and it's there her magic is unearthly.

But this thing she's talking about is different. It doesn't fit into any category: preternatural or the norm.

"Listen," I begin. "Jillian's idea is a bit, well, over the top."

"So, what else is new?"

I scowl at him long and hard, have to force myself not to chant the words of a nasty spell. Recalling the vision of his hairless exposed chest last night, sprouting excessive thick and curly body hair sounds like a good idea. I restrain myself, only just. "Listen," I try again, gritting my teeth. "You know what people think around here. If I tell you Jillian's plan, how can I be sure you won't go spreading it across the mountain?"

He looks seriously offended, and stops walking. "What do you think I am? For heaven's sake, Kate, I wouldn't do that. I like Jillian. I wouldn't do anything to hurt her."

As we start walking again I mumble half to myself, "I'll hold you to that."

"What did you say?"

I start biting on my lower lip again, then stop myself. "Look, I don't want Jillian hurt. She means everything to me. Do you understand, Jarrod?"

He nods but remains quiet.

I stare at our dusty shoes. "She's more than just my grandmother. She . . . she loves me."

"I can see that," he says softly.

There's more I need to say, I just don't know how. "She didn't . . ."

"What is it, Kate?"

"She didn't abandon me, all right?" I hope this is enough. We walk the rest of the way in silence.

It turns out Jillian isn't home, the Crystal Forest temporarily closed, the sign reads. I take Jarrod round the back through the herb garden, under the bare wisteria vines that weave through the back veranda. Once there I hunt for the key I know is here somewhere. Jillian is mostly always home. I guess her absence now is related to her plan. She locks up only because of the valuable pieces, crystals, and irreplaceable antique books and equipment in her room, not for anything she has in her shop, that's mostly costume stuff, for tourists.

At last I find the key, but Jarrod is sitting on a stone pillar at the edge of the veranda that backs on to the rain forest, watching the currawongs, bower birds, and brush turkeys come to feed on the scraps Jillian put out earlier. Jillian loves the forest too. Our backyard is the forest, a place where birds know they can always find food, water, and a safe haven.

He looks so comfortable, at peace with himself for a change, I don't want to spoil the image with Jillian's far-fetched scheme. I pull up a pinewood garden stool and sit quietly opposite him, enjoying the play of afternoon sun on the giant buttressed trees, palms, ferns, and eucalyptus that make up the vast majority of forest up here.

"You're so lucky to have this, Kate," he says softly.

"I know."

He drags his eyes away from the array of bird life spread out before him and locks into mine. "Your self-assurance scares me."

"That's only because you don't have any."

"I admit it, I'm a gutless coward. You deserve so much better."

This last statement surprises me. It sounds as if he's thought about, perhaps even considered me a prospective girlfriend. I feel empathy for him, but his self-pity is still disgusting. "If you accepted the gift, Jarrod, your self-confidence would improve like out of this world."

His expression changes from awe to exasperation. "You're not going to start on that again, are you?"

I almost stomp my feet, the frustration is so real. "If only there was some way to prove it to you. I could make you angry enough to spark that temper of yours, but because you don't know how to handle your strength, your mind triggers some sort of catatonic trance and you don't remember very much. So there's no point in destroying my home and Jillian's livelihood just to prove a point you might easily brush off with one of your ridiculous explanations."

"We know this is a dead end conversation, Kate, so tell me Jillian's idea."

"It's crazy." I'm totally honest.

"Okay, so what is it?"

I can't look at him. I don't want to see the smirk I know will follow, so I pretend fascination in the squawking currawongs arguing over a few remaining food scraps. "To stop the curse from being affixed on your family in the first place." I flick him a quick glance. His eyes are narrow, his elbows resting on his knees. He leans forward, hanging on my every word.

"Jillian thinks the curse has created a link so strong it surpasses time and space and matter. She thinks she can generate a spell that will physically forge you back to the time and place the curse was first created. Or near enough." I choose to use simple language so he will grasp the idea quickly and I won't need to repeat myself with long explanations. I also rush this before I lose my nerve. "Simply put, Jillian believes she can take you back in time and place. Back to Britain during the Middle Ages, to that same spot up near the border of Scotland where the first family in your father's heritage book lived."

He stares at me, a funny little crooked smile playing around his lips as if he wants to ask something but wouldn't dare in case it encourages insanity. Sometimes it's there, and a hint of a dimple appears in one cheek to complement the hint of cleft in his chin, then it disappears as his eyes roll upward. "Swing it past me again, will you?"

He doesn't believe me. Well, what a surprise. *I* don't even believe it's possible, and I've witnessed Jillian do amazing things. I groan. "That first family listed as your ancestors is littered with controversy—deceit, abduction, illegitimacy— you name it. Even sorcery. It has to be through them the curse originated. Jillian thinks so too. She's been studying your heritage book day and night."

Jarrod's finger leans toward me, bouncing back and forth in midair. "Not that part." He sounds as if he's talking to a stupid child. "The other bit. The *insane* part about time and space and matter."

I'm not going to repeat what he obviously takes for lunacy. Even though I don't believe in Jillian's theory myself, I take the defensive immediately. "How do you know it's insane? What better ideas have you come up with other than suicide? Are you always so ungrateful when people are just trying to help?"

"Don't get heavy with me, Kate. Do you know how ridiculous you sound? No wonder you're worried about what people might think. But don't worry that I might tell someone, 'cause I know that if I did they'd arrange beds for you and Jillian at the nearest psychiatric hospital."

It's such a nasty thing to say I want to hit him. "You're a jerk."

"Yeah, well explain to me how Jillian's going to perform this miraculous feat? Her theory does include a return journey, doesn't it? Or what would be the point?"

"I'd be wasting my breath."

He shrugs. "Have it your way."

"Look, you don't understand. Jillian's got the gift too. She comes from a long line. And it's *Old Magic*, Jarrod. It's different. It's powerful."

"Just tell me the plan, Kate. I can make up my own mind."

I decide, against my better judgment, to take the chance. What the heck? Things couldn't get any worse. He already thinks Jillian and I are crazy, what more damage can I do? Just maybe, and I cling to this hope, with a little more explaining he might start to believe. . . . "It's got to do with the forest."

"How?"

"Links."

"I don't understand."

"Jillian believes you're linked to the past through the curse. And because the curse is still active, still working through you, taking you back would be easy. The difficulty is returning you."

He nods at this, so I continue explaining enough, without going into every detail. "She's working on an amulet that has the ingredients that will link you to the forest.

Her magic, old as time itself, will take you back; the amulet, with its strong link to the forest, is supposed to return you."

"What's in this amulet?"

"It's something to do with the trees—the oldest and newest." I'm losing him again, it's in his doubting expression, so I sum up quickly. "It doesn't matter how she does it, all you have to do is trust."

He laughs at this. "You don't believe her, so why should I?"

He has me there. My teeth dig into my lip again as I try to think of a plausible reply.

He scoffs. "Don't bother. I really don't want to hear it. Actually, I don't want to hear another crazy word."

I don't get the chance to retaliate as I hear Jillian's car drive into the garage. We're both quiet while Jillian lets herself in through the shop front. She starts singing a Scottish tune. I wonder where she picked this up. "Jillian's home," I mumble, even though I know he knows. Suddenly, I wish I was anywhere else but here, even Pecs's bedroom would be better at this moment. "I hope you can at least be civil," I grind out between gnashing teeth.

She comes practically flying through the back door, her hands full of bits of crumbled bread mixed with wild bird seed. We have to duck low as bits of food fly toward us. She sees us too late. "Oops, where did you two come from?" The surprise has her miscalculating her aim, and the seed and bread crumbs come tumbling down over the top of us instead of her original aim of the backyard. "Oh, sorry. Look what I've done. You'd better brush that off before you come inside or the birds will follow you."

I believe this easily as I've seen a variety of wild birds on occasion trying to get through the door.

We stand and brush seeds and bread bits out of our hair and clothes. "It's all right, Jillian," Jarrod says softly. "No harm's done."

I glance swiftly at him, quietly impressed. He really does like Jillian. He has himself completely under control.

"Come on then, the least I can do is fix you a drink."

We follow her into the kitchen and sit around the table while Jillian pours three glasses of iced water, carves up a fresh green lime, and squirts a little juice in each drink. As she does this the tension in the room keeps mounting with long awkward silences. Jillian asks Jarrod how Casey is, and how long before his brother will be returning to school.

Jarrod politely replies but I can see, and feel, he's uncomfortable. He'd rather be anywhere right now than sitting here pretending politeness.

It doesn't take Jillian long to comprehend. Her fingers slide all the way round her glass, while her eyes lift and settle quietly on Jarrod's frowning face. "I see Kate has told you my theory."

He swallows, hard. I watch his Adam's apple bob deeply up then down. I wonder if he can maintain the calm, polite facade much longer. "I don't believe it's possible, Jillian," he says.

At least he didn't call her a crazy mad woman.

She smiles, nods her head understandingly. "You don't believe in very much, do you, Jarrod?"

He takes the defensive. "Look, I believe Kate has certain talents. Some things are undeniable. I feel her in my head sometimes—"

Jillian shoots me a reprimanding look. "Kate, you haven't. I thought I taught you better than that."

"Sorry, Jillian," I mutter.

"That's intrusive, darling."

"I know. I don't do it often. Really, I don't," I add at her disbelieving look.

"It's all right, Jillian," Jarrod says quietly. "Most of the time I don't mind. It doesn't hurt or anything. I can block her out if I want to."

"Really?" Jillian queries. "That's impressive, Jarrod. Most people can't detect she's even there, let alone forge a block against the intrusion."

Jarrod's lips shut tightly. He looks annoyed, probably thinks he's been manipulated into an admission of some sort. The water and juice in our glasses starts fizzing furiously. Jillian notices and slips me an interesting look.

"Don't you start too, Jillian. I've explained to Kate she's on the wrong track about this gift rubbish."

"You don't have to get nasty, Jarrod," I snap.

He stands and his chair falls backward, hitting the timber floor with a loud crash. "Look, I've had it, okay. So forget your . . . your crazy plans. I'm out of here." He turns and rights his chair, then looks for my eyes. When he finds them he says slowly, making sure I understand the meaning behind every word, "I've gone along with your theories, Kate. Hell, I even started believing them. And now my head's all messed up." He drives a hand roughly through his hair. "But this time travel stuff, it crosses a line with me. I want nothing to do with it. I'm leaving now, and I'm not coming back, Kate. *Never!*"

His words hurt. The thought of Jarrod not ever talking to me again, or coming over and doing stuff together, rips into me. He has no need for specifics, I understand what he's telling me clearly enough: If I approach him, he will ignore me, pretend we're strangers. I want to hate him. I want to cry. But Jillian is watching and I feel sympathy pouring out—a thing I despise. So I just say quietly while my voice is still under some form of control, "That's fine with me. You know your way out."

He turns and leaves.

The second the front door tingles shut, the water and juice in all three glasses fizzes over the sides and spills onto the tablecloth.

Kate

The next day Jarrod misses school. I don't know what to make of this, just hope nothing else has happened. At first I try to tell myself I don't care, but as the day progresses a dreadful sense of foreboding kicks in that no amount of mental distraction can shake. By the end of the day the feeling of impending doom is so real I can't concentrate. I feel wasted. Even Hannah is steering clear.

Walking home I come to the fork in the road and fight the temptation to take the asphalt track to Jarrod's. After all, I could be dead wrong and Jarrod could simply have missed school for any number of insignificant reasons. Maybe he's got a cold, or a headache, or goodness knows what. If I turn up at his front door and nothing tragic's happened, I will look like a complete idiot, or worse—he'll think I'm obsessed. His message yesterday was humiliatingly clear—*Stay out of my life!*

So I trudge home and decide to check with Jillian to see if she's heard anything.

She hasn't, but says she's been thinking of Jarrod and his family all day too, harboring a strong sense of prophetic gloom. She tries to put it down to the unpleasant scene in the kitchen yesterday but admits she doesn't often get such strong feelings.

There is nothing we can do, so Jillian finishes off the medieval garments she's been working on, deciding to make a shop front display out of them. "Someone might want them for the fancy dress party coming up."

"Good idea," I mutter, but can't work up much enthusiasm, not the way I'm feeling.

While Jillian finishes stitching, I prepare the evening meal of vegetable pasta. Both Jillian and I are vegetarians. We eat a lot of salads, but today has been our coldest day so far this year and preparing all the vegetables gives me something to do, anything to take my mind off Jarrod.

I almost phone him several times but can't go through with it in the end. He doesn't want me in his life. I have to accept this. Just after nine I talk Jillian into phoning. It will be all right coming from her. All she has to do is inquire into Casey's recovery.

Jillian phones but no one answers.

"Please, Jillian, let it ring out this time."

"I did, Kate. There's no one home."

"At this time of night?"

Jillian glances at the white-faced digital clock on the wall. "It's only nine twenty, darling. Maybe they went to the theater."

"It's not Friday."

She pats my shoulder comfortingly and starts clearing dishes.

"I'll do it," I say irritably, needing something else mundane and laborious to fill in time.

Washing dishes for two takes a whole twelve minutes, even after scrubbing the bench top three times. There is nothing left but to go to bed. Homework doesn't even come into it, I couldn't concentrate anyway. I say good night to Jillian and go to my room.

I hear the thumps on the shop front door just as I make it to the top of the stairs. I tear back down, calling out to Jillian as I go, "I'll get it!"

It has to be Jarrod, I just know it. So I yank open the door, my heart thudding somewhere in the vicinity of my tonsils. When I see him, he looks so distraught, I can't help but scream a kind of strangled gasp. It's as if he's been to hell and couldn't find his way back, except via a sewer system. "Jarrod, what happened?"

He can hardly speak, his eyes sunken half into his skull, vicious dark circles surrounding them, his skin ashen gray. He doesn't say much, except, "Dad tried to kill himself."

"Oh, God, is he . . . ?"

"In the hospital."

I drag him out of the freezing cold. He's shivering and damp all over. He didn't even bother to grab a jacket. In this weather it's unthinkable. "How?"

"Overdosed on antidepressants."

I remember Jarrod telling me once how depressed his father's been, especially since the accident, and how his depression sparked the idea to move to Ashpeak—an attempt to lift his spirits, rejuvenate him. "I'm so sorry. What do the doctors say?"

His chest heaves. "He'll be okay. But he has to have therapy. They're worried he might try it again. They're talking of institutionalizing him."

Unconsciously, my mouth drops open. If this happens it will be very hard on them all. They're such a close-knit family. They've been through so much already. I dread to think, emotionally, what this new problem will do to them. "How's your mom coping?"

"She's hanging in. It's all she's ever done. It's not fair, Kate. Why?"

I don't think it's an appropriate time to start spouting curses to him, so I just shrug and offer a lame smile. "Come and sit by the heater." We have one of those glass-encased wood burners in the living room. They're great up here, heat spreads through the entire house, right up to my bedroom, even on really cold nights like this one.

But he doesn't move. His head falls back, his eyes slide shut as he gulps in huge raking breaths. I wait silently while he attempts to pull himself together. When he does, he looks at me, his head tilted, and says, "I want a shot at Jillian's plan."

My stomach does a funny sort of somersault. "Sure," I tentatively agree, suddenly very nervous. Jarrod looks desperate. What if Jillian's plan doesn't work? Chances are it won't. Logic suggests it won't. *I* don't think it's possible to go back in time and place. How disappointed will Jarrod be then? "Sure," I repeat, stalling for time.

I become aware of Jillian, waiting silently nearby. Now she steps toward us. "I'm sorry, Jarrod, about your father."

He nods, acknowledging Jillian's sympathy. Then, "When can we do it?"

He means Jillian's plan, but taking one look at Jarrod's distressed state has my nerves jumping again. If it does work, it could turn out a harrowing event. We haven't even talked about the details, what can go wrong, what to do when we get there. If we get there.

'Tonight all right?" Jarrod asks.

I glance at Jillian. "Look at his condition, Jillian. Wouldn't he need his strength about him for this sort of thing?"

Jillian's face distorts as she thinks about this. "Strength is certainly important, Kate, but so are emotions, and Jarrod's are highly charged right now. In this state he's probably psychologically more accepting."

"What are you saying? That we should do this thing now?"

"Well, I have everything prepared."

I stare at them both in turn. Things are happening too fast. Surely more thought has to go into this decision.

"I'm ready, Jillian," Jarrod says softly. His deep green eyes find mine, remaining steady, determined, challenging, as if defying my idea of him being a spineless gutless wonder.

"I'll let your mother know you're staying the night."

Jillian goes to phone Mrs. Thornton, and I grab the moment to explain that I think he should wait a few days, one at least. But Jarrod rejects every point I make. Even suggesting his mother needs him at home while his father is ill in the hospital makes no difference.

"Something else could happen, Kate," he reasons. "If there's something I can do tonight, right now, to stop this craziness, then I have to try. No matter the consequences."

He means his own death. And I know what he's thinking. If he can't lift the curse and dies trying, at least his family will be rid of the curse for this generation. Of course he isn't thinking how devastated they'd be at losing him. So I remind him of how much they need him at home, how much they've already been through; but he can only see that, should he fail, his family would be better off.

Jarrod is so adamant that all I can do in the end is agree and support his decision. I hand him the medieval garments Jillian prepared, explaining how to put them on. Nothing too difficult, a pair of tight woollen hose for his legs, a fine linen shirt, a long pleated tunic with padded shoulders, which belts at the waist with a buckle, and soft brown leather boots. He nods and I leave the room while he changes.

I go to my own room and change also. Jarrod doesn't know this yet, but Jillian's plan includes me. It's the only sure way of knowing we can get Jarrod back to this time and place safely. He could possibly do it himself if he accepted that he has the gift, but he hasn't yet, and maybe never will. So we can't chance his going alone.

I step into my woollen stockings and flinch at the rough feel that makes me suddenly want to scratch. Maybe I could do without them? But, no . . . to succeed, it will have to be done right, to the smallest detail. The undergarment is next, soft and full length, with buttoned long sleeves from elbow to wrist. Over the top of this I pull on a long full robe, the top half snugly fitting my bust and waist with quite a flare to the floor. It has vertical slits at my hips to slip my hands through to lift the long undergarment. There are thirty-six annoying buttons down the back, and elbow-length sleeves that hang almost to the ground. My boots are also leather, not that you can even glimpse them underneath all this fabric. I brush my long hair, then braid it into two coils over each ear.

I practice slipping my hands through the dress slits to lift the undergarment as I descend the stairs. I'm concentrating so hard on not tripping on the long hem that I walk right through to the kitchen, where my subconscious mind registers Jarrod's and Jillian's voices, before looking up.

It's the dead silence that hits me first. Both Jarrod and Jillian are staring at me. I hear Jillian's breath suck in sharply while Jarrod just looks stunned, his mouth hanging slightly open as his eyes take it all in from my medieval hairstyle to the full-length beige-colored garment. "You look brilliant," he says softly, then adds, "but why are *you* dressed up?"

It's time to tell him, obviously Jillian hasn't. I mentally thank her for this and take two small steps forward, conscious again of the full-length skirts and how they sway when I walk. "Didn't I tell you? I never grew out of playing dress-up," I joke, trying to inject some humor. He doesn't say anything, just keeps staring. "I'm going with you, of course."

He leans forward, locking his fingers firmly around my wrist. "No."

I send Jillian a pleading look.

"She has to accompany you, Jarrod."

He spins toward her. "Do you think I can't do this without Kate?"

I snort at this, yanking my wrist out of his hold. Typical male pride. "This isn't meant to be a cut to your ego."

He snaps his head back to mine, eyes blazing at the insult. "I wasn't thinking that. I'm actually thinking of you. Of the dangers."

The lights overhead flicker. "Calm down," I reprimand. "I apologize."

He seems content with that and his eyes soften.

Jillian asks, "Do you think I *want* to send Kate on this journey?"

He frowns and I think he's beginning to understand where Jillian's coming from.

"She's not just my granddaughter, Jarrod. Kate is my *daughter* in every sense of the word. Her mother abandoned both of us years ago, and Kate is very dear to me. But I care for you, too, and you may find this difficult to understand, but I sense there is something very special about you. I want to help you get rid of this curse so that you will be free to be the person you were meant to be."

She sighs and puts a hand on Jarrod's shoulder,

locking eyes with him. I know this stance, it's captivating. There's no way he will be able to resist this pull. "Jarrod, Kate will help you in your quest, and you may need her talents to return home. Remember, it's a big task to deal with a powerful alchemist's magic. If you don't realize your own powers, then you have no choice but to accept Kate's generous offer."

He quiets down submissively. "I'm sorry. I just don't want anyone else getting hurt on my behalf."

"Kate can take care of herself. I trust her completely."

My eyes mist at Jillian's words. I give her a hug and feel her warmth. "Thanks, Jillian." I pull back and look at Jarrod. "It may take the strengths of the two of us together to beat this thing. Besides"—I shrug lightly, adjusting to the bulky feel of the garments—"how can I pass up an opportunity like this? If Jillian's magic works, then I get to experience firsthand medieval life. The idea is nerve-racking but exciting at the same time. Don't you feel it? And besides, I've always been fascinated with that part of history."

"I don't share your enthusiasm," Jarrod replies cynically. "I can hardly think of anything worse. I enjoy history too. It's my favorite subject. But *living* it? I'll be glad if we make it back in one piece."

I try to lighten his mood, "Don't be so morbid, Jarrod. Remember, we're going back to do a job, not rally an army and invade a country. We may even enjoy the experience . . . if the magic works, of course," I add, airing my doubts.

"Well," Jillian says, opening the back door and letting in a gust of pure icy wind. "Let's see for ourselves, shall we?"

We follow Jillian into the forest. She heads straight for the creek, I know exactly the spot. It's my favorite place, where I attempted the cleansing spell on Jarrod. It's also the place where I was conceived many years ago, so my link to this particular part of the forest is strong. Jillian knows this. It's why she's chosen this spot.

We carry little with us, except the medieval clothes we're wearing, and a box that has Jillian's equipment. I wonder what strength and form of magic this will take.

I have to lift my skirts high off the ground not to trip over the broken logs, hanging vines, and jutting roots. But eventually we arrive and Jillian makes us sit on an overturned log while she prepares the area. It's dark so we're using a flashlight, but it won't be for long. Jillian carefully lays out a hundred short white candles in a circle large enough for two. When the circle is complete she stands back, closes her eyes, and concentrates. Her hands stretch out and I hear a dull hum. Out of the corner of my eye I watch Jarrod's reaction. I've seen Jillian do this a hundred times, but each time the thrill is the same. Jarrod is mesmerized, watching Jillian. He can tell something very special is about to happen. The sense of it surrounds us.

Jillian begins to chant in Latin, and though it's very dark, we see her clearly. She is glowing softly, her skin a golden hue that seems to come from inside, like she's creating her own unique energy. Suddenly she stops chanting, her eyes fly open, and Jarrod gasps. They're glowing bright red.

"Kate?" His whisper is sheer panic.

"Relax," I whisper back.

And then it happens. One hundred candles ignite, simultaneously. There's no smoke, just leaping blue flames that soon settle into small gold ones. The air is electric.

The small spell complete, the circle cast and protected, Jillian's eyes return to their normal dark blue and she turns to us, keen to get on with it. "There are some important things you must remember." She draws out of the box two necklaces, strung from leather, and puts one around each of our necks. "Protect these with your lives, their power combined will return you home swiftly."

Jarrod nods and catches my eye, remembering my earlier brief explanation but needing to know more. "What are they exactly?"

"The amulets are a combination of elements of the forest. I've been very lucky to obtain the unborn fetuses of twin marsupial mice. Their mother was hit by the car of a camper the other night. They brought her to me, but she had already died. There was no way to save these developing fetuses. That's when it occurred to me. They were conceived in the forest and robbed of their right to live in it. But their non-births will not be in vain. One has been forged with the sap of the oldest tree, the other with sap extracted from one of the new seedlings. So now they are both encased in amber crystal. Don't doubt their abilities; together they are a strong bond."

My fingers wrap around the amulet with reverence for a long moment. Jarrod is staring at his, as if trying to make out the shape inside the amber crystal. He hasn't got a chance, the fetuses are too small. Finally we tuck them inside our clothes, close to our skin.

"Do not take anything more than absolutely necessary from this world into the past," Jillian warns. And pointing to Jarrod's watch she says, "Especially these." He unclasps the black leather strap of his watch, then pulls out his glasses.

"I'll miss those," he remarks, pointing to the glasses.

His worry has me wondering how much he relies on them to move around. I know he needs them for reading, but in the past, I doubt this will cause too much of a problem. And though he wears them a lot, I've seen him walking around without them plenty of times.

Jarrod runs a hand down the front of his tunic. "What

about these clothes? They look authentic, but—"

"They'll be fine," Jillian says confidently. "They're hand-stitched and hand-dyed from the same quality of fabric that was around in those days." Her voice hardens. "But remember this: If you make an implement to help you, then destroy it before you leave. When in the past you must publicly use only the knowledge and wisdom known to that era and nothing more. I'm relying on you, Kate, you've studied medieval history in great depth, so you will understand what's right and what's wrong here. Do you both understand this warning?"

We nod: We are to complete a task, not bring future technology into the past. We have to be careful about this.

Jillian sorts through her box and returns with a ring for each of us. She slips one on my ring finger, a ruby set in antique gold. Jarrod's is similar, except solid gold, no gem, just three interlocking bands. "They're both worth a lot, but don't worry, if you need money, use them."

I stare at our hands: Jarrod's are strangely calm, mine are trembling. He remains unaffected by what we're doing. Which is odd for Jarrod. Worry, I realize, for his family, has overtaken his natural reluctance to believe. This is what Jillian sensed, why she judged it a good time to go ahead. Tomorrow he could be his usual disbelieving self.

"Also," Jillian continues seriously. "By all accounts, Jarrod, you come from a wealthy family, a king's knight no less. The clothes you both wear fit that nobility status. But I'm not confident where you two will end up, how far from the family estate. Though these clothes give you social standing, the peasants may scorn you. If you end up in a village, a poor village at that, you will have to be extremely careful, find appropriate clothing so that you don't stand out."

There is a lot to remember. I hope none of it is lost during the course of the transposition spell.

"What about our language, how will we communicate?" Jarrod asks.

Jillian smiles at this, and I know she is remembering Jarrod's perfect enunciation when he read her ancient manuscript. I'm glad now, as this night suddenly becomes frighteningly real, that I took the time and effort to learn the ancient tongue myself. "Don't worry about that, there's enough magic here tonight to refresh your language skills."

But Jarrod remains unconvinced. "I don't know, Jillian. How can you do that? Suddenly make me understand and speak a foreign language?"

"Don't you think that if I can weave magic strong enough to take you physically back, it might also be strong enough to refresh the ancient language skills that are already inside you? This magic, Jarrod, will strengthen your link with the past, including the skills you already have. Trust me, and trust yourself, everything will fall into place."

She hugs us both and tears shimmer in her eyes that she quickly blinks away. Finally she steps back and indicates the ring of burning golden flames. We step into the circle at her direction, carefully protecting our clothes. We turn to face Jillian but Jarrod has more questions. "How is this magic going to work? Will we feel anything?"

"I will draw on the elements of earth and nature, to power the link which is already established by the curse."

"I don't have to wear dirt, and drink the creek again, do I?" he asks distastefully.

Jillian spins me a startled look; heat tears up my spine. "You tried a cleansing spell, Kate?"

I play with a fold in my full skirt. "It was better than contemplating suicide."

Jillian's eyebrows lift almost to her hairline as her eyes shift to Jarrod.

"Let's not get into that," he mumbles.

"Do you have any more questions?" Jillian asks softly. We shake our heads. "Then let's begin by learning the words you'll need to recite when ready to return home. They shouldn't be too hard to remember." She takes a deep breath and says, *"Ad silvam redire."*

It's Latin.

"It just means, 'Return to the forest,'" Jillian explains.

"But the amulets must be together as one, or it won't work."

We repeat the short chant several times, until Jillian is happy the words are carved into our brains.

"Good," she says, pleased with our progress. "Now I want you to start breathing slowly and deeply."

We remain quiet and still, breathing as Jillian requests, deeply from our abdomens. Jarrod takes my hand into his. It's cold yet steady. "See you in the borderlands of England," he whispers. "And I hope those Scots are behaving themselves."

I nod, and try not to think about neighborhood squabbles or what period in history we are entering. Unconsciously my mouth moves with Jillian's words. She calls on the elements individually to work their magic, starting with air and earth, ending with the circle of fire surrounding us. There is power in her voice and deep emotion.

She follows this with a few specially selected ancient words. As she murmurs the enchantment the short white candles explode into screaming blue flames, leaping and thrusting into the air as high as our bodies. Heat and energy tear at me, dance through me, fighting a battle with every one of my cells.

I cling to Jarrod as blue fire swirls around us, knowing at this moment that Jillian's spell will work.

A crushing feeling starts in my head. My hands begin

shaking uncontrollably, quickly spreading. Jarrod's body is also shaking; his grip on my arms punishing. My nails dig into his back.

Something is happening really fast now. The crushing in my head grows with such intensity I think my mind is going to explode. I lean right into Jarrod's chest, his head comes down over the top of mine, shaking violently. Then a pulling starts, almost gently at first, as if my body is turning liquid and someone is sucking me upward, into a spinning rainbow chasm. The pace accelerates, and with it the colors. They become vivid, almost blinding in strength, obscure in pattern. Color becomes my world. It is everywhere. Floating. Swirling. Spinning. My body seems to stretch beyond the norm of what blood, bones, and tissue are supposedly capable of doing. A thought occurs that I will never live through this. It saddens me.

It is the last thought I have.

Part Two
JOURNEY

Kate

Everything aches. From my toes to the very roots of my hair. My head particularly feels as if it exploded and was frantically put back together, with the bits not quite matching. I'm lying on my back, skirts hitched up to my thighs, small rocks poking into my back. Stunned, I tenderly run fingers over my face to check the condition of my head. It is, apparently, all there.

"K-kate?"

I hear Jarrod through the fog in my slowly reawakening brain, but it's a distant sound. I lift my head and open my eyes. Night is descending, but it's only a guess. I'm totally disoriented.

I remember now what happened. Jillian linked us,

through the curse, with the past. For a second my heart stops. It must have worked!

Sitting up, I look eagerly around and can hardly believe what I see. For one thing the rain forest is *nowhere*! I'm sitting on a road that is really no more than a worn dirt track. One end disappears into woodland for a while, but I pick it up again as the landscape starts rising toward a headland in the distance. There are buildings that look like they might be made of stone taking up the whole top point. Could it be a *castle?* I wonder at this in awe.

Peering at this landscape I make out two peaks with an ocean beyond. I can smell it. There's a mist coming in, and it's salty on my lips. The second peak of this strange-looking landscape stretches away across to another jutting headland, and it too has a building on it, but it's getting too dark to make out any features.

If those two buildings are stone keeps —*castles!*—then Jillian's magic was dead on.

As I think about this my body starts repairing itself, so I try standing, carefully, my head doing a slow throb, and look for Jarrod. We must have been thrown apart some-how during the leap. He's alive though, I did hear him.

"Jarrod?" I spin around on this dirt road and take in the different view. Here there are fields divided into long strips. Some have been recently ploughed, others have crops that look as if they've been roughly hacked at.

As I stand contemplating, Jarrod comes up beside me, brushing dirt off his tunic. "Where do you think we are?"

I glance up at him, his negative attitude, as always, leaves me bewildered. His gray tunic is covered in dirt all over one side, right up to his face. I help him get some of it off.

"Can you believe it?" I say as the throbbing in my head eases and excitement replaces it. "We're here, Jarrod! In medieval Britain! Where else do you think?"

His head comes up, his eyes narrow as his gaze does a full 360-degree circle, pausing for a second on the distant buildings, like he's assessing them. "I have no idea. We could be anywhere."

"Come on, Jarrod, have some faith." My mind starts spinning, not with pain now but adrenalin. Excitement accelerates, making me light-headed. I start laughing, dancing around in circles, lifting my skirts, brushing the dirt out of them with a couple of good shakes. "This is so unbelievable! I'm the luckiest person who ever lived!"

Jarrod's face creases in a deep frown, his eyes flat and unemotional. I want to probe his mind, feel what he is feeling. But it isn't necessary, I guess. He's been distraught ever since his father's attempted suicide, worried like hell about his family. But he's here now, and soon we'll find the reason for the curse, and somehow stop it. At least that's our plan. I lower my skirts and smile at him, offering encouragement. "C'mon, Oh-Great-One-of-Disbelief, let's find some shelter before it gets dark." I hook my arm through his, content that I have enough enthusiasm for us both.

We head off in the direction of the twin peaks. Of course those buildings are too distant to reach before dark, but if we're lucky, we'll find a cottage, storehouse, or some other structure on the way that will offer protection. I'm guessing by the chilly air it's going to be a freezing cold night.

We walk and keep walking as dark clouds roll over our heads, snatching any remaining light with it. The air grows even colder, and without coats we're both feeling it and start to shiver. But at last we hear noises, the low hum of voices, and grunting, rumbling sounds.

The road leads us straight into a ramshackle village, little more than a group of huts haphazardly thrown together among a scatter of trees. The first thing I notice is the smoke. You'd think the cottages were on fire. Smoke is billowing out of holes in the top of thatched roofs, pouring out of windows. There are no chimneys.

We stand still at the sight, overwhelmed. There's no denying it now: We are actually standing on the outskirts of a peasant village in early Britain. Not that we can tell the exact date from the cottages. Our link to the past is through the curse. We can't say for sure when the curse was generated, we could be years before or after the event, though either should do as long as Jillian isn't too far off the mark.

The thought that I am now *living* history sets my heart pounding. But I have to control my enthusiasm. This is not a game, our lives could be in danger if we get careless.

I glance up at Jarrod. His mouth is hanging open, his green eyes enormous. He looks as if he's gone into shock. "We should find shelter," I prod, pointing toward the third cottage on the left side of the dirt road. "It's the only cottage that has no smoke. What do you think?"

His gaze follows my finger and I'm glad to hear he still has a voice. "Could be a trap."

I stare at him intensely. "Don't be ridiculous. No one's expecting us."

He seems to calm at this, hauling in a ragged breath. "Yes, of course." He sounds embarrassed. "I suppose no one's in it then."

We decide to take the chance, but walking directly into the center of the village seems foolish. We'd probably be heard, and spotted too, through the wooden shutters or window openings. A dog barks from inside one of the cottages and there are muffled voices of humans and animals mixed together. We skirt silently around the small buildings.

The cottages are full of life. It's incredible to think they are filled with people who know nothing of computerized technology, nor even running water, sewage systems, or electricity. And yet here they live. Surviving.

We edge our way around the outside of the first cottage without any trouble. There's only one window, closed with timber shutters, which we avoid. As we approach the rear of the second cottage, we hear a distinctive male voice, gruff and too close.

Not ready to make our first appearance, we hide behind the trunk of a huge tree, probably an elm, thickly losing its leaves. As the rough voice nears, so too do other noises, scurrying sounds and angry grunts. Dirt and the scent of moist earth and grass hits my nostrils, making me want to sneeze. A short thick man with hunched shoulders and a roughly cut beard suddenly appears, panting, and cursing at a dozen or so grizzling pigs. He is apparently attempting to herd them *into* the cottage with a crooked wooden staff. Unfortunately for him the pigs, with minds of their own, decide they'd rather stay outside. One moment the herd veers toward the cottage opening, when all of a sudden it races around the back again.

I stop breathing in case the slightest noise gives us away. But hiding proves useless in the end, as one particularly thoughtless swine starts acting individually, and charges into our hiding tree. Both of us jump back with the impact, startled. The man's head swivels at the sound, suddenly alert. His hunched shoulders straighten as much as they can, and the stick begins to resemble a lethal weapon.

"Who's out there?" he calls.

Uncertainty has us tongue-tied.

"Show yourselves," the man draws nearer, his swine, now that they aren't being chased, gather around their master, snorting and grunting. "'Tis cold and late to be out, unless ye're a pair of lovers delighting in a moonlight tryst." The man glances up at the heavy bank of dark clouds totally obscuring the night sky. "'Twill rain, sure it is."

He has almost reached us at this stage. His breathing, now that he isn't chasing his pigs, starts slowing down. I realize this means the man has his wind back, and will be in a better position to defend himself if he feels the need.

I grab Jarrod's hand, taking the lead. Hiding like thieves or lovers only raises this man's suspicions. Together we step from behind the tree. "We're weary travelers from afar." Jarrod's head swings to mine, his face registering surprise at my fluency of the ancient language.

The man is carrying a burning flashlight. He steps nearer, raising the flashlight to our faces. His gaze, narrow and suspicious, slides astutely over the two of us from head to foot. It has my pulse leaping wildly. Jarrod's hand in mine is icy cold.

"Where are ye headed? Surely not this village, by the looks of them fancy clothes."

"We're looking for Thornton Keep."

The man's head lifts and turns in the direction of the dual-peaked headland, his eyes practically bulging from their sockets. "I knew it," he mutters, his rough voice filled heavier with scorn. In a sudden gesture that takes us completely by surprise he grabs our joined hands, lifts and examines them closely. "Look at this."

We glance alarmingly at our hands thinking they must somehow give us away. Just how much could hands change in eight hundred years?

Then he says, "Not a day's work in either of them." With these words he flings back our hands as if they burned his callused fingers. "What is your business with the Lord?"

Lord? This stuns us a bit. Then I remember Jillian's warning about Jarrod's family being wealthy and how the poorer townspeople might scorn us.

"If it's coin ye're after, ye'd have better luck with the devil himself."

Jarrod's head lifts and shifts backward. I can't blame him. Besides rancid breath, this pigman breathes hatred, but we need information on where we can find Jarrod's ancestors. "Can you tell us where to find Lord Thornton? We're distant relatives."

"Relatives!" He splutters the word as if he's just swallowed poison. It starts sprinkling, icy cold droplets. The pigs grunt and run about again. The man curses them, but I feel it's meant

more for us. I wish now I hadn't mentioned being a relative.

The pigman starts waving his stick about as one pig runs off, then he comes right up to Jarrod and looks him straight in the eye, even though he is well below Jarrod's eye level. "Aye, ye have the look of them," he mutters angrily. And then he spits, a huge gulp of steaming saliva, right in Jarrod's face.

I am totally stunned. The pigman switches his glance to me and my reflexes have me cowering and shielding my face. I do not want this man's spittle on me. But he doesn't do it, he just stares, unblinking. Then he says, "Thorntyne Keep stands alone on the southern peak. And beware, the northern peak is not for strangers."

Even though he has given us the information we need, I'm seething inside, and have to squash a growing urge to thump the barbarian, except the action might put our plans at risk. I can't wait to get away from him and his foul breath. Jarrod finishes wiping warm saliva off his face with his tunic sleeve. My stomach lurches at the sight, glad at this moment that Jarrod is holding on to his temper, even while a part of me wishes he would release it and plant this man somewhere among his precious pigs.

The pigman turns to leave, then swings back. "If ye were naught Thorntyne blood, I would invite ye to stay the night at me hearth. Ye are not welcome. Spit on all of yours."

With these affectionate words he starts rounding up

his pigs, and this time they do almost as ordered, eventually racing round to the front of the cottage with their master.

I tug on Jarrod's arm. He's gone very still. I glance up into his face. Droplets of rain start gathering across his brow but he does nothing to stop them from tumbling around his eyes and down his face. And he's shivering. "Hey!" I call. "You okay?"

"That man," he says softly, "did you hear him?"

"Of course I heard him, I'm not deaf."

"He hates my ancestors. No, he *detests* them."

"Oh really? What gives you that idea?"

"It's not funny, Kate."

"I know this, Jarrod. But don't worry so much. So the guy hates the Thorntons. Who cares? At least he told us where to find them. And we learned to add an *I* in the pronunciation of your ancestral name. Actually I'm beginning to feel quite pleased about all this. He may not have liked us, thanks to your ancestors, but our authenticity wasn't questioned. That's a real bonus."

The rain thickens. I tug on Jarrod's arm, leading him toward the smoke-free cottage up ahead. "Let's find some shelter, who knows where we'll be sleeping tomorrow night."

Jarrod

Kate makes sense. The pig herder obviously has a hate thing going on with my ancestors. It has me wondering what kind of people they are. A *lord*, he said. I recall what that means. All the people in the village slave away from dawn till dusk working his fields, while he sits in a castle being waited on by servants that are probably underfed. Of course he has his part to play, overlord and protector with an army of trained knights. But only when the need arises. I guess, as my ancestors live near the Scottish border, the need might very well arise on occasion. I hope now is not one of those times.

I did a research assignment on life in the Middle Ages only last year. I found the era fascinating, all that chivalry and court romance. But I never pictured anything as poor as this village. This is the pits. There's no romance here, definitely no chivalry. And it stinks—of sweat and smoke and sewage.

The fact that I'm actually here in the past, scurrying through the back of a medieval peasant village, confirms one thing for sure—the status of Kate's grandmother. She really is a witch. The genuine article. One that can actually work magic. Still, I'll have to be careful before admitting too much. Kate would soon be thinking I believe her theory about *me* having hidden powers. What does she call it: *the gift*. Sure, I accept Kate's probably right about the curse, but that's as far as I go. But a gift? Me? That's absurd.

I just hope we can do our job quickly and get back home all right. Once we get rid of the curse, the link that brought us here will no longer exist. In a kind of sudden mad panic I search under my vestments for Jillian's amulet. She stressed its importance over and over—our link home. When the time comes we have to crush the two together, joining the sap of the oldest tree to that of the youngest. I feel the small crystal. Thank goodness, I didn't lose it during our forge with the past.

The cottage has life in it, but it's not human. A cow, a half-dozen grunting, snorting pigs, and a few chickens are crudely barricaded off to one side. Not that the cottage is large enough to house animals *and* humans. It's just one room. The only light is coming from a few candles, or so Kate calls them. I try to remember how they're made— simple reeds dipped in animal fat, I think. They have a putrid odor, but Kate says our senses will soon adjust.

There is a place where a fire is usually lit, in the center of the room. A scalded iron pot hangs over it.

After acknowledging the animals, Kate explains that the pot is where the woman does her cooking, and that it must be winter, or near enough, as the cooking is normally done outside the cottage in the warmer months. She has a real interest in this period, is incredibly knowledgeable on the subject. There's burning enthusiasm in her eyes. She's ecstatic about being here. It gives me an eerie feeling she might like this era too much.

The little smoke from the candles just hovers inside the cottage. There's no raging fire like the other cottages must have. The room is miserable with damp. I'm still shivering from that cold sprinkling of rain and wish we did have a raging fire in here so I could dry off.

I take a good look around. Dragging my still stunned gaze away from the restless, offensive-smelling animals, I notice the cottage has only one window. I yank on the wooden shutters and close it, lessening the chill. The walls are sooty black; the room itself has little furniture. There is a pile of straw in a corner with a couple of dirty rags on top that might be animal skins, apparently where the inhabitants sleep. There are a couple of low crude-looking stools, a table with some stale black bread on top that feels like a brick, a few wooden plates, and a box with raglike clothes inside.

Kate's excitement is so real it's spooky. She has no fear, and marvels at everything her eyes focus on, her fingers adoringly caressing even the tiniest details. Nothing escapes her passionate attention.

Even though I liked doing the research project, I don't have Kate's eagerness for this era. The very idea itself, of being here, not only in a stranger's house uninvited, but in another time, for goodness' sake!

"This is unreal, Jarrod!"

I stare at her. "It stinks."

She just laughs, shaking her head as if she's tolerating the ravings of an idiot child.

It begins to rain hard. As it pelts down on the roof I worry it will fall in; it's already dripping. My mind shifts to the sound of scurrying feet splashing around outside. People are running fast. It soon becomes apparent they're running toward *this* cottage. Any second and we'll be discovered.

"Here." Kate grabs my hand.

We climb over the barricade and dive through startled animals. Chickens scatter noisily as we make for the farthest, darkest corner. Squatting, hugging knees to chests, we try to slow our breathing, and will the chickens to settle down quickly. A pig comes over to give us a sniff. His face hovers close to mine. I keep my eyes averted and try to slow the pace of my pounding heart.

Two women with five small children between them come rushing into the cottage. The children start tearing around, chasing each other, except for the baby, who is clinging to one woman's hip. This woman is the elder of the two and has gray-brown hair poking out from beneath a sopping white scarf. "Is it true, Edwina?"

The woman called Edwina looks about twenty at the most, and is rake thin. She holds her arms out to one of the children, a small boy, who eagerly hops up. "Every word."

They stand just inside the open doorway as the rain incredibly thickens outside and the ceiling drips increase. "He's a cruel lord, there's no doubt about it, but this . . ." The older woman shakes her head in a disbelieving manner, and loosens the dripping white scarf with her free hand. "Can he really do it? Can he turf ye out of your home, strip ye of your land?"

Edwina fights back tears. There is sorrowful pride in her eyes. "A woman's no good to her lord with no husband, bless poor William's soul. Who will work the land? Who will work the lord's stupid fields?"

"There's no kindness in that man's soul. He should take ye in at the castle, that's what."

"He says nay. He says he has enough lazy servants."

The older woman's face contorts into a disgusted frown. "What will ye do?"

"On the morrow we head south to the streets of London. Eventually I hope to find servant's work there. If not, I will do all I can to survive. I have me little ones to think of, even if I have to beg."

The older woman peers around the single room, her eyes moist with compassion, and for a second I swear she pauses as she glances into our dark corner. My own eyes shut tight as if I can will myself to disappear. A long breathless moment later I hear feet shuffle. Taking a quick look I see her attentions are taken by an older child clinging to her leg. She pats his small red head, straightening his hair. "This house is too cold, Edwina. Ye have no fire tonight. And that rain dripping in will make it difficult to start. Come, stay with me. We'll drink to your sorrows. Aye, Thomas has plenty of ale to see us through till morning. Now don't ye worry none. Lord Baron Thorntyne's day will come and I will be there to spit on his grave."

"Make sure ye spit on it for me, too." They laugh together and their conversation shifts to the children as another little one seeks attention.

Eventually the rain eases and the women, children clinging to their long skirts, leave.

We're finally alone but neither of us seems inclined to move. I don't know about Kate, but I'm still ingesting the women's conversation, beginning to get the picture now. My ancestor, Lord Thorntyne, is throwing an entire family out of their home because the man of the house died and can no longer work his fields. I cringe at the harsh and callous act.

"Your relative is a complete monster."

"He certainly wouldn't win any popularity awards." We help each other stand, our limbs stiff, and are careful to keep our clothes away from the animal dung that litters this end of the room. As the woman and her young family are not returning tonight, it seems safe to climb over the animal barricade. It's cleaner in the other part of the room, although impossible to find relief from the stench of wet animals and their droppings.

Kate adeptly makes a bed out of the straw. "It's kind of Edwina to leave us her cottage for the night."

I follow Kate down. "Just wonderful." I burrow beneath the foul-smelling rugs and wonder what insects I'm sharing the night with. The temperature drops with the lifting of rain. It's soon completely dark as the candles burn away to nothing. Even the animals settle into sleep. Other than the stench, there's nothing but silence—deep and empty.

Though exhausted, I can't sleep. I start thinking of the enormous task ahead. "How on earth are we going to find the person responsible for this curse?" I ask Kate. "Do you still think it's the illegitimate half-brother?"

She answers with a sleepy slur, "We'll know him when

we meet him, Jarrod. I'm pretty sure he'll stand out."

"What about the people here in the village? They hate the Thornton name so much maybe they did the curse. We've only been here a few hours and already have three suspects."

"Hmm? What are you going on about? These poor peasants don't have the skills to procure a curse."

I feel her shiver and snuggle in close, seeking physical warmth. It takes all my effort to remember what I'm talking about. I shrug; Kate tugging right in under my arm is doing strange things to my senses—all of them. She burrows down so that her damp head lies on my chest, one arm wrapping snugly around my waist. In seconds she is sleeping. I can tell by her slow steady breathing.

Positioned like this, Kate lying asleep in my arms, so close, even the stink from the animals fades. I thread my fingers into Kate's hair. Though still plaited, the coils have come apart. It feels like silk, just as I thought it would.

Sleep nears; I feel its druglike pull, yet I fight it for as long as possible, enjoying the feel of Kate's warm body next to mine. But it's no good, the day with all its unbelievable events has drained my energy.

I let myself fall into the mental peace sleep offers. Dawn, and all the challenges it brings with it, will arrive soon enough.

At least, for this moment, we're safe.

Kate

Something wakes me. Outside, someone is moving about. It's not quite dawn yet, though the sky is beginning to change. I stir and feel Jarrod's warm body beside me. I move, instantly waking him, though he remains groggy for a minute. It gives me time to crawl out. God, how did we end up in that position, entangled arms and legs? My hair between his fingers?

Sitting up, I adjust my clothes. They're a mess, just like the rest of me. I need a drink to clear the cotton in my mouth. I also need to relieve myself, but that I guess will have to wait until we're on the road. I miss not having a mirror, comb, and especially a toothbrush and have to rub my finger over my teeth.

Instinctively we both know we have to get out of the cottage before the entire village wakes and starts doing whatever it usually does at this time of morning.

We learned from the man with the pigs last night where the Thorntyne family lives—on the southern peak of the headland we saw yesterday. About a morning's walk and we should be there.

Without saying a word, in case we're heard in the still, early dawn silence, Jarrod and I creep silently outside, round the back of the cottage, avoiding the early risers and skirting the village much in the way we came in last night. With the dawn the weather changes, giving us all the cover we need. Fog, thick and moist, rolls in from the ocean. It's quite eerie watching it, a vaporized white sheet concealing everything it touches.

Luckily, the road appears straightforward, heading in one direction, the twin peaks on the ocean edge. Still, the farther we travel, the thicker the surrounding woodland becomes, so we're careful not to deviate from it, and risk getting lost. The road itself proves hard on our feet, cold as if the earth froze overnight, and slick with patches of icy mud. Our boots are not enough protection, the soles too soft. I miss my springy sneakers.

We travel only a short distance when Jarrod almost walks straight into a water trough sitting on the roadside, probably used by thirsty cows or travelers' horses.

We stare at it, trying to measure up just how desperate we are for the stuff.

Jarrod's mouth looks dry. "I really need a drink, but . . ."

"It's been raining, so it should be fairly clean," I suggest.

Jarrod looks at me. "What about that plague? Bubonic, wasn't it?"

This comment actually has me laughing, relieving some of the tension. "You're such a negative creature, aren't you?" I whack his arm lightly. "Assuming Jillian's got it right, we should be a good hundred years too early for the Black Death. I guess that's not a bad margin for error."

Still, jokes and all, I too am reluctant to drink from the animal trough. But thirst in the end pushes aside any other doubts. "It's not like we've got a lot of choice here."

Jarrod scours around for something to break the ice-covered surface. He finds a small rock that satisfactorily does the job. I plunge my hand into the icy water and drink. It's not too bad.

Jarrod drinks and we move on, a little more comfortably. I ignore my growling stomach, food is another thing that will have to wait. Hopefully we'll be made welcome at Thorntyne Keep. I try not to think about how much can go wrong. While walking we revise our plan, airing doubts, double-checking our story. We're only going to have one chance to get it right. If they don't believe our first story they're not going to sit and wait for us to come up with another, more plausible version.

Finally the fog lifts, freeing the sun, allowing it to

shed a little warmth. We keep walking, the road inclining noticeably now. But it's around noon before we get to the foot of the steeply rising headland. Together we stand and stare straight up at the castle.

"It's for real," Jarrod mutters like it's only now sinking in where and *when* we are.

"Of course it is. I told you Jillian was good."

We're silent for a minute, taking it all in. I sigh in absolute awe, and wonder at the job it took to build the thing. It stands high on the top of the hill, a square tower from the main keep's back corner reaching farther into the sky. What a laborious task it must have been for the peasants to haul the massive amounts of stone up that headland. It would have taken years for sure. "Wow," I can't help saying. "It's magnificent. Just look at that wall and how it circles the entire peak. And those battlements. There are soldiers up there, you know, probably looking at us right now."

Jarrod gives me a shrinking look. "Thank you, I needed to know that."

We decide to take a moment and rest our backs up against a tree trunk. The weedy grass is wet from last night's soaking. I can't be bothered worrying about my clothes anymore, the whole lower half is mud.

I glance at Jarrod, and without even trying, feel his doubts. "Just stick to our story, we'll be fine."

His eyes roll. "What if they don't buy our story?"

"Stop being so negative. We can always go home."

He attempts a smile, but it's really pathetic. Going home before we've dealt with the curse would mean this whole exercise was a waste of time, and Jarrod would still have his problems.

"Look," I try to lighten his mood. To carry this off, Jarrod needs to approach his ancestors with confidence, not cowardice. "They're not going to expect visitors from another time. They wouldn't even understand the concept. And thanks to Jillian, we're suitably clothed in period costume, jewelry and all." I hold out my hand, fingers splayed, the ruby and gold ring gleams as if in confirmation. "So what if our accents are a little off? We're supposed to have come from a distant country, remember? I swear, Jarrod, they won't suspect a thing. Besides, didn't that pigman say you look just like them?"

Jarrod's eyes swing to mine, a glimmer of strength brightening them. "Yes, you're right. Even though it's probably no more than a coincidence."

I pull myself up, eager to get this initial meeting over and done with. "Coincidence or hereditary makes no difference at this stage. As long as they buy it."

We're both weary, having walked all morning without food, and little water. But this is the last part of our journey, which gives us an energy boost. We don't talk much, are content with our own thoughts, battling our own doubts. Soon speech becomes difficult anyway as we struggle with the climb in our mud-heavy clothes.

As we near the apex the castle walls become clearer. I glimpse a portcullis, the iron bars forming even crosses, set within high stone walls. In front of this is a raised drawbridge, which creates a barricade to the entrance of the castle. On top stands a stone structure like a cabin. This has to be the gatehouse. There are guards—knights, I assume, and these are the ones that have been observing us, no doubt. It's an irritating feeling, knowing they're just standing there, watching, and armed. Glancing back down I see that from here there is a perfect view of the whole road, all the way across to the village in the distance. I see now why the castle was built on this hill, so close to the ocean. It's perfect, strategically, and easy to defend from invading armies.

The view is actually quite spectacular. The far side of the keep drops away sharply to a thrashing blue-green ocean, which seems to go on forever. To the north, on the twin peak stands another keep, also on a cliff edge. I can't seem to draw my eyes away from it. It looks isolated and strangely sinister. The tallest point is a circular tower that stretches so high, rumbling dark clouds threaten to obscure it.

The eerie sight causes goose bumps to break out everywhere on my skin. "I wonder who lives there?"

Jarrod's eyes shift sideways, and he shrugs. "Who cares?"

"It looks dark and spooky. And didn't that pigman warn us not to go near it? Why is that, do you think?"

Jarrod gives me a bit of a disbelieving look, then inclines his head toward the castle so close now, only a few meters to the smelly stagnant moat. "Are you suggesting Thorntyne Keep looks friendly or inviting? Look at those high walls."

He's right, both buildings look uninviting. And even though Jarrod still carries the name, these people are strangers. But I want to keep his thoughts light. "They're your relatives," I remind him.

His face forms into a sarcastic sneer. "Yeah, right. Like eight centuries ago."

Jokes aside, I can't shrug off an unnatural feeling emanating from that dark neighboring castle. It scares me.

As we near the gatehouse of Thorntyne Keep, a deep male voice demands to know our business.

"We are weary travelers from a faraway land, once of Thorntyne," Jarrod announces with a calm I know he doesn't feel inside. But we've rehearsed his lines many times on the road, and he's doing well.

"*Thorntyne!* Who are you to claim the Thorntyne name?"

"My name is Jarrod. I am the lord of Thorntyne's

eldest brother's son," Jarrod returns. We had to rehearse this line the most.

The man gasps and swears. A lot of murmured discussion from the guards in the gatehouse follows. My skin starts tingling like a thousand ants are chasing each other across it. Finally the soldiers move away from the battlements to obtain a clearer view of the youth who claims to be the son of the lost Thorntyne brother.

I see the man in charge clearly for a minute. He's largely built, with broad straight shoulders and a full head of dull red hair going gray. He would have been a striking man in his day, and still is, though I can only guess his age to be around the mid or late forties. He's wearing leather bands, wrapped around his lower legs, a beige tunic with a full skirt to his knees, and a cloak with a rectangular mantle pinned on his right shoulder. He's not wearing chain mail, but his companions are, and the sight of them is breathtaking. I wish I wasn't so nervous.

He's probably a knight of some high order. He moves back and starts descending the inside stairs, looking formidable. The knight has made a decision.

An order reverberates through the gatehouse, and the portcullis starts sliding gratingly upward, then the drawbridge lowers. The knight is accompanied by a soldier on each side of him, one young, one much older. They make an awesome sight. I can't help but stare as they cross the bridge and head toward Jarrod, who is standing a little way in front of me. My pulse is racing, my palms sweating, and I'm glad at this moment that I lingered behind a little looking at the castle on the other peak. I hope Jarrod handles this just like we rehearsed. He looks scared. He can't stop wiping his palms on his tunic and flicking me quick worried glances. He looks like a wild pony that wants to bolt.

The knight stands directly in front of Jarrod and studies him carefully with narrowed eyes. He's clearly suspicious, taking in every detail, from the rust tints in Jarrod's hair to the creamy color of his skin. But it's Jarrod's eyes the knight lingers over the most. And then he surprises both of us when his own eyes go all watery, and a huge grin splits his rugged face almost in two. He looks at the two soldiers flanking him for a quick second, grinning and nodding. In one lightning movement the knight turns back, grunts loudly, spreads his arms wide, and smothers Jarrod in an almighty bear hug that lifts him completely off the ground.

After swinging Jarrod around full circle a couple of times the big man reluctantly puts him down, then starts thumping his back with great big guffaws. Jarrod is trying hard to maintain his balance. "Welcome, nephew. Welcome," the big man announces between powerful thumps. "I knew this day would come. I dreamed of it many nights since your father left."

The word, *nephew*, sticks in my head. This man isn't just a knight, or one of the lord's soldiers, he is Lord Baron Thorntyne himself. And he has accepted Jarrod's explanation simply by looking at him. Just as I start wondering how much Jarrod must resemble his ancestors it suddenly dawns on me that if they cast so much heed to looks, then our planned story just disintegrated. Too late to think of anything else now, my heart starts hammering madly in my chest.

I look again at the lord of Thorntyne, master of his castle and all its people. The warm way he's greeting Jarrod isn't at all how I imagined he'd be, especially after what those villagers said of him.

The other two soldiers welcome Jarrod too, though one of them remains coolly reserved. The lord introduces him as Malcolm, his twenty-year-old son, but remains oblivious in his own joy to notice his son's chilly reception. The older soldier is Thomas, apparently a lifelong friend of Jarrod's "father." Thomas can't take his eyes off Jarrod, keeps shaking his head, touching Jarrod's shoulder, and grinning.

An elegantly dressed woman suddenly pushes through a gathering crowd at the front gates. "Richard," she calls the lord. "What's going on? We can hear the ruckus from inside the Great Hall."

"Isabel, my love," Lord Richard says excitedly, draping

one of his arms around the slender woman's waist. "It's Lionel's son, returned to us from a distant land."

Isabel's eyes widen, instantly on alert, skepticism fighting hospitality on her refined yet delicate face. She studies Jarrod closely. "Aye, he certainly resembles a Thorntyne, but not Lionel directly."

This last comment worries me. If not Lionel, who is apparently the long lost brother, then who?

"Geoffrey," she decides.

"Geoffrey?" Jarrod queries tactfully. Earlier we decided that if we needed information, family names and such, we would have to make the inquiry sound casual. Jarrod's is perfect.

Isabel, apparently content now with Jarrod's claim to ancestry, links an arm through his, explaining, "Of course you wouldn't know him, and your father, bless him, should have told you about your heritage. Geoffrey was your grandfather. He passed away long before you were born, my dear." She peers studiously at him. "But you're too young to be Lionel's firstborn."

Jarrod quickly explains, "I'm not. I have a brother before me." He's good, I breathe in slight relief. But the show's not over yet, the major hurdle is yet to come—me.

"He is well, but I had an urge to see my homeland," Jarrod continues carefully.

We have to be careful not to release any information

we're not sure of, and that is really just about everything we know. Jillian warned us not to disturb any
future destinies, not to do anything, or say anything that
might lead to changing history. We know that Lionel's
real firstborn son will return one day to claim his rightful inheritance.

Others join them, a girl about my age, introduced as
Jarrod's cousin, Emmeline, who can't take her eyes off her
newfound cousin, smiling at him with a mixture of shyness
and slyness. I dislike her instantly. There is another child,
maybe six or seven, attached to a woman's leg, who turns
out to be Isabel and Lord Richard's youngest son, John.
The woman that shelters him is Isabel's maid and, apparently, not worthy of introduction.

While all this is going on, I am momentarily forgotten.
I don't mind though, it gives me a chance to evaluate everything. If it wasn't for Jarrod's uncanny resemblance to his
Thorntyne ancestors I doubt our first meeting would have
gone so smoothly. But my presence is yet to be explained.
And this is where we're going to have a problem. Why
were we so stupid?

They begin moving across the drawbridge into the bailey, when Jarrod turns for me. He doesn't get a chance to
speak though. Lord Richard starts babbling apologies for
his rudeness.

He puts his arm around my shoulders urging me forward. Once inside the castle walls we have to stop as a large group of curious people gather in number. Richard proudly introduces Jarrod to the crowd as if the prodigal son himself has returned. There is wild cheering and Jarrod almost drowns in their welcome.

Among all the ruckus Lord Richard angles his head down to me and says, "Who is this lovely noblewoman?" And the crowd goes quiet.

Jarrod is supposed to say his *sister*, which was, of course, our plan. His eyes connect with mine, troubled. What should he say now?

Isabel frowns at me and says, "Of course she's not a Thorntyne, just look at her pale skin, the color of her hair, like ebony, and those eyes, so light yet incredibly still blue and . . . such an unusual shape."

"They're shaped like a cat's," Malcolm tosses in.

I try not to stare at him, even though I wouldn't mind turning him into a cat right now.

To me Isabel adds, "My dear, from what lands do you hail?"

I stare back at her numbly.

Lord Richard, who is still holding my shoulder, glances across at Jarrod for an explanation, his head inclined with impatience. Obviously, he's not a man used to waiting.

I know exactly when the idea hits him. His fingers go all hard, digging into my arm a little, not so that they hurt, but I can tell he isn't pleased. My heart beats faster. What can he be thinking? Something offensive, I'll bet. I don't dare probe his brain, Jillian warned me about this. These people live with magic but in a fearful way, with less understanding. If they think I practice witchcraft, I will most probably be killed.

Then he says, "Surely, Jarrod, this exotic creature does not travel with you unchaperoned?"

Jarrod appears completely dumbfounded, not expecting this sudden twist. Damn, we should have prepared an alternative story. Of course I look different to them, with my black hair and unusual almond-shaped eyes. Something we should have realized earlier. Too late now as everyone is waiting for Jarrod to explain. I sense it has to come from him. They wouldn't accept our "sister" plan now, that's for sure.

"Jarrod? Who is this lady?"

"She, um," Jarrod starts. "Her name is Kate—'

"Katherine," I say quickly as the shortened version isn't popular yet.

But this is not an explanation and the crowd waits for more. Lord Richard's fingers tighten around my shoulder, his thoughts diving again. His head swivels to Jarrod's, looking at him sharply. "Tell me you have not stolen Lady Katherine's innocence and made her your mistress?" His voice grows louder and the crowd thickens around us. "Your father, my dear brother," he continues, shaking his head, "would stand for none of this if he knew."

I don't like what's happening. In an instant our welcome has turned threatening. I suddenly visualize the dungeons these castles reputedly have — literally windowless holes in the ground. Sure, as everything else around here, I'd like to see them, but my curiosity stops there. Every pair of eyes zeroes in on me. My face is in flames. I urge Jarrod to say something, *anything*, to get us out of this unfortunate twist.

And so he says, "Katherine comes from . . . an island, far away from here. She . . . she is . . ." He drags in a deep breath. "She is my wife."

A collected relieved sigh escapes from the crowd, and the lord's tight hold around my shoulder eases. In fact, he drops his arm and lifts my hand, as if searching for something. When he finds what he's searching for he holds my hand up high so everyone can see. It's my ring, the ruby and gold one Jillian gave me, that has everyone's attention.

"It's true then," Isabel announces, coming up and giving me a welcoming hug. "How lovely, my dear. Come, you must be hungry." She glances at my soiled skirts and messy hair. "And when you have both eaten, I will arrange hot baths and a comfortable bed." Here she glances at her husband, Lord Richard, with one fine eyebrow raised in query. As if by familiar silent communication they agree on something, and Isabel says, "We can't have you sleeping with the servants in the Great Hall, so you two can sleep in the tower room. It hasn't been used since Lionel wed his young bride."

A room of our own. This is quite an accomplishment. Other than the lord and his lady the rest of these people would normally sleep in the Great Hall on beds of straw. This privacy is just what we need.

Isabel's glance slides to Jarrod, her voice whisper-soft. "It's their room you see. Your father had it built especially for Eloise as a wedding gift. It's the room your parents slept in when they lived here, before . . ." Her pause is met with an electric silence. The air practically ignites with tension. Even though Jillian warned me sternly against it, I have to do it, just one time. Isabel is hiding something. If I can decipher some of her fears, I might understand the why of it. And why the idea of sleeping in this tower room has suddenly taken on an unsavory feel. So I probe, very gently, Isabel's mind. What I feel there shakes me up a bit. This seemingly strong, very in control woman, is scared. Of course, we know from Jarrod's heritage book that the young bride was kidnapped. But as I understand it, the bride was returned only hours after the event. An unrequited lover's vengeful prank. But, glancing at the gathered crowd, I see fear in their faces. There is definitely more to this story. Something dark and sinister happened to the young married couple, Jarrod's supposed "parents." Though it happened possibly twenty or more years ago, it still has the power to affect all those who remember it, even their children. And it happened in the tower room. That much is clear.

A sudden chill hits every one of my senses. The thought of sleeping in this room now gives me the creeps. I withdraw from Isabel's head, but the fearful sensations remain, too strong to subside.

Jarrod

Lord Richard insists on showing us around the keep, which takes the rest of a very short afternoon. It's amazing seeing how many people live inside the castle walls. There are cottages along the inside, with soldiers on guard on the ramparts, while servants and retainers, workmen like the blacksmith, their families, even priests, all hurry around, going about their business. There are animals too—pigs, dogs, hens.

Kate is loving every moment, though I must remember to call her Katherine. She is in absolute awe.

We have dinner in the Great Hall. There is so much smoke from the central fire I'm glad I've never been asthmatic. How do people live in these conditions? The fire is necessary, otherwise the Hall, the whole castle in fact, would be cold and drafty. But there's nowhere for the smoke to go. There are windows high up on another level, narrow arched slits really, without glass, but the smoke takes forever to get up there.

Kate and I are seated at a long table on a slightly raised timber platform. Everyone that lives or works in the castle is here dining together, but the soldiers and servants sit at makeshift tables farther down the hall. Our food is served on thick slabs of stale dark bread. There are wooden knives and spoons, no forks, but everyone is eating with their fingers. Kate almost gags at the sight of all the food, especially when a whole pig's head is proudly placed before us. I'm sure Kate feels like spewing. The only thing that's saving her is her empty stomach.

Most of the food is salted meats. There's an eel pie, some spicy sauces, and more heavy dark bread. There's no water, but plenty of red wine. Unfortunately it's really coarse stuff. Not that I'm a connoisseur or anything, but I've had it a couple of times at home. Dad drinks it a bit to help him sleep. This stuff is really harsh. The most I can do is sip it to ease my thirst. And I can't eat much either, my stomach simply refuses. Kate nibbles on some spiced apple and that's about all. To avoid insulting Lord Richard we both complain of severe exhaustion from our travels, explaining we suffered from a mild dose of food poisoning on the roads.

It's funny really, I wouldn't say these people are gullible, but they swallow our stories without question.

They're keen to hear every detail we can recall of our journey. I guess they really hang out for news from travelers. They wouldn't get many up here. We're careful, though, not to say too much. Kate is better at it. I leave most of the conversation to her.

She tells them how we lost all our belongings in London, including our horses. This explains why we arrived on foot, with only the soiled clothes we're wearing.

"I was there last spring," Richard easily agrees, nodding, his eyes wide. The wine, I realize by his rosy cheeks, has started to kick in. "'Tis a city riddled with beggars and thieves."

This thought has me remembering the woman called Edwina, who he is about to toss into the streets simply because she lost her husband and can't work his fields anymore. Lord Richard is proving quite contradictory. He can't have been more welcoming to us, whom he believes are family, yet to his peasants he's cruel and unjust.

Dinner ends and Isabel grabs a lighted flashlight out of a wall bracket, ordering two girls to have hot baths waiting for us in the tower room. I start thinking ahead. It looks as if Kate and I are going to be sharing a room, probably with one bed and not much else. My body is tingling with the thought of sharing a proper bed with Kate. My palms are sweating so much I have to wipe them down the side of my grubby tunic.

We follow Isabel up a dark spiral staircase that never seems to end. Finally, at the very top of the tower, we arrive at a single room. By day I imagine it would be well-lit, as there are actual windows on both sides, but the sun disappeared a long while back, and an icy chill has set in.

Before Isabel leaves she orders the maids to see to the fire and rushlights, and arrange suitable clothes for us. The baths are already half filled, with hot buckets arriving every few minutes.

The maids get the fire going and light the rushlights and some candles, which give the room instant warmth and a soft, though smoky, glow. Kate is standing by one of the tall arched windows, looking north. I come up beside her and see that she is looking across at the castle on the northern peak, silhouetted against the darkness by a single glowing light from one of its tallest towers.

"Who lives there?" she asks one of the maids, the one Isabel introduced as our own personal servant, Morgana. The other, a little older and thicker set, is Glenys.

Morgana, who's placing another rushlight in a wall bracket, goes very still, her young face clouding over worriedly. "His name is Rhauk, my lady. His castle is called Blacklands."

She doesn't say anything, but I can tell what Kate is doing to Morgana. Kate picked up on Morgana's fear and is now probing the poor young girl's mind, picking her brain for emotions. I hope she doesn't go too far, as we have to be careful. But probing minds is second nature to Kate. I doubt she could ever live without it.

"Why are you afraid of this man called Rhauk?"

Morgana goes straight over to the huge four-poster bed, her long skirts swishing with every step. She pulls back the bedding and fluffs the pillows. "Everyone is, my lady. Even the lord."

"Why?" Kate asks softly.

Morgana pauses, pillow in hand. When she looks up her eyes look glazed. "They say he is descended from the devil and that father and son talk often."

"Do you believe these rumors?"

It's the older girl, Glenys, that answers. "We know nothing, my lady. Naught has ever happened in our lifetimes. These are but childhood stories, exaggerated to make a wee child scared enough to go to bed."

I smile at this, instantly liking Glenys's sensible mind, and glance at Kate. She doesn't pursue the subject, yet I can see she's still disturbed.

The last steaming buckets fill the two wooden tubs that sit side by side in the middle of the room. Morgana finishes laying out our night clothes, long white gowns, across the bed. Glenys taps the rim of the nearest steaming bath. "I'll see to your soiled clothes after Morgana helps you with your baths."

She means for us to take off our clothes. Now. And step into the baths. Immediately Morgana starts working the buttons at the back of Kate's dress. Kate jerks uncomfortably aside, and catches my eye. It's apparent the maids intend staying while Kate and I bathe simultaneously.

I quietly observe Kate's eyes. I don't need any so-called gift to feel her discomfort. Her wide-eyed look urges me to say something, but honestly, I don't mind the idea at all, and it's amusing watching Kate look uneasy for a change. I watch a hot blush spread across her pale skin, darkening it. The hard part is trying not to laugh.

"Jarrod!" Kate hisses between clenched teeth. She can tell I'm enjoying myself and she's totally unimpressed. *"Do something!"*

I shrug, and pull off my tunic.

She hisses. Really. Like a snake. I'm sure she's thinking of some nasty spell to put me under.

It's a relief to yank off the too tight muddy boots. Kate's shoulders spring back.

"My lady," says Morgana softly, picking up on Kate's sudden change in temperament. "It would be easier if you allowed me to disrobe you."

I have to hand it to her. Inhaling a long steadying breath, Kate drags an amazing smile to her face and says calmly, "Morgana, if you don't mind, Jarrod and I will tend to our own baths."

I'm sure Kate isn't prepared for young Morgana's outrage, or her steely determination. The young maid practically squeals and there's real fear in her voice. "Oh no, my lady. We cannot leave you unattended. The lord, you see, he would beat us till our bones are skinless."

From what I heard in the village I don't doubt Morgana's words for a second. And neither does Kate, but she hasn't finished trying. She puts her arm around Morgana's much smaller shoulders and leads her toward the door. "Now, don't worry, either of you." Her gaze includes the older Glenys. "I'll assure Lord Richard personally what wonderful servants you were, tending to all our needs. You have my word."

Morgana glances at Glenys, looking for advice. But Glenys is shaking her head. "You don't know the lord, my lady. If he found out you had no one to tend to your bath, it'll be our hides that bear the brunt of his anger."

Kate's tolerance collapses. It's the closest I've seen her come to pure panic. She must be exhausted, I know I am. And even though it's amusing to see her squirm, I decide not to stand by and watch her lose it completely and risk our plans because of this small hiccup. So I try a different angle with the maids. "Glenys," I start, for she's obviously the one who makes the decisions. "The reason my lady is so close to tanning your hides herself, is that she likes to attend to my bath *personally* . . . and, well, *privately*." I smile, find Kate's eyes, which have grown huge, and add, "We are newly married, after all."

Morgana has the grace to blush profusely, giggling behind her hand, Glenys just huffs stubbornly, but does at last agree to leave, promising to return at a suitable time to put out the lights and collect our soiled clothes.

They leave and Kate spins on me. "You enjoyed that, didn't you?"

I laugh and toss her the rough towel. "Allow me to be your chivalrous knight. You go first."

She stares at me for a long moment, waiting.

"What?"

She begins waving at me. I get the message and turn around. When I hear water splash onto the floor I turn back. She is submerged all the way to her chin. Her hand goes straight to the amulet that is now floating in water. I understand the gesture, having felt for mine several times during the day. It's our link home, something we have to protect, no matter what.

While Kate bathes I examine the wildness of the ocean through the open window. Waves pound into solid rock far below. It reminds me of the time we lived at a beach-side caravan park on the south coast of New South Wales. Dad had a friend who ran a fishing business, and who gave him a job on his trawler. You couldn't see the ocean from where our rented van was, but the sound at night was *all* you heard. Mom was pregnant with Casey, and Dad was away every night. But the job lasted only a couple of months as their catches were the worst on record and Dad's friend had to sell the business.

Tonight there's no moon, at least not yet, but I can still make out the foamy white tips like little sailboats rhythmically tacking to shore. The familiarity of sound, scent, even the taste of salt wafting up this high is somehow comforting. Finally Kate finishes her bath, dries herself, and gets into bed, running fingers through her hair.

"Your turn," she says, doing up the last button of her gown right up to her throat.

I get behind the bath, which comes to about waist level and strip off. Kate has taken so long with her bath, my own bath water is barely tepid. Still, I enjoy it. Who knows when I'll have the luxury of another. I don't think these people bathe every day, probably less than once a month. There's no soap, so I have to scrub hard at the caked-on mud.

I finish bathing and slide on the long white nightshirt. My limbs are sore and tired and the bed looks comfortable and very inviting, especially with Kate in it. This thought, after the incredible day, has my head spinning. And suddenly all that amused bravado I had shown earlier disappears on me. I wouldn't mind being able to probe inside Kate's head for a change, see, *feel*, exactly what she's feeling. But I can't do that, so I'm left guessing. My instincts tell me she wouldn't mind if I tried to kiss her, but she's acting so modestlike, I don't know what to make of it.

It's perfect timing, for as soon as I slip into bed, Glenys and Morgana return with two male servants. They take some time, but eventually empty the baths and remove them. The maids clear away our clothes, lay clean ones out on a wooden chest for us to wear in the morning. Just before they leave they stoke the fire and extinguish the rushlights.

Finally we're alone. Completely. Especially considering the location of this specific room, isolated high up in the tower. I glance at Kate. She's curled up as far on her side of the bed as possible without falling out. "Kate."

"I'm going to sleep!" she snaps.

My jaw falls open. Hey, what does she think? That I'm going to . . . to . . . what? Try to . . . ?

Annoyed at her attitude, I roll far to the other side. Even though I'm sore and tired and mentally drained, sleep doesn't come easily.

I can't take my mind off Kate.

Kate

I don't know what Jarrod can possibly think of me now. What an idiot. I find myself playing the terrified virgin maiden role. It's not anything Jarrod's done. It's me. And where we are. In bed together! My feelings for Jarrod are pretty intense, but I don't trust he can return these feelings. At least, not yet. So I'm wary of taking a major step toward intimacy. If we kissed or anything, would it stop there? I don't quite trust myself, especially considering we're alone up here, and well, living in circumstances where we're actually *playing* a married couple. And here, now, in this time and place, it isn't right.

Besides, I don't want to end up a teenage single parent. My mother was, and couldn't cope. What if I couldn't either?

So I pretend to sleep, which doesn't happen for a long time. I'm on edge anyway, sleeping in the tower where

Lionel and his young bride, Eloise, once slept. Something sinister happened here, and I can feel a strange energy pulsing eerily from the dark castle called Blacklands. This pulse is like a slow heavy beat in my chest, totally synchronized with my heart. And I'm pretty sure no one else feels it. Jarrod surely doesn't. And this freaks me out. Who lives there? Morgana said it was a man named Rhauk. Could he be the illegitimate half-brother with sorcerer powers?

Eventually I guess I do sleep. When I wake it's early dawn. Hazily I realize what woke me — a loud squawking noise. I search for the sound and find a huge black crow sitting eerily on the windowsill, looking at Jarrod and me, curled up on opposite sides of the bed. I swear the bird is wearing a satisfied smirk on its face, its black beady eyes, almost humanlike, appear intelligent in a way a crow's eyes never should.

I decide my sleepless night has affected my sanity. A bird, from any century, is just that — a bird. "What are you looking at?" I snap at it. It squawks loudly and flies away.

Jarrod rolls over, waking groggily. "What? Who are you talking to?"

"A crow."

"What?"

I get out of bed and start dressing, slipping the stockings on first. The fire died sometime during the night and it's freezing up here now. "Forget it. We're so high up the birds think this is their home."

I finish dressing without once looking back to see what Jarrod is doing, or even where he's looking. My restless night has put me in a foul mood, and I can still feel yesterday's eerie vibes shoot through me. Jarrod and I are here for a specific reason, the sooner we accomplish our business, the better. Not that I mind being here really, having this opportunity to experience the past, something that absolutely fascinates me.

Breakfast is apparently served in the Great Hall. Even though I'm starving I'm skeptical about eating any of the food. Last night it just looked so . . . unhygienic. Being vegetarian I don't eat meat anyway, so my choices are narrow at best.

As we start down the spiral staircase all thought of food disappears. Someone is screaming, a young female voice filled with such fear it echoes through the stone corridors like the screams of a tortured ghost. It has us running through the passageways right into the Great Hall.

It's Morgana, the smallest and youngest of the maids who prepared the room last night. Jarrod and I glance quickly at each other, wondering if we're to blame for the maid's beating, for not letting her deal with our baths last night. We recall how worried she was at the thought that Lord Richard might find out.

"What's going on?" I ask immediately. "What has this child done?"

I'm ready to take the blame, explain that it was my choice not to allow the maid to attend our baths last night. My sympathy pours out to her. She's doubled over with pain, Lord Richard himself striking her with the back of his fist. Morgana is so small, each of Richard's knocks has her physically reeling back against the wall. Morgana's face is red on both sides and already beginning to swell. There are others—Isabel; Emmeline, her niece; Malcolm, her eldest son, who's wearing a certain smug look in his dark green eyes; and Thomas, Richard's closest and most loyal knight—but they're just looking on with casual interest. Servant bashing is apparently something that happens regularly. Malcolm catches my eye and one eyebrow lifts. Evidently he's amused at my distress. Emmeline, the cousin, is oblivious. Her gaze switches to Jarrod, and stays there, longingly. She reminds me of Tasha Daniels. I can't believe my luck.

Lord Richard finally notices my concern. "Stupid girl," he mutters angrily, his hand still raised ready to strike the next blow. "Look at my tunic." He points to a slowly spreading liquid stain on his front that goes from his chest to a little below his waist, soiling what could only be the family crest—two white doves hovering over a purple rose inside a crimson diamond. "She spilled ale all over me." He looks back at her angrily, and Morgana cowers into a small ball. "I'll teach her to be so careless." With that he strikes her, once again, sending her flying backward.

"My lord!" I can't help but interfere. My heart hardens at the unjustness of the penalty. "I require the services of this maid. Do not damage her to the point that she will be useless to my needs."

His head swings toward me, and for a second I think perhaps I've overstepped my mark. But his face finally softens, and he withdraws his hand. "Quite right, Lady Katherine. I dare say the wench has learned her lesson now anyway." With this he dismisses Morgana, who sends me a grateful look as she quickly escapes the room.

After this incident I find I have no stomach at all for food. We move around the table and Jarrod bumps his leg on the corner. I grab his elbow, making sure he clears it this time. On top of being normally clumsy, he's probably missing his glasses. I make a mental note to watch for inadvertent obstacles in his way. Jarrod nudges me, mumbling a subtle thanks. We sit and he offers me a slab of dark bread. Reluctantly I accept, aware that I need the physical strength food offers.

And the jam doesn't look too bad. At least it smells all right, no little blue bits of mold. Fresh berries would have been better, but, as we discovered last night, it's only a few weeks to winter, so there's little if any fresh fruit or vegetables around, only dried, preserved, or far worse—heavily salted stuff that is so close to being poisonous I don't even want to stand too close in case it spreads infection.

The jam turns out better than I thought, and I lather it on the thick bread. I have to concentrate though to block out the rough images of the others wolfing down their food, yanking off chicken legs with greasy fingers, slopping ale into wooden mugs, dripping it down their chins, which they wipe with the backs of their sleeves.

And while they eat, Lord Richard boasts about his cruelty to the villeins that work his fields. Thomas and Malcolm grin and nod, and this attitude is shared by soldiers at the other tables who think their lord's ugly deeds are comical. My appetite disappears altogether when they start laughing over the fate of the peasant woman who recently lost her husband in a battle to help save the keep from falling into the hands of a neighboring Scottish lord. He was, apparently, a hard worker. This woman is Edwina, and I wish I'd never met her now. They discuss how she'll probably turn to a life of thievery, or begging, or prostitution to survive.

I almost gag on the food that refuses to go down my throat. Jarrod sends me a sympathetic look, but he knows, as I know, there's nothing either of us can do about that woman and her family. I have to let it be. If only I could use a little magic, I find myself thinking.

It's just as I think of magic that a commotion outside

the Great Hall seizes everyone's attention. It seems Lord Richard has an unannounced visitor. A tall impressive-looking man strides in, wearing all black. He bears an even more striking resemblance to Jarrod than Richard, except he's taller and thicker set. He has Jarrod's hair color too, dark blond with russet tints, except this man's eyes are jet black. And I realize with a start where that eerie pulsing energy is coming from.

So I guess who it is even before Lord Richard mentions his name. Only a powerful magician can emanate energy like this. It isn't a warm welcome he receives either. "How is it, Rhauk"—Richard's voice is cold and hostile—"that you always get through my guards, without anyone ever seeing you?"

The man, Rhauk, simply smiles. Slowly. He walks straight up to Richard, giving me his profile. "Is that any way to treat your brother, Richard?"

"Bah!" Richard scoffs. "You are no brother of mine. My father never acknowledged your birth. Never. Not even with his dying breath."

"That may be, but he never denied it either. But I don't want to get into that today," he replies, seemingly bored. "I've more important things to do."

"Well, what do you want this time?"

Ignoring Lord Richard, as if it's beneath him to reply, Rhauk's head shifts sideways, searching. His eyes find mine, and lock. *"Eloise,"* he whispers. Shivers hit me in waves.

For starters, I can't possibly *look* like Eloise—these people would have noticed and reacted differently when they first saw me. I don't look anything like these people, and because they don't travel, they've never seen someone who looks quite like me before. My eyes are way too oval-shaped, my hair true black.

Rhauk seems to collect himself and smiles again. This time the smile has an element of cunning. He nods at me, and it's as if he's acknowledging that I'm what he's come for. "What an exquisite creature," he purrs like a feline. "Introduce us, Richard."

Lord Richard is clearly uncomfortable, and coughs a little to clear his throat, I suspect, to buy himself some time. Rhauk's reaction has him confused. "Er, this noble-woman is Lady Katherine. She comes a great distance to be with us. She has nothing to do with you, so keep your eyes off and stay well away."

As the two discuss me I feel another energy pulse in the room. At first I don't recognize it, until an almost familiar wind starts up. It quickly turns chillingly cold. It's Jarrod. And he's looking at Rhauk with eyes of absolute steel.

"Easy, Jarrod," I say softly, suddenly seeing the huge problem in front of us. We've found the instigator of the curse, but Jarrod hasn't acknowledged his gift yet and so can't control his powers, let alone use them.

Rhauk senses another strength in the hall too. His

nostrils flare, his head comes up just a little, black eyes drawing into slits. Slowly he turns to face Jarrod. Then he smiles that slow unnerving smile again.

Their eyes hold fast, and the wind inside the Great Hall picks up to gale force. Another power has entered the storm—Rhauk's. Emmeline screams, yet I hardly hear it as the wind keeps growing violently. She clings to Isabel, who's after answers, but her Lord Richard doesn't have any. He's struggling just to stay upright. Neither Jarrod nor Rhauk move. Their eyes remain locked.

The wind thrashes everything, tables empty, stools upturn, tapestries fly across the room. Everywhere is chaos.

Rhauk finally breaks the spell, swings his eyes to mine, and says softly, "How very interesting."

The wind dies as quickly, and Jarrod stumbles to his knees, grasping his head. Richard demands to know what happened, but Rhauk ignores him. Instead he says to me, "Blacklands is on the northern peak. I'm sure you've seen it, Lady Katherine." He pauses so that I understand his meaning. "You have a clear view of it from the tower."

My eyes widen with surprise. He knows I slept in the tower last night. It gives me the creeps. *He* gives me the creeps. It's exactly what he wants, to let me know how strong he is. So with an attempt at calm I reply, "So you noticed the rushlights were lit. How observant of you."

His laugh is sarcastic. "Clever girl. I like your humor. Please, join me for dinner tonight, at dusk."

Before I have a chance to reply, Richard interrupts. "Forget it, Rhauk. You can't get your claws into this one. Lady Katherine is already married."

Rhauk's eyebrows shoot up at this. He glances at Jarrod and scoffs loudly. "To you!" He laughs as if he's cracked a hilarious private joke. "Oh well, I guess you'd better come too."

He leaves a trail of devastation behind him, and a lot of nervous conversation. I help Jarrod, who remains unsteady and dazed, to his feet. I pull up a chair in which he gratefully sits.

As servants start straightening the chaos I think about Rhauk. Sensing Jarrod's powers, he showed some of his own. But he was only playing with Jarrod, trying to gauge his strength.

And it didn't take much for Rhauk to sum Jarrod up as being no challenge at all.

Jarrod

I recall the look in Rhauk's eyes the moment he spotted Kate. It will stay with me forever, carved into my brain like an engraving on a headstone. It's as if he found something he treasured, something he's been looking for all his life.

He wants Kate, all right. But I have to wonder why? What is going on here? It's more than just an instant attraction. It runs much deeper. This is what's wrong.

This unusual man has to be the one we're looking for. The one who cursed my family. He has a certain strength about him; the Great Hall is a shambles. Richard is running around like a headless chicken while servants and soldiers alike rush about at his orders straightening the mess. The mess can go to hell for all I care, I just want to get to the bottom of Rhauk's vengeance. He spoke to Richard under the assumption of a blood link. I know part of this history already, but it's still a good place to start.

"Why does Rhauk say he is your brother?" I ask Richard.

Richard pauses in the middle of issuing orders to his soldiers and looks at me. "Unfortunately, nephew, it is what he mistakenly believes."

"Is that why he's so resentful?" Kate asks, putting a hand on my shoulder, encouraging this line of conversation.

Richard's chest lifts and expands. He holds this breath for a long moment, then collapses into his high-back chair. "I have something he thinks belongs to him."

"What would that be?" I prod at his lengthy pause.

"Our castle, of course," Isabel replies. "And all our lands and incomes."

"Was Rhauk first born?" Kate asks.

"No!" Richard yells, thumping a heavy fist on the table just righted before him. "Rhauk may claim he is Geoffrey's true firstborn son, but Rhauk's birth was never acknowledged by my father."

Kate frowns. "He doesn't look old enough to be . . ." Her voice fades.

Richard lifts his gaze to hers, his voice oddly hoarse. "It's his magic, my dear. It's rumored Rhauk's mother was a true-born witch."

I can see Kate thinking: This will explain Rhauk's unearthly powers, his ability to place a curse on the family that denied him, the family that shut him out. And Richard

is a hard man, and cruel, he would never hand over owner-
ship of his castle and lands.

"Couldn't Rhauk's mother confirm his parentage?"
Kate asks.

"Aha!" Richard glances briefly at Isabel, who stands
beside him, her hand comfortingly patting his arm. She is
his rock, and this big man is not embarrassed to lean on
her. Another quirk to his colorful nature.

"Her parents died in a fire. She came to Blacklands for
food and shelter. The nuns took her in but already she was
with child. It was strongly rumored she had been seduced
by the *devil*," Isabel hisses. "She remained at Blacklands
until the birthing. The nuns knew of her evil sorcery and
tried to cleanse her, but even her own magic wasn't enough
to save her life."

"She died?" I ask.

"Yes, in childbirth."

Kate swears, softly under her breath. Both Richard
and Isabel's eyes fly to hers. They are not used to such
words coming out of the mouth of a lady. Thankfully, Kate
recovers quickly and mutters, "Such a shame. The baby, I
mean. To be motherless at birth. Who raised him?"

Their attention successfully diverted, Richard says,
"Ah, now that is another mystery."

Again Isabel takes up the explanation, "Some say he
was raised by the crows that feed out of Blacklands. But of

course this is nonsense. Others believe the nuns raised him before he ravaged and killed them all while still a youth, claiming their convent for himself."

I'm going for the nuns' story, even though both stories have the feel of exaggeration. These people sure are a superstitious lot. They're so isolated up here, they probably believe anything, and make up half the stories themselves for pure amusement.

"How can you not know the truth?" I ask. "After all, the two castles are neighbors."

"The nuns were self-sufficient and lived reclusive lives. Years could pass before anyone saw or heard from them," Isabel explains.

"One thing is certain," Richard's voice is suddenly deadly serious. "Rhauk is powerful and evil. I strongly advise you do not accept his invitation to dinner. Not only does he want our lands, the income we gain from them, but he has a personal vendetta with our family."

Now we're getting somewhere.

As Richard relates the tale, the room falls silent. He looks at me. "Did your father ever tell you why he moved away? Relinquishing his title and lands to me?"

I shake my head, eager for him to explain it all. "Your mother, Eloise, was a beautiful young woman. Many desired her, but none as much as your father—*and* Rhauk."

Kate finds another chair, pulling it up beside me. "Both

courted her, and it was clear she had affection for them both, but when forced into a decision, she chose your father. Rhauk could not accept her decision, and on their wedding night your father claimed Rhauk kidnapped his virgin bride. No one saw Rhauk do it. I was on guard duty that night myself and didn't see a thing. No one broke through our defenses. Yet your father slipped into a state of shock, muttering for days a crazy story about Rhauk's eyes. No one could make much sense of his words. By first light Eloise had wandered back, dazed and somewhat mindless for days afterward."

Moisture glistens in Richard's eyes, and Isabel leans down with comforting arms around his neck. The tears help me glimpse in him a softer side. To members of his family he is loyal and compassionate. And I sense he is carrying a guilty conscience at what happened the night of his elder brother's wedding, especially considering he was on guard duty. Perhaps he thinks he should have protected them better. A thought hits me: Considering it was the evening of a celebration, maybe Richard was a drunken guard that night. And now *he* is Lord of Thorntyne Castle and all its estates, while his brother hides himself somewhere in a foreign land.

"It was rumored that Rhauk seeded Eloise with child, for the infant born nine months later strongly resembled Rhauk. The rumors cut deeply and Lionel took his young family far away." Richard's eyes clear and focus on mine. "How goes your brother?"

My "brother" is supposed to return to claim his rightful inheritance sometime in the future, there's a battle described in the heritage book, so at least I know of him, and that he lives. "He is well."

"You have seen Rhauk. Who does your brother resemble, now that he is a man?"

This is a tricky question. I don't have any idea. I shrug, as if I don't care. "I know him only as my brother."

This seems to satisfy Richard, who stands suddenly as if tired of the conversation. He looks about him, observing the quietness in the room, and starts bellowing orders to continue with the cleanup.

Kate and I go out into the bailey. We need to hash over everything we have learned. Rhauk is obviously the one we want. And I think Jillian's timing is perfect. But we need to discuss tactics. How are we going to stop this man?

One thing is certain, no matter Richard's warning, we will have to go to dinner.

Blacklands awaits us, and all Rhauk's mysteries.

Kate

Richard arranges an escort to Blacklands by a dozen of his best knights. The horses stand massive in front of us, neighing and fidgeting restlessly. We're supposed to be competent riders, but I've never ridden a horse before, and from the wary wide-eyed look on Jarrod's face, I guess he hasn't either, at least not successfully. But these people believe we rode horses as far as London, and probably for most of our lives.

It turns out easier for me as one of Richard's strongest knights helps me to the saddle by lifting me effortlessly from the waist. Being female, no one it seems, expects perfection. All I have to do is sit oddly, both legs on one side of the animal's broad back, and hold the reins without falling off. Yeah, right.

It turns out to be much more difficult for Jarrod. For starters, without his glasses his vision is a little blurred, and he's clumsy anyway. He's also been allocated a stallion! A handsome white and speckled gray creature. This is supposed to be a compliment, but I don't think Jarrod sees it this way. When he tries to mount the massive white restless stallion, he goes straight over the other side, descending headfirst into the hard dusty earth. He stumbles near the stallion's foreleg, making it shy and fidget. And it looks as if Jarrod's bruised his shoulder in the fall. The poor thing.

Out of respect for their lord, the mounted knights try hard not to laugh at this bumbling nephew, but I can hear their snickers anyway. Only Malcolm makes a comment, and it's a nasty snide remark about Jarrod's incompetence. It makes me think of another bully in another time. I guess certain things don't ever change.

Malcolm looks at me and my skin crawls. And even though I know I shouldn't, but because I sense I'm looking at the face of an enemy, I decide to probe inside his head.

Malcolm is filled with resentment, envy, and surprisingly, even fear. Suddenly it hits me. Malcolm is Lord Richard's eldest son. He stands to inherit Thorntyne Keep and all its estates, including the title. Now Jarrod's come along, son of the eldest Thorntyne, who can lay claim to the lands himself. So Malcolm sees Jarrod as a threat.

He will have to be watched.

Malcolm's eyes narrow, studying me. I'm careful not

to make eye contact, especially while still in his head. Not that he can feel me, it just makes me uncomfortable. It adds an element of intimacy.

Jarrod's next attempt is still pathetic, but at least this time he doesn't fall off. He grabs the reins as if his life depends on his not hitting the ground again. His face deepens to colorful shades of red. Finally, with a lot of grunting and heavy breathing, he straightens and grips the horse's reins. If we were in class right now, they'd all be cheering.

We approach Blacklands at dusk, as invited. The knights remain outside the gatehouse, clearly unsettled just being this close to the dark stone and timber walls. Only Malcolm is calm and relaxed.

The high gates suddenly swing open, though no one appears to be around. Jarrod and I dismount, leaving our horses with Malcolm and the other knights, walking into the bailey on our own. No one greets us, or shows us the way. The castle itself is complicated, with several connecting buildings, not, as most castles of the times, with one large keep. Much of it consists of timber, plaster, and thatched roofs. Then I remember it was once a convent. Now it is lifeless and unnerving.

A door opens to the first building and Rhauk is standing beneath a high stone arch. Again, he is dressed all in black, tights, undershirt high up to his throat, tunic, and boots. There are sprinklings of gold in a braid around the edge of his high-necked undershirt, and on his belt, which supports a buckle made completely of gold. It intrigues me. My eyes fasten on the shiny object. Closer I see it clearly, and my heart jerks, throwing me unexpectedly. The buckle is a maze of snakes, scores of them, weaving in and out of each other's bodies, only their heads and beady eyes clearly visible.

I recall Jillian's vision of the snakes around Jarrod's upper body, and how Jarrod hates snakes. I watch Jarrod's reaction. He sees them, squirms uncomfortably, probably remembering Jillian's vision too.

We follow Rhauk down a covered cobbled walkway, up a spiral staircase, into a sparsely furnished room, except for a magnificent timber dining table at one end. There's a fire in the center that sheds warmth and light to the dying day. The smoke, I notice, isn't as bad here as in Thorntyne Keep, so I follow to see where it's going. There are air vents, long vertical slits in the roof, a mini-tower covering them, so smoke can escape, while rain can't get in. It's clever, considering chimneys aren't invented yet.

Rhauk is watching me. He gives me the shivers. Even as he lays platters of food on the table, his eyes dance with mine. He's flirting, I realize. Bold and obvious. And it's hard to remember he's more than double the age he looks. His skin is flawless, unmarked with age, his hair still deeply russet, his body lithe and youthful-looking. Occasionally his black eyes shift sideways to Jarrod, who's trying hard to hang on to his patience. I warned him earlier—we come tonight seeking information, clues of any type that might help us solve the problem of the curse. Perhaps observing Rhauk in his own habitat will give us a lead. Losing control could blow everything. But Rhauk is teasing Jarrod. I just hope Jarrod can see through him, and not be blind to Rhauk's games.

We sit down to dinner and my eyes bulge at the sight. There appears to be no one in the castle except for Rhauk, yet he's prepared a luscious feast. Mostly fresh foods, berries and grapes, pears, apples, sweet corn, even light grain bread. There's plenty to drink too, cider and sweet red wine, not coarse and rough, like at Thorntyne Keep. It has to be near impossible to grow all these things at this time of year. The aroma is strong and overwhelming. I'm hungry but skeptical. Who wouldn't be?

"Is the food not to your taste?" Rhauk frowns.

"It's just that, well . . . ," I mutter, then opt for a direct line with this man. Anything less he wouldn't respect. "It's almost winter. There are few fresh fruits at this time of year."

He smiles at me, laughs a little. "Nothing is impossible at Blacklands. I have my own gardens. Would you like to see them, Lady Katherine?"

His voice is like velvet, smooth and sensual. I glance at Jarrod, wanting to see his reaction to Rhauk's invitation that leaves him out specifically. Thankfully, though he looks annoyed, he's keeping control. I glance back at Rhauk. "We might like that later, thank you."

Rhauk, if anything, looks smug and amused. He's playing with us. It's all a game to him. Well, I can play games too. I just wish the rules were clearer, and the stakes understood.

Rhauk carves up a pheasant, places a few slices of breast on Jarrod's wooden plate. On mine and his own he serves a slice of the hot blackberry pie. His look challenges me. It says he knows I'm vegetarian, or at least that I favor fruits to meats. But how can he know this?

"How goes my dear brother?"

Both Jarrod and I look up at Rhauk, startled. Who exactly is he asking about? Confusion throws us for a moment. We're being paranoid, I realize.

"Your father." His voice is mocking. "Or has your long journey dimmed your memory of the man who raised you?"

Softly, thankfully not taking the bait, Jarrod replies, "He is well."

"And your beautiful mother?"

Jarrod stares at him, but can't hold Rhauk's gaze. Damn. Don't give away clues, I silently curse. Stare him down, if you have to.

"Fine."

"Hmm, fine you say." Rhauk looks bored, then adds, "Memory recalls Eloise a striking woman, yet . . . not quite as striking as you, *Kate.*"

My eyes fly to his in astonishment at the way he says my name. How does he know so much? Instinct? Or magic? They lock with his, and I'm trapped. Caught by the claws of something eerily strong, not from this world.

Jarrod feels the tension, his patience thinning. "Leave her alone."

Slowly, Rhauk releases me, and his eyes move to Jarrod's. "Why? I'm enjoying this conversation."

Jarrod's voice tightens. "Katherine is my wife."

Rhauk laughs from deep within his chest. "You are a very poor liar."

"I'm not lying," Jarrod denies Rhauk's accusation, but his voice hasn't the conviction necessary to pull it off.

Rhauk's head leans forward, his black eyes narrow slits. "Young lovers don't sleep on opposite sides of the bed," he hisses.

"How . . . ?" I hold this thought as I struggle not to look surprised or give our true marital status away. No matter his suspicions, or how clever this man is, Rhauk can only be guessing. Jarrod throws me a worried look.

A grizzly squawking sound draws our attention to the arched window slits. A black crow is perched there.

I study it, wondering if it's the same one that was perched on our window ledge this morning. Rhauk calls to the bird with a slight flick of his head, and the crow flies over, landing gently on Rhauk's extended elbow. Rhauk croons to the bird, who soulfully responds, his arrow-shaped head inclining in an affectionate manner to one side.

I can't drag my eyes away from the crow, understanding that I'm looking at no ordinary bird. Yet, I can't accept that this crow somehow communicated to Rhauk our sleeping arrangement. It isn't possible.

Rhauk feeds the bird a wedge of juicy apple, and the crow flies back to the window ledge, apparently satisfied. But it doesn't fly away. The crow remains there throughout the entire meal, hauntingly watching.

It becomes fully night and Rhauk lights more rushlights, placing them in brackets around the large lonely room. My stomach tightens and I want to leave. Darkness at Blacklands is scary. But we really haven't learned much yet, so I decide to speed things up. Rhauk begins serving sweet cakes. As he leans over my shoulder to offer me the platter I say, "We know about your plan for revenge."

He pauses, going momentarily still. Shivers flutter across my sensitized skin. "Of course you do. This is why Jarrod has made his long journey here."

I wonder how much he really knows about us. I have

to find out without giving too much away. "So you know we're here to stop you."

He straightens. "You may attempt to, but seriously"— he glances at Jarrod as if seeing nothing more than a pesky fly—"you will only waste your time, and no doubt, die in the process." He returns to his seat at the end of the table and looks across at me. His eyes are like rocks of coal. "My dear Kate, I have a vision for you." He rubs his hands together like an excited little boy.

Jarrod climbs to his feet. "You have no business with Katherine."

Rhauk also rises and stares at Jarrod. "You, Jarrod, have come to protect your family. I respect that, though, in the end, respect means nothing to me. And, though you do not know this, you have brought the Lady Katherine with you because this is where she belongs."

"What!" Jarrod hisses.

"An injustice was done to me many years ago by your father. He stole my lady, persuading her against me with cowardly lies and outrageous rumors. Bringing me your wife is recompense. What was once stolen will now be returned." Here he glances pointedly at me, and a chilling smile spreads slowly across his face. "What a delightful addition you will make to Blacklands, Lady Katherine. Just like Eloise would have."

"You have it wrong," I try to tell him, dread settling

tightly in my chest. "I'm not a replacement for Eloise."

"Ah, but that's where *you're* wrong," he denies. "All is going as it should. I knew this day would come."

"Katherine is not staying here!"

Jarrod is losing it, fast. I tug on his arm and whisper, "Don't fall for it, he's only goading you. He wants to test your powers."

Rhauk laughs and says smugly, "Clever, Kate. But you're only half right."

I yank Jarrod backward, away from the raw energy emanating from Rhauk. "We'd better leave."

Jarrod calms a little at this idea and nods.

But Rhauk hasn't finished playing with us. "Don't be in such a hurry. Why, I haven't told you my plans yet. Isn't this why you came?"

Just as he knew it would, his words stop our retreat. I breathe in deeply, my nerves rattling on a dangerous edge.

Once he's sure of our attention Rhauk explains. "Jarrod's fears for his family are certainly not unfounded. Right now, in the solar tower, I am preparing a fright-ful curse. Every seventh-born Thorntyne son will know its wrath from now to eternity. Fools they will be, born clumsy, while evil and misfortune will befall every member of their family."

"So," I try to gain a little more specific information.

"This curse you speak of is not complete yet?"

He pauses, his eyes staring straight through me, like he's deciding on his answer. Then he says, "Alas, it lacks but one ingredient. The sweet root of a winter-flowering herb."

Since it's late autumn we have only a little time to act. We'll have to use it wisely, somehow find a way into the tower, destroy the brewing curse, then deal with Rhauk so that he won't brew another curse. Just how hard this will be is anyone's guess. At least now we have a starting point.

It's time to leave.

Jarrod is just as keen. He takes my hand in his and brings it to his mouth. Against the back of my palm he mumbles, "Let's get out of here, fast."

We make to move toward the spiraling staircase, but the look on Rhauk's face stops us. His pupils have done a full dilation. I wonder what's caused this stunned reaction. His unblinking eyes drift down to where Jarrod is still holding my hand.

"We're leaving, Rhauk," Jarrod says into the chilling silence.

Rhauk blinks and seems to regather his senses. "Oh, but you can't leave without a parting gift."

As he speaks a heavy wooden door slams shut the entrance to the stairwell, blocking our retreat. The thundering sound echoes through the empty corridors. Startled, we glance back at Rhauk, in time to see him throw a shimmering silver ball high into the air. The ball explodes, the entire area surrounding us fills with silver and light as thousands of tiny shards of sharply pointed, needlelike projectiles fall around us in an eerie shower. I try to protect my face with my arm, but the needles are plentiful and sharp.

They sting, piercing the skin, right through our garments. "Jarrod, do something!"

He screams back, "What, Kate! How do I fight this?"

I shield my eyes while trying to look up at him, pleading with him to realize his gift and use its powers. "You can stop this, Jarrod! Reach inside!"

He stares at me, openmouthed, his head shaking. "I don't know how. . . ."

He can't help. It's what Rhauk wants, to see for himself, to measure Jarrod's weakness.

I glance up quickly to see if there's any end in sight to the silver rain. I try to tell myself it's just magic, it's just an illusion, but blood is now staining my long-sleeved tunic and my scalp is stinging from the needles lodged there. There is so much silver light the entire room is glowing with this strange unnatural energy. And in this moment of understanding I realize that Rhauk will stop at nothing to have his revenge. A revenge on his half-brother for stealing the girl he loved, and his deceased father for not acknowledging his rightful heritage. He will even resort to murder, if Jarrod or I stand in his way.

I hate him for this. And I can't just stand here and do nothing, letting Rhauk get it all his own way. Jarrod may not be in a position to use his gift, but nothing is stopping me. So, not thinking of the risks I take exposing my knowledge of magic to this dangerous man, I straighten in the face of the shower of silver needles and lay my arms gently by my side. I concentrate deeply, slowing my breathing and trying to ignore the stinging pain. In my mind I see the silver projectiles change into harmless shapes, their pointed ends softening, curving, molding, floating.

Before I'm even aware that my trick has worked, I hear Jarrod's sharp intake of breath. Opening my eyes, I blink to clear my vision, put my hands out and watch, unable to stop a smile forming as, instead of the shower of silver needles, hundreds of white dove feathers drift around me, collecting in my open palms.

When I look up, I realize sickeningly that I've just made a fatal error. I've shown Rhauk something of my own powers. And now he will want me more than ever. The joy is written in his face. He starts clapping, ecstatically, both eyebrows rising half into his forehead.

When he stops clapping he walks over and stands directly in my space, grinning, his eyes sparkling. "We will make a formidable couple, you and I, Lady Katherine."

I shake my head wordlessly and step backward, avoiding eye contact.

He simply laughs. "Yes. Imagine it—your power and mine! The world will be ours. Who would dare! No one could better us!"

From my side Jarrod flinches. "She's not staying with *you*!"

Rhauk stares at Jarrod. "In the end she will choose. To be fair, Jarrod, Kate must have an understanding of what could be hers, of what I can give her. She must glimpse both worlds." He shifts his focus back to me quickly, catching my eyes before I have a chance to look away. His voice is velvet again, hypnotic. "Will you stay, Lady Katherine? *Kate?* Here, with me, at Blacklands?"

Jarrod stares at me, a kind of shocked look on his face. He's wondering why I haven't answered yet. Why I haven't given an abrupt "No" to Rhauk's outrageous proposal. He doesn't understand that when Rhauk's hypnotic eyes bore into mine, when Rhauk's overwhelming energy swamps my senses, I can't easily break this hold. And right now the pressure is intense. I blink several times quickly, it helps to draw me away from him. Finally the spell of his hold releases me.

I glance up at Jarrod, mentally drained, and say softly, "Take me home."

He grabs my elbow, supporting me. "You heard her decision, Rhauk. Let us out."

As the heavy wooden door creaks open, the black crow squawks and flies straight between us so that we have to duck to the side, coming to rest on Rhauk's extended elbow. It's eerie how it seems to look at us with scorn. I don't have time to think about this, I just want to get out. The darkened staircase is so close now, allowing us a route of escape. Just before we reach it, Rhauk's voice washes through us, chillingly, "You leave me no choice, my lady . . ."

I make my feet keep moving, though nothing can stop his words, as they chase us down the staircase. "I will have to come for you." My entire body starts shaking, his words an ominous warning. "Watch the darkness, for I will be the shadow, coming for you." And then, in a hushed sort of whisper, *"Sleep tight, my lady."*

Sure. Just the thought of staying in Blacklands overnight with Rhauk terrifies me. At last in the bailey, I can't hear his words anymore, but the image of his eyes, small, black, and cold, remains vividly clear. I wonder if I will ever sleep again.

Jarrod

Dinner at Blacklands with Rhauk really unnerved Kate. We're on our way back to Thorntyne Keep and she's quiet and sullen, her eyes huge ovals. She's trembling all over, hands clasped tightly together in an attempt to stop the shaking. It doesn't.

Lord Richard greets us in the bailey and walks us to the tower room as the rest of the castle sleeps. After telling him a little of our evening with Rhauk, content that we survived intact, he bids us good night. The servants have prepared the room, giving us a warm glowing fire.

Kate looks numb. With mechanical movements she sits on the bed, lifts her nightgown to her face, unconsciously inhaling the smell of it. Her eyes lift to mine. "You know you're going to have to fight him."

I stare at her. She means Rhauk and she has to be joking. "Are you crazy?"

She sighs a kind of weary disappointment. "Well, I can't see any other way."

"Really? So how exactly am I supposed to do this?" She knows just how incapable I am of fighting anyone, let alone Rhauk with his tricky magic. I cringe remembering tonight's display with the needles. "Had I known your plan I would have brought along a semiautomatic machine gun."

"This is not a joke, Jarrod."

Her comment stings. "I know." But I'm annoyed with myself more than with Kate. After all, she's here for my sake. And I realize that I disappoint her. "I just don't know what you expect of me."

She groans, tugging the nightshirt up to her face again, this time completely burying her nose in it and taking a deep exhilarating breath. She does this sort of thing all the time, with the heavy drapes, or a tapestry on a wall, even the candleholders. This morning I saw her inhaling the scent of a washing bowl! She loves this era and she loves being here. I think it's more than just the opportunity to live history. Maybe it's because she has no history herself. Not knowing her mother, not even knowing who her father is.

Lowering the nightgown, Kate traces adoring fingers gently over the hand-stitched embroidery. "You *have* to acknowledge your gift." Her eyes find mine across the room and her voice hardens. "Because you have to use your *powers* to defeat him!"

"Kate . . . Don't start . . ."

She tosses the nightgown to the bed angrily. "How can you *not* believe in yourself after all we've been through? Look at where we are! A real-life castle in medieval Britain! Doesn't that tell you something? You have to admit now that Jillian *can* perform magic and yes, there is a curse on you. You just spent the evening with the man who created it!" She pauses while I absorb this. "Stop and think, Jarrod. *Let* yourself believe. I've been right so far, all the way. Just maybe I'm right about your gift, too!"

I try to do what she says, *let* myself believe. But it's just so hard. My life has been one hard knock after another, how can I suddenly start believing that I'm endowed with incredible magical powers? The idea is beyond me.

"Look," she tries again. "It could be possible that you have inherited Rhauk's own powers."

I glance at her earnestly. What *is* she saying?

"That could make you at least as powerful, if not more so. The possibility is there."

"Why Rhauk?"

She looks exasperated. "Remember your father's heritage book. You are directly descended from these people. If Rhauk did kidnap Lionel's young bride and seduced or raped her, and you descended from that union . . ." She lets the rest fade.

It's enough though to make me see what she means. There is sorcery in my ancestry. I saw it tonight with my own eyes. "God, you could be right."

She smiles, motions for me to turn around. While I do. I hear her changing into her nightgown. When I turn around she's climbed into bed. The fire is dying and the air is getting chilly. I change briskly and climb in beside her.

This time something's different. She doesn't cringe or anything, neither does she roll toward the farthest side of the bed. I don't think she wants to be alone tonight. Rhauk really shook her up. And if it's just company she's after, someone to comfort her when the fire dies and the shadows lengthen, then that's fine with me.

So we sit with our backs against the magnificently carved timber headpiece, quietly aware of each other but in a comfortable way. "If I do have these powers, how would I, um, tap into them?"

She lifts my hand between both of hers. Her fingers are warm. "All you have to do is concentrate."

"That sounds easy enough."

Kate's lips curve downward. "Well, it's not really. It takes time and a lot of practice. You have to train. Hard."

This makes sense, only I wonder just how much time do we have?

I feel her probe, gently at first, inside my head. She's trying to sense my feelings. It will be easy to feel the doubts and fears. Her probe deepens. I reach a point where I want to block her, and this realization suddenly hits me — I've blocked her before, and Jillian said that most people can't even tell Kate is in their heads. I can, and I can block her if I want to. Is this proof that I have abilities beyond the norm?

I look into her eyes and feel her probe deepen. She doesn't look away, and the moment becomes intense. It's an amazing feeling, having Kate in my head, sensing my emotions while maintaining eye contact. It's like we're naked or something, our emotional secrets lying bare to each other's observation. Wordlessly we continue to share our feelings. And the intensity increases.

Finally she speaks, and her voice is croaky. "You'd better kiss me."

I nod and swallow the sudden lump in my throat.

We kiss and slide down the pillows and keep kissing, forgetting everything — where we are, *when* we are, what we're supposed to be doing here. Kate feels fantastic. I acknowledge on some higher level that we are made for each other.

"Jarrod," she murmurs.

"Hmm?"

"I'm afraid."

Her words make me stop. For starters, they're so out of character. Kate is always in control, even when she's upset or angry. She never loses her head. I understand she's really worried. She's thinking of Rhauk's parting words. I wish there was something I could say to make her feel better, safer. I glance up into her face. Her beautiful crystalline eyes look large and frightened. She reminds me of a newborn foal, all wobbly legs and unsure of itself. Her pale skin is even paler than usual, almost translucent in the dying light of the fire. I lightly brush my lips across her eyelids, her cheeks, overwhelmed with a fierce feeling of wanting to protect.

"I need you to hold me," she says softly. "All night, okay?"

I promise with my eyes 'cause I know my voice is unreliable right now.

"Promise you won't let me go, Jarrod. Not for a second."

Her words move me in a way I've never felt before. I lean over her, my hands on either side of her head, and kiss her mouth. "I promise," I croak, meaning every word.

A distant squawk pierces the still night, but neither of us recognizes the sound as danger at first. Somewhere in the depths of my mind I register the noise, but it's only when the demanding squawking sounds come from *inside* our tower room a few moments later that I understand. It's the crow. Rhauk's. Peering at us from the window ledge, making angry noises to get our attention.

I stare at this obtrusive intruder. "Kate, it's Rhauk's crow."

Its head lowers slightly, tilting sideways as if listening to—and comprehending—our conversation.

"No," Kate whispers, her lips trembling. "I don't think . . ."

The crow moves closer. "Have you ever seen anything so large!"

Kate's eyes never leave the massive crow. "The eyes . . . ," she whispers.

The fire is almost out, so light in the tower room is dim, filled with flickering shadows, but nothing can disguise the crow's eyes. For they are not crow's eyes at all. But human. Too much like Rhauk's. Black and cold.

Before either of us moves, the large crow with Rhauk's knowing eyes lunges. I throw myself completely over Kate. The crow's talons dig into my back, ripping my nightshirt to shreds in a vicious assault to move me. I try to shake it off, without shifting from Kate, but the bird beats at me with its sharp talons and flapping wings, all the while squawking and shrieking. My senses fill with its scent—birdlike, yet impassioned with human revenge. Blood oozes out of my back where its talons dig deeply. I hit at it with my elbows, back, head, kick at it with my heels. Anything to shake it off. This far up the tower I wonder if anyone can hear what's going on and come to help.

A wind starts that soon becomes fierce. At first I think this wind is exactly what we need, but I soon realize it has no effect on the attacking bird. If anything, it seems to incite it.

Kate squirms beneath me, tries throwing her fists at the monstrous thing at my back. It grins at our attempts, seeing them as feeble, and starts intensely now, pecking with its pointed beak at an artery in my throat. It doesn't once harm Kate, yet its purpose is clear. *It's trying to get to Kate.*

Blood trickles from my throat, onto Kate's white night-gown. She screams at the sight. "Jarrod, you're bleeding!"

"I'm all right, don't struggle. I won't let it get to you."

"It might want *me*, but it doesn't mind killing *you* in the process. You have to do something!"

"What, for goodness' sake?"

"Use your *gift*!"

"I don't know how!"

Panic is not going to help. I jerk my arm and shoulder trying to dislodge the thing off my back, the hole in my neck now spurting out blood. The crow lifts momentarily, giving me a much needed second to breathe, but then it dives, catches me under my shoulder and in one powerful thrust, knocks me to the ground.

In my heart I realize that I've lost this battle. That I've lost Kate. The massive crow takes my place over Kate. I throw my body's weight at it, trying to wrench it off, but nothing works. It's like the bird is made of steel and I am made of feathers. Kate screams, and the sound resounds in my skull like the echo of a thousand chimes clanging together. The wind increases, becomes cyclonic. Hissing, it works against me, pushing me back. I have to fight through it to get to them. The crow's wings spread wide and embrace Kate, covering her. Like steel braces, the crow's wings close completely around Kate's body and lift her. The crow hovers for just a second over the bed, its black eyes locking with mine, gloating. Then it moves in a graceful motion, through a north-facing window, Kate tucked neatly within its wings.

Although it should be too awkward and cumbersome, the crow flies like this, with Kate trapped inside its incredible wings. I race to the window, reaching out to the escaping bird, lunging until I half fall out. For a second I have her feet, but they slip through my fingers. Kate's screams recede as the crow flies in the direction of Blacklands.

My head falls back, a feeling of utter despair pulses through me. The door smashes open. Richard with Isabel, the young maid, Morgana, Malcolm, Thomas, and Emmeline burst through all in stages of undress, demanding to know what is going on. They heard Kate's screams, tried to climb the tower's spiral staircase, but hundreds of bats attacked them on the way, stalling them, Isabel explains.

It's Rhauk's magic, I realize. "He took Kate—Katherine," I finally breathe, dropping to the bed, depleted. There is so much blood smeared over my back, neck, and chest, it's difficult to tell from where exactly it is coming.

"How could this happen?" Isabel cries. "We doubled the watch tonight, with extra guards posted around the bailey."

Weak with loss of blood, I sway toward the floor, grab the bedpost, and lean my head against it. "He was the crow."

"Then it is true," Richard hisses, crossing himself, his eyes shifting in the direction of Blacklands, looking dazed. "For many years we knew of his evil and trickery." His focus comes back to me. "That night he kidnapped your mother, Lionel said it was a crow. Black, with Rhauk's eyes. None of us believed him, just thought Lionel had temporarily lost his wits." He shakes his head wearily. "What sort of brother am I? I should have given my body and soul to protect them. And now my nephew follows the same fate."

I shake my head at the man, unable to share his pain

of guilt. My own thoughts are with Kate. Her fate, at the hands of a dangerous madman.

Morgana comes to me with a bowl of water and bits of rag. She takes a piece, dips it in the water, and attempts to wipe away some of the blood. I brush her away, unable to deal with anything other than the pain she can't get to. Inside. "How can I think of myself when Katherine is with Rhauk right now?"

"You have to let us treat your wounds, Jarrod," some soothing female voice croons. Emmeline's, I realize. "Morgana knows what to do. She's the best healer in the highlands. And you can't tackle Rhauk if you bleed to death first. What good would you be to Katherine then? You'll need all your strength to rescue her."

The girl is right, even though her voice sounds really false. I suddenly recall the force of that wind. It's gone now, so I concentrate, just like Kate said. It starts, slowly at first, but enough for me to finally understand—*the wind is mine*!

Some internal strength I can't as yet pinpoint has created it.

I focus even more intently. In seconds the wind gathers in magnitude until it ravages the room with the force of a hurricane. Nothing remains of the bedding, tapestries rip to shreds, Morgana's slight body flies across the room, bowls and ornaments thrash about. *I really do have a gift!* This recognition is unbelievable, strengthening my concentration, and the wind increases amazingly more.

"What's happening!" Richard cries, grasping a bed-post tightly to stop from being tossed around the room like the others.

I'll have to tell them eventually as I'll need their help, but I don't want to scare them. And I don't have the tolerance or knowledge to explain things I'm not even sure about myself. I'll have to think of a way that won't alarm them. But there's only one thought in my head right now. Getting Kate back.

I push through the wind to the north-facing window and stand before it. *"I will bring her back!"* I shout into the darkness.

I do this because I know Rhauk will be listening.

Kate

Even before I open my eyes I can tell it's morning as the sun is bright, though weak with the chill of late autumn. There is a strong taste of salt in the air, the sound of crashing waves loud in my head. If only last night had been a dream—a nightmare. I could live with that. But as I force my eyes to reluctantly open, I see I'm not in the tower at Thorntyne Keep and Jarrod is nowhere to be seen.

Of course it wasn't a dream. Who was I kidding? Scratches from last night's battle with the crow are raised and red on the skin of my arm and on one side of my face. There's blood on the front of my nightgown. Jarrod's.

The room is quite beautiful really. The bed is covered in white satin. There are deep blue drapes at the windows, a wall-size tapestry of a hunting scene—horses, hounds, and a black knight in full mail riding proudly on the back of a massive black stallion. It almost covers the entire opposite stone wall. There is a square of carpet on the floor beside a magnificent four-poster bed and a matching table with stool beneath the vivid tapestry. A ceramic washing bowl and urn adorn the table top.

I run to the window to see if there is any way I can climb down or jump. But it's a straight drop, about three stories high, over a jagged cliff face. The ocean, deep blue-green, smashes against sharp rocks below.

I sense Rhauk. The perception deep in my stomach scares me. Why am I so aware of him like this? Instinctively I understand that he knows I've woken and that he too is aware of me. Shivers break across my skin that have nothing to do with the fact that I'm only wearing a night-gown on a chilly autumn morning.

I spin around at the sound of his footsteps on the smooth timber floor. He has two pewter chalices in his hands. He sips from one, a drop of ruby red liquid hangs for a moment on his bottom lip, the other he extends to me, his voice sickeningly smug. "A celebration."

Frowning, puzzled, I cross my arms over my chest. "Go to hell."

His eyebrows lift as he draws near enough so that I can accept his offer of wine, and smell his pungent breath. "Not without you, my dear."

Air forces itself out of my lungs; his determination is so steely. For a flash of a second I recall the pigman and his not-so-warm greeting on finding out Jarrod was a relative of Lord Richard's. Pretending acceptance, I take the pewter chalice, draw in a mouthful of Rhauk's sweet red wine, and spit it back in his face.

For a flash of a second Rhauk looks surprised and angry. I think he's going to hit me, which doesn't particularly worry me at this moment. I'm so worked up I'll just hit him straight back, where it hurts, as hard as I can.

But he doesn't react predictably at all. Instead he laughs, deep from his chest, pulls out a square of black satin from his tunic, and wipes his face without shaking the smirk. "We will make a formidable pair, you and I, my Lady."

"I want no part of your schemes. I won't stay at Blacklands. Whatever you do to me, I'll find a way to deceive you."

"No doubt you would."

For a second his acknowledgment throws me. Is he acceding defeat? I doubt it. Obviously he has something devious planned. He walks across the room, places his pewter chalice on the table, studies the ceramic urn with such concentration you would think it was a photograph of his mother, then his penetrating eyes slide sideways. "There is only one way that Jarrod will stop me from generating my very clever curse."

Skeptical, I agree to listen. "Go on."

"It's simple really. A small swap."

Dread tightens the air passages to my lungs. "What sort of swap?"

A cunning smile forms slowly on his determined face. "You, for the curse."

"No."

"A little more thought on it, I think, my pretty."

"I don't have to think about it. And don't call me that."

He scoffs, amused. "I will call you whatever I want. You have no say in it. You belong to me now."

He moves closer, runs an ice-cold finger down the side of my face. I yank my head backward. "Stay away from me."

"Oh I will, for now. You see, I will have to get over my disappointment. At first sight, I swore you were a virgin. Just like my Eloise was."

I force myself not to react, not to break his illusion. Rhauk has superior senses, but must never find out Jarrod and I are not really married, nor even lovers. "So, now you know the truth, why do you still want me? Why not some innocent girl from the village?"

"That's simple, my lady. I've had plenty of those and they bore me. But you, now that I've had a taste of your talents, take on new meaning for me. You will make the perfect Queen for Blacklands."

He unnerves me completely. "How-how-how long will I have to stay with you?"

His smirk is an ugly grin. "I don't take you for being naive, Lady Kate. This curse is for eternity. I only want you for the rest of your life." His black eyes bore into mine. "Sounds fair, don't you think?"

I snort loudly. "What if I don't agree?"

He shrugs. "Oh well, Jarrod will die."

I can hardly breathe. My chest is aching. How I hate this man. He doesn't just represent evil, he is evil. Maybe the rumors about him are true, and the devil's blood does run in his veins.

"He will come for you," he continues smugly. "It will be in the form of a challenge. Already he's been making a nuisance of himself outside the gatehouse. But he is too weak, physically, and well, you know . . . in his mind."

"Jarrod was here?"

He looks bored. "He soon understood his pathetic attempts were useless. Not without something stronger than a handful of soldiers. His magic is unknown to his will, unexercised by his mind. His inexperience will be his downfall. That is, if he cares for you enough to make a challenge—one-on-one. Of course, there is always his delightful cousin to amuse him."

He means Emmeline. Rhauk is still playing his games. I try to ignore this comment by staying silent.

His hand sneaks out and grabs my chin. "A challenge is the only way he can draw me out of my castle." His fingers are like icy claws. "If you accept my offer, my lady, this boy who plays at being a man is free to return home, unharmed. He is a nuisance. I don't want him here. But of course he can only leave *without* you."

The pewter chalice in my fingers shakes as tremors wash through me. I clutch the goblet with both hands. Rhauk's fingers drop so I can reply. "How do I know you won't generate this curse whether I stay or not?"

"You'll be here to make sure of it."

As I think about this, he continues explaining, "Of course, the fool boy may still decide to challenge me, even after you have convinced him of your desire to stay at Blacklands. Either way I will uphold my end of the bargain. I won't produce the curse if you stay. It will be up to you to stop Jarrod from issuing the challenge. If he does, then so be it—I will have no choice but to kill him anyway."

Wordlessly I stare at him. He asks too much. My life, sacrificed to this madman, in exchange for not putting the curse on Jarrod's family. Either way, Jarrod could still die. Not fair.

Rhauk watches me carefully. "I want your answer by sunset. In the meantime, come," he offers his elbow. "Let me make your decision easier. I will show you Blacklands, the wonder of it, the *power* that can be ours."

I shrug off his offer of an elbow, and take a long swig of the wine instead. When the chalice is empty I toss it to the floor.

He seems pleased, a knowing smile slices his face. "Ah, that spirit. You present to me my greatest challenge. But you *will* be mine."

I hate him even more. But as I have the day to think on his proposition, I decide to make the most of my situation. Maybe the more I see of Blacklands, the better chance I have of spotting its weaknesses. "Show me the curse."

"Come," he says softly, appreciatively.

I follow him down a long dark corridor to a spiral staircase that climbs halfway to heaven. The solar tower is circular, unusual for this period in history, and bright, yet cold and draughty. Windows, many of them, open arched slits, surround us. I start to shiver in my thin nightgown, the chill breeze blowing through to my bones. Rhauk seems oblivious of the icy wind.

My feathery acquaintance, the crow, this one the smaller version, sits perched on a bar suspended on chains from the sharply pointed roof. Rhauk fishes something out from his tunic. The crow nibbles at it, then swallows greedily, inclining its head for a caress from its master as if saying thank you.

I glance around the room, dazed at the chaotic mess. It's stuffed with benches and haphazard shelves, containers overflowing with powders, crystals, and stones of all colors including black obsidian, all shades of red and brilliant blues. There are strange colored liquids and wizard's tools—an assortment of bells, wands, a dagger that has an unusually long blade. And of course the traditional work book—the *Book of Shadows*. There's an assortment of crude brewing apparatus as well, but I presume it's sophisticated equipment for this period in time. The floor has small holes and burnt areas where dripping chemical combinations have left their marks, probably during one of many of Rhauk's experiments.

One particular cauldron interests me. I feel drawn to it. Rhauk's eyes follow me around the room. I sense I have the curse at my fingertips, and wonder how difficult it is to brew, what ingredients stir inside it. Jillian would be able to tell me.

I step right up to the cauldron for a closer look. At first I'm disappointed. It's only red wine. Rhauk is making red wine up here. I look at him. "Where's the curse? You said you were brewing it."

"You are looking at it, my dear."

I point into the cauldron. "That's red wine."

"Ah, yes, so it is."

My brow furrows deeply as I study his smug attitude. I look again at the wine, and it hits me. "My God, it's the wine. You brewed the curse into the wine." It stuns me.

He laughs with boyish excitement. "You are clever. But never as clever as me, my Lady. This wine will quench the thirst of Thorntyne blood for generations. It's the quality you see," he explains, gloating. "Ahh, it is so smooth, so sweet, only Lord Richard himself, his immediate family, and perhaps a few treasured guests along the way, will be honored to drink it."

I know this plan will work. After all, this is the curse that goes on to haunt Thorntyne generations for more than eight hundred years. Its simplicity is superb. The wine at Thorntyne Keep is rough and very dry. Lord Richard will treasure this brew, hoarding it for himself and the only other thing he loves — his family. There's just one thing I want to know. "What makes you think Lord Richard will accept this wine from you? Won't he be suspicious?"

"My dimwitted half-brother will think this wine is a gift from the king."

"You have everything covered, don't you?"

He arches one eyebrow high, tilting his head at me. *"Everything."*

He's including me. I turn away to one of the many windows. This one looks south, Thorntyne Keep directly in its view. I wonder what Jarrod is doing right now, what he's thinking. He was outside the gatehouse early this morning. I crane my neck to see, but there's no one there now, the long track to Thorntyne Keep empty of travelers, disappearing into thick woods. I try a mind probe, needing to feel Jarrod's strength, assess his condition, but distance has me draw a blank. The thought occurs, maybe he died, from the wounds the crow inflicted last night. They could have festered and poisoned him. I remember in a sudden panic how much blood is on my nightgown. My fingers automatically trace the now dry stains.

"He lives," Rhauk suddenly says, startling me. For a second I think he can read my mind. But then I realize my emotions are there on my face as I gaze across to Thorntyne Keep. I glare at Rhauk, hating him with my eyes. He ignores me. "But the fool boy wasted his energy trying to reclaim you this morning after he lost so much blood last night. Richard should have warned him there is no way into Blacklands without an invitation."

My anger simmers over. "You did this to him!"

"Tsk, tsk," he croons, stroking the crow's face lovingly. "It was not me, my lady, but the crow. You must remember."

"That crow last night was you!"

He pretends a shocked look, his mouth hanging open. "Surely you jest."

"How did you do it?" My skin prickles with the knowledge that only the most powerful sorcerers of legend have this ability. Even though I grew up with magic, just thinking about the art of shapeshifting makes me shudder. It isn't human. "How did you transform into the shape of a crow?"

His black eyes glow eerily for a second. "Stay with me, Kate, and I will show you. No! I will *teach* you."

I shiver at the mere thought. "I don't want to turn into a bird, or anything else thank you."

"Ah, well, ultimately the choice will be yours." He turns his back and reaches for something on the bench top. It's a full length brown cloak. He throws it at me. "You have till sunset to make your decision. For now," he bows down at the waist, extending his arm in a mock gesture of greeting royalty, "you are my honored guest. Let us break our fast, then I will show you the rest of Blacklands."

Numb, I follow, throwing the cloak around my shivering shoulders, grateful for its warmth and protection as I accompany Rhauk.

It's not until much later that I find myself alone in my room. There are clothes laid out on the bed, a simple blue gown, but elegant in its simplicity, the fabric soft and silky. There are underthings as well, and soft leather boots. I'm reluctant to put anything on that belongs to Rhauk, but I need the clothes, if only to make myself more comfortable in Rhauk's presence.

I change and lie down on the bed, weary. I spend the last part of the day reflecting on everything I have seen and everything Rhauk has said. The man is not only a talented magician, he is tainted with madness. The proof of his magic is everywhere. I can't dismiss it. His gardens are unbelievable, rows upon rows of exotic fruits and vegetables, most of which grow out of season, some that have no rights at all growing under a cold British sun. And how clever to invent a cursed wine. A sweet wine for a stingy Lord; Richard's own greed the family's eventual downfall. Thorntyne family members will drink the wine regularly for the rest of their lives, oblivious to the fact that it has in it the ability to affect their very genes, causing inherent clumsiness in generations to follow. But the real power in the curse is its ability to lie dormant until the seventh-born son. That is the magic in it, and the misfortune that accompanies that child and all his family members.

It's this very reason Jarrod and I are here in this time period. But what price will we have to pay to stop this curse? Our lives? Jarrod will surely die if he challenges Rhauk. And I, well, my whole life will be a total waste. I'll never be able to return home. Never see Jillian again. The very thought of living the rest of my life at Blacklands, with Rhauk, is so unbearable it brings tears to my eyes. I blink and sniff them away.

The sun is rapidly sinking behind a distant gold-streaked horizon. Rhauk will soon come for my answer. I have to make a choice, but what choice do I have really? In my heart I realize there is only one way. I just have to convince Jarrod to return home to Jillian—without me. At least this way the curse will be stopped, and one of us can continue with our normal lives.

A part of me inside dies with this realisation. But what other way is there to stop this dangerous curse? Rhauk's powers are too strong for either Jarrod or me. But choosing to stay here at Blacklands satisfies Rhauk's need for revenge.

He will not give the gift of wine.

The price for Jarrod's freedom is to be my imprisonment.

Jarrod

Richard is right. He warned me that Blacklands is protected by Rhauk's witchcraft. Still, he did accompany me this morning, along with Malcolm, Thomas, and a dozen of his best knights. But it turned out a pointless exercise. Blacklands' gates will not open without Rhauk's permission, the gates and walls are warded under a protective spell.

On returning to Thorntyne Keep, Richard talks me into breaking our fast in the Great Hall. I have no appetite but last night's battle has left me weak. Morgana stitched the wound in my neck where the Rhauk-Crow dug his beak, and put herbal antiseptic on the talon scratches on my back.

I'm so worried about Kate in Rhauk's castle, my stomach can't stop churning. I can think of nothing except getting her back. Food is like cardboard in my mouth. But

I force myself to eat to build my strength. Of course I know that physical strength alone is not going to be enough to get Kate back. I need the strength my gift can give me. And it has to be more than just the ability to create strong wind. I need *magic*.

Kate believes I have it. It's time now for me to face the truth, accept my gift, and train. And for this I must have Richard's understanding. These people are deeply suspicious of the paranormal. It's part of the reason they hate Rhauk so much. Besides the fact that he wants their lands, they know he's an accomplished sorcerer of the black arts, and this terrifies them. I don't want to end up in their dungeon, or worse, dead, leaving Kate stranded at Blacklands forever.

I begin tentatively. "I have to challenge Rhauk."

Richard thumps his fist on the table while still holding a pig's shank. "Impossible! Do you think we have not tried?"

I sense his concern for me. I'm family, and that means a lot to him. I hope he remembers this after I explain. "With your help, my lord, I can beat him at his own game."

"Rhauk is a sorcerer!" Malcolm is sitting on his father's other side. "How do you suppose to outwit him, cousin?"

It's the opening I need. "With his own fire. Magic."

The table goes dead still. Even Isabel, who joins us for some conversation, looks startled. "Surely, you jest."

I look at both Richard and Isabel. Even though Richard is the lord, he looks to his wife for many decisions. "I don't mean to frighten anyone. I understand my gift now and I would never harm you. I just want to fight Rhauk and get Katherine back."

Malcolm pushes out from the table and glares at me, pointing a long finger. "Sorcerer! You're the one who caused the windstorms! One time here in the Hall, and last night in the tower."

"Yes," I agree, struggling to explain before Malcolm stirs up trouble for me. "But I didn't understand my powers then. I do now. Please, I need your help. I want to destroy Rhauk. I *have* to destroy him."

"And destroy us in the process!" Malcolm's voice now has the attention of others still lingering in the Hall.

"No! I only want *Rhauk*."

Malcolm's hand flies to his sword. Only Richard's quick action stops him from withdrawing it. "Stop, Malcolm. As your father and lord, I command it!"

Malcolm seethes, his eyes emerald daggers.

Richard looks thoughtful. "What are you capable of?" he asks me.

I shrug. "I'm not sure, that's the problem. I need to find out. But I don't want to frighten anyone. If you understand that what I do is not meant to harm, then I can go ahead and train myself."

"I may be able to help."

"What! Father, are you mad?"

"Be quiet, Malcolm! I've lived in Rhauk's shadow all my life, and one day, as lord of this manor, you will too. Only another adept in the black arts has a fighting chance with that devil."

My pulse is racing, but Richard's support is encouraging.

"What say you, my dear?" he asks his wife.

She is thoughtful for a long time, looking at me with a frown. "I have come to trust in Jarrod's good manner and loyalty. I think you should give him all the support he needs."

I smile a relieved thanks.

"My lady, this is an outrage!" Malcolm yells at his mother. "You are giving this heretic my inheritance on a platter! If we help this scoundrel, and he becomes powerful, more so perhaps than Rhauk, what's to stop him taking Thorntyne Keep for himself?"

Both Lady Isabel and Lord Richard anxiously await my counter-reply. I try to keep my voice calm and confident. "You have my word," I say. "As a Thorntyne."

I hope it is enough.

Kate

I start out for Thorntyne Keep at dawn the following morning on the back of Rhauk's black stallion—Ebony Prince. He is a massive animal, but, incredibly, easy to ride. He has a broad, powerful back, yet is surprisingly calm and steady. As if programmed, he knows exactly where he's going, and leads me straight to Thorntyne Keep's gatehouse.

Malcolm is on guard, with several other soldiers including Thomas, who can't hide his relief, assuring himself I'm unharmed. A very tense Malcolm announces he will take me to Jarrod. I follow him into the bailey to a private courtyard where Jarrod, bare to the waist, stands quietly staring at the drifting petals of a purple rose.

I gasp softly at the wounds on his back, one especially long row of stitches on the side of his neck. They look angry and I have to stop myself from running to him. I tell myself the wounds are freshly made and probably normal-looking considering. At least someone with healing skills has sewn him up, and for that I should be grateful. My fingers automatically slip to my chest; feeling the amulet of late gives me comfort. I'll be sorry to part with it.

Malcolm clears his throat and Jarrod spins around, Jillian's amulet reflecting the morning sun. "Kate!"

It's only one word but it's filled with so much—surprise, relief, passion. I have to work hard at schooling my features into something that resembles calm control, even disinterest. "Jarrod, I hope your wounds are healing all right."

"Morgana's a gifted healer. Your grandmother would enjoy a conversation with her."

It's my expression that stops him from running at me and spinning me around in his arms. I can see—*feel*—it's what he wants to do. I keep my shoulders stiff, my chin tilted high in a superior, standoffish manner. It's hard, but if I'm going to pull this off, Jarrod has to believe every word. Malcolm nods and leaves us.

"Did he hurt you?" he asks, taking one step closer now that we're alone.

"Not at all, he's really quite the charmer," I lie and lie and lie.

"Really? Well, your face is all scratched."

I stop my fingers from racing over the scratches I know are there. "It was the crow."

"It was Rhauk!"

With difficulty, I try ignoring his hostile tone. "He is a very clever man."

"He is evil."

I agree, but let none of it show. "Actually, Jarrod, his magic intrigues me."

One eyebrow shoots straight up. "What! How much?"

This is my cue. "So much that I've decided to stay with him."

He stares, motionless. And finally, just when I think I'm about to crack under his glare, he says, "You're lying."

Of course I am, but I can't let Jarrod know this. His freedom and his life depend on my being convincing. So I turn away, pretend an interest in the rose bushes that have recently been pruned and wonder fleetingly where the single purple rose came from. My eyes, I know, will be his key to seeing into my soul. "He offered to make me his Queen. He wants to share his powers with me, teach me all he knows. It's an opportunity I can't—"

"This is rubbish, Kate! It's all lies! How can you fall for it? He's just using you."

"No, he's not. He wants me."

His voice is whisper-soft, but I hear every word. "I want you too."

I harden my face, swallow the sudden lump in my

throat. "Well," I spin around to face him, determined to make this work, "I want Rhauk." And before I lose my nerve, I slip off the amulet that hangs from my neck and quickly place it in Jarrod's hand. "You'll need this to get home. Remember the words."

He stares at me, his head shaking with astonished disbelief. "You can't be serious."

"I am, Jarrod. Deadly serious." For this is how I feel, dead inside.

"And what has Rhauk promised in return? To stop the curse?"

I fight to hide my surprise, battle to keep my face smooth and appropriately bored. "But of course. It's a fair exchange."

"Your life is more important, Kate, than an exchange of promises that you have no way of knowing he is even going to keep!"

"He will keep his promise, Jarrod. I'll be there to make sure of it."

"Is that why you're staying?"

"No!" God, he's so close to the truth. "I want to stay."

"You're lying."

This time I have to convince him. "Look, I know this is difficult to accept, especially after, well . . . the other night." I feel my face heat up, remembering how his hands had felt. I force the memories away. "I've finally found a place for myself in this world with Rhauk. You know in that other world I'm a social outcast. I can't practice any magic. I have no freedom, nothing like the freedom I could have here with Rhauk. He's a master, Jarrod. And I'm sick of the way they treat me in that other world. I want to live where I'm welcome, where I'm accepted. Surely you can understand that concept."

And I know this will hurt, but I have to do it. I try to make my voice brim with hatred. "You were worse than all of them, with your pretend interest. I thought you were my friend, but did you ever acknowledge our friendship in public?"

Inside I cringe at the total look of self-disgust that fills his face.

"I don't want to live like that, Jarrod. Here, with Rhauk, I don't have to. And I can work my magic, and learn from a true magician."

"I will still challenge him."

"Aren't you listening?" Panic fills me. "There's no need. You're free. Use the amulets, say the words Jillian taught us. You could be home in minutes, and things will be different now. Your family will be normal again, not jinxed with one disaster after another. Don't they deserve this chance? And what about you? Think about this, Jarrod: You can return to the world of Tasha and Jessica and Pecs and Ryan, and enjoy the life you were meant to have."

"Do you really think I'm that shallow, Kate? How can I return knowing that I've left you here with this monster? On my behalf?"

"I *want* this. I don't want what you can offer."

This time my words have the effect I'm looking for. But then his eyes flicker with disbelief, and I can sense his doubts resurfacing. "I will still challenge him," he repeats stubbornly.

God, how can this be so hard! I struggle to stop myself from screaming at him. "For goodness' sake, Jarrod, aren't you listening!"

His eyes narrow as he looks at me astutely. "Why are you so edgy? Why is it so important that I return home?"

Because it will all be for nothing if you die! I shrug. Aiming for unconcern, I give myself a moment to invent something that will drive him away from me without remorse. And then it hits me. I spin around and look him straight in the face. "I'm worried that someone might get hurt."

His face fills with relief and a tremulous smile forms, followed by a gentle hand that reaches out to me.

I ignore it. "It's possible, now that you realize your gift, that you could hurt him."

His entire body freezes. *"Him?"*

I nod, my mouth desert-dry.

His hand falls to his side, bunches into a white fist. *"Rhauk!* Are you protecting Rhauk now!"

I try to work moisture into my mouth. "Of course. Who else?"

His eyes grow round, his mouth hanging open. Then he collects himself, emotions and all. "Do you love him?"

My chest tightens. I swallow hard. "He is my life now. I want no other."

There is nothing else to say. I can't stand here and look on Jarrod's stricken face one second longer without breaking down and telling him everything. I spin on my heels and walk away. Back to Ebony Prince. Back to Rhauk. But I will never forget the look on Jarrod's face.

He was devastated. And angry. I hope he'll grow even angrier, so much that he will grab those amulets, smash the amber crystal that surrounds our link home, and chant the Latin words lodged in our brains—before he stops to think.

I need him to do this, to give my sacrifice purpose.

Jarrod

I can't believe it. Kate came back. I could've squeezed her to death; couldn't put a name to the emotions I felt. Malcolm brought her to me, still looking bitter and resentful. I ignored his attitude as I sensed straight away something about Kate was odd. Malcolm left us alone, but still I couldn't go to her. She had this don't-touch-me, don't-come-anywhere-near-me kind of look. At first I thought it was because Rhauk hurt her, physically, emotionally, or both. So I was careful not to rush at her. But it turned out he hadn't hurt her, at least that's the story she gave.

It's hard to believe any of it was true, but she was so convincing.

She's leaving now. I want to run after her and grab her, bring her back, but my legs won't move. I feel shattered inside. I want to hate her. What's even more shocking, I want to put my hands around her throat and shake some reality into her brain. I squeeze my hands into tight fists, and feel Kate's amulet dig into my palm. I pull it over my head, wrapping my hand around the two of them together. One hard squeeze will be enough to rupture the amber crystal. I could be home in minutes.

But I can't do it. Not yet at least. Not until I'm sure of Kate's motives. If she didn't love this period so much, if she didn't love her magic so much, I'd say for sure she's just doing this for me. How can I tell what's the truth? She was very convincing. Yet, as long as there is even one chance she's sacrificing her life for me, I could never turn my back on her. I would rather die.

And die I might when I challenge Rhauk. But I'm not so stupid as to try before I spend some time harnessing, training my powers. What little I've learned is enough to control the flow of energy when I lose my temper. Winds that have often been gale force, cyclonic even, don't happen anymore, at least not unless I want them to. It's a small achievement, but one that tells me I can train my gift. This morning I played with Isabel's garden. She'd only just pruned her roses. I made a bud form, then watched it bloom and die, all in the space of one or two breaths.

"Jarrod?"

It's Emmeline. I groan. Not again. The girl is bored out of her mind. Stitching tapestries all day, who wouldn't be? Unfortunately, there's nothing I can do to help her. A handheld computer game is out of the question. "Emmeline, what is it this time?"

She sits on a stone bench, gathering her long mauve silks around her ankles, pretending to accidentally lift them so that her ankles and a good part of her pale-skinned calf is left showing. I could laugh as a vision of a group of girls sunbathing in brief two-piece swimsuits flashes through my head.

"A small request," she murmurs silkily.

I sit beside her trying not to groan too loudly. "Go on."

"When you leave here, I want you to take me with you."

"But—"

She lifts a hand to shut me off. "Wait, Jarrod. Listen, please. You don't know what it's like living here. I want to travel, I want to see the world. Your world."

"What makes you think it's any better where I come from?"

"Of course it is. Look at you, how worldly you are, knowledgeable."

"I'm sorry, Emmeline. When Katherine and I leave here, we're not going where you think we are."

"Are you not going home?"

I don't want to lie, but I can't tell her the truth either. "Not exactly."

She moans dramatically. "It doesn't matter where you take me. I can't stand living here anymore. I am going slowly mad. And you will want company on your journey, Jarrod. Company that will keep you warm at night."

I look at her, hard. She's definitely in the wrong time period. Unfortunately, that's her tough luck. "I have Katherine."

She twists her lips. "Yes, of course. What was I thinking?" She stands to leave, shaking her skirts into order.

"I *will* get her back, Emmeline."

"Hmm, perhaps she will grow to like Blacklands. I've heard much gossip from the village. The young maidens say Rhauk is not without charm."

I tower over her, wanting at this moment to strangle the girl. I wonder fleetingly what difference this might make to history. I can't take the chance even if I did surprise myself and do it. She doesn't even flinch, just brushes her fingernails across the skin of my shoulder so that they leave thin red streaks, and smiles demurely, provocatively. Her message is clear. It makes me want to spew.

"Maybe *you* should try him," I suggest.

Malcolm arrives, his eyebrows lifting with interest when he sees Emmeline's eyes on me. She sees him and waves a loose wrist. To me she throws a cunning smile that doesn't reach her eyes. Then she laughs, short and cynical.

She leaves me with the impression that where Rhauk is concerned, she knows it all already.

"What was that all about?" Malcolm asks.

"She's bored. You should take her hunting."

He scoffs. "She finds riding distasteful. Court life would suit that wench."

"She wants to leave here."

"When I am lord she will, if not before. Father is aware of my wishes, as I am aware of her seductive games. She's tried them with me as well, Jarrod. Being a cousin makes no difference to that wench." His voice drops. "Be wary, she'll force herself between you and Katherine."

I cringe, wishing there was something between Kate and me that would warrant forcing. But his remarks about being lord one day remind me there are some things we need to discuss. His hostility toward me is coming from seeing me as a threat. "You will be Lord of Thorntyne Keep one day, Malcolm."

"Not if you have anything to do with it, cousin."

I put my hand on his shoulder, trying to assure him my words are sincere. "I do not want Thorntyne Keep."

He brushes my hand away. "Bah! For what other reason are you here?"

He will tell if I'm lying, so I can't just give him any excuse. "It's hard to explain my reasons, except that where I come from we've heard of Rhauk and his evil ways."

His eyebrows shoot up. "His reputation is far-reaching for sure."

"And as I have . . . strange abilities—"

'Witchcraft!"

"In a way, I guess," I acknowledge reluctantly. "It was decided I could help rid my relatives of Rhauk's evil powers."

I see with relief Malcolm is actually considering this explanation. I need him as a friend, not an enemy. "There's something in what you say."

I breathe easier, and feel aligned with him tentatively. "There is something else you should know. It's about my brother."

He peers at me with a frown.

"He's going to challenge you one day. I can't say when, but I know it is his intention."

"Does he gather an army as we speak?"

This I don't know. But when the challenge arrives I do know that after a difficult battle, Malcolm will win. I wish I could tell him this, but it might make him cocky, not prepare properly. And if this makes him lose the battle, then Thorntyne history will change. Jillian's warning not to interfere rings in my ears. "He's very strong. You should prepare thoroughly, and always be on alert."

His green eyes shimmer with thanks. I think I've just made a friend.

The next couple of weeks pass in a blur. I become frantic for news of Kate. She remains at Blacklands with Rhauk. And I *feel* him now, his aura, his energy— something impossible to my imagination a short while ago. He grows edgy. I guess that's because he can sense my powers growing. It makes him uneasy.

Every day I train. Richard and Malcolm help me, pushing me into new areas of magic as soon as I accomplish one aspect or trick. Morgana helps too, as she has a talent of her own, not psychic or anything, a kind of mellow magic, healing with herbs her specialty. And thanks to Morgana my wounds are healing nicely. She removed the stitches from my neck only this morning. Both of us were pleased to see the earlier signs of infection disappearing.

Unfortunately Emmeline watches me train too, ever eager to find an excuse to be near me. I try to ignore her advances. I don't want to be responsible for hurting her feelings, but as I get to know her better, I realize, the girl doesn't have any, except for her own beauty and desire to have her sexual appetite satisfied.

I'm even growing closer to Richard and Isabel, especially now that they accept the evidence of my "witchcraft." The feelings are returned. If there is one loyalty that Richard has, it's to his family; except Rhauk, with whom he adamantly denies any blood link. To do so would mean to lose Thorntyne Keep; Rhauk as the eldest son, would inherit all. Richard will never let this happen, his love for his lands, his castle, his family, are the things that drive him.

At times I try to make him think about his loyalty to his village, the peasants and workers there. But he scoffs at this, and I remember I shouldn't interfere. To Richard there is a clear line between noblemen and women, his family, his knights, and the lower class of crafts people and farm workers. He sees them only as peasants, scum of the earth.

It seems I can't work spells like Kate, my magic is all from my head. A kind of thought projection that actually changes things. Nature is the easiest for me to work with. I've made Isabel's precious roses bloom double in size on every bush, and withered her herb garden with one concentrated look. She tells me off, but with affection, and hugs me when I return her garden to thriving health.

I have a long way to go, but I sense Rhauk's restlessness. I just hope he can hold on to his temper until I've learned enough skills to better him. It's possible, of course, that I may never have enough strength. Even knowing this, it will not stop me from fighting him. It has turned into more than a battle to save my family and future descendants from a frightful curse now. It has become a personal battle.

For Kate.

And I go crazy every day I don't hear anything. As

I improve in the paranormal arts, I also improve in the physical. I need to know how to wield a sword, and fight with my hands if necessary. I've had many volunteers helping me in these areas. Today it's Malcolm. My worry for Kate comes up in conversation as I deflect a lunge from his sword.

"I have an idea about this," he says and explains himself.

His plan is good; I consider its merits. After a long discussion the plan is fine-tuned and ready to put into action.

It will prove to be a test of Malcolm's friendship.

Kate

It's been almost three weeks and Jarrod hasn't returned home. Rhauk refuses to teach me anything until he rids himself of Jarrod, one way or another; but Rhauk is aware of Jarrod's presence. So I know Jarrod is still at Thorntyne Keep. Every day he remains, Rhauk grows more restless, peevish. He has a foul black temper. I've only to mention Jarrod's name and the man goes insane on me. I've learned to shut my mouth. Most of the time, anyway. But sometimes I just can't help it. My perverse side enjoys seeing Rhauk lose control.

Time is passing agonizingly slowly. I have so little to do. Mostly I'm confined to my room, looking out over the inhospitable ocean. I spend many hours just thinking: How easy would it be to lean across the stone window ledge far enough to lose my balance? My pain would end, but what else would this achieve? There would be no one then to watch Rhauk, to keep him to his promises.

He storms into my room in a fit of temper, the darkest I've seen yet. As usual he wears all black, this time only a ribbon of silver rims the edges of his tunic and undershirt. "He leaves me no choice, my lady!"

I pull away from the window ledge and face him. "What are you talking about? Who leaves you no choice?"

He jerks an extended arm, pointing vaguely in the direction of Thorntyne Keep. A shower of gold sparks smashes into the stone wall to my left. "Your lover!"

I don't correct him, letting him believe his fantasy. As long as he thinks Jarrod and I are lovers, he leaves me alone, sexually at least. Besides this bonus, the idea positively irritates Rhauk. Something that gives me immense pleasure.

"What is Jarrod doing that so upsets you?"

His black eyes narrow, but he remains silent. He isn't going to tell me. Whatever it is, though, has got him in a real spin. With a sudden insight that nearly knocks me over, I understand. My mouth drops open, then transforms into a smile I can't stop from spreading across my face. "He's training, isn't he?" Rhauk doesn't reply. He doesn't have to. I can smell his disapproval. So Rhauk knows Jarrod's gift is truly immense, and now that Jarrod is learning how to use it, Rhauk is getting nervous. My pulse starts racing. "Jarrod's getting stronger, isn't he?"

Silence.

"My God, his powers are growing so strong, he's scaring you."

"Shut up, wench!"

His icy tone doesn't scare me like it probably should. I'm too hyped up with the knowledge of what Jarrod's been doing with his time—accepting the gift, harnessing his powers. "You're afraid of him," I dare. "You're panicking!"

He flies across the room and hits me all in the space of one heartbeat. If only I'd been paying more attention to his mood, I might have been able to avoid the connection. Instead, Rhauk's fist smashes into the right side of my jaw. Sharp pain throbs from ear to chin. Something falls onto my tongue, small and solid. A tooth, I soon realize, and spit it out. There is blood too. I taste it. The bastard.

I would try a quick spell, but there's no point. Rhauk would only be amused. The spells I have tried over the past few weeks have proved useless. He's aware of everything I do. He outsmarts me. I detest him.

He heads for the door, but turns just before it with an afterthought. "Jarrod must be gone by morning. Right now I am going to pluck my sweet little herb out of the ground by its roots and extract the oil I need that way to finish this damn curse. This close to winter the strength of its poison will be sufficient, and will make no difference to the sweet taste of my wine."

"You would break your promise?"

He laughs coarsely. "My lady, did you really think I would keep it?"

"But . . . you said . . . if I stayed—"

"I lied."

"Why? I lived up to my end of the bargain. I came back to you!"

"And I gave you what you wanted—freedom for your lover to return from wherever he came. It's *your* fault he didn't leave. You obviously didn't try hard enough to convince him."

Nausea hits me. I sway and grab the bedpost nearby. "But the curse, you promised to destroy it. It was part of the deal!"

"If I hadn't promised, would you still have chosen *me*?"

This does not require an answer. He knows I would never have, and this explains the reason for his lies. He tricked me. Just like he thinks Eloise had been tricked into choosing Lionel instead of him all those years back. And Jarrod will probably still die, and I'm trapped in this cold and drafty hell-hole with a dangerous lunatic for the rest of my life. It's all been for nothing. The curse will still go ahead. And there is no way Jarrod will be gone by sunrise. The thought hits me that I will never see Jillian again.

I have to try something; panic threatens to suffocate my lungs. How can this have happened? I watch, my soul filled with black, passion-fueled hatred, as Rhauk moves toward the door. "If you go ahead with the curse—breaking your promise to me—I will jump out of this window, taking my chances with the cliffs below."

This seizes Rhauk's attention. His eyebrows lift, black eyes shift to the only window in the room, the one that overlooks the cliff, contemplating, assessing the weight of my threat. Would I really go through with it? When he turns back, he searches for my eyes, and locks with them. He is too fast, the effect hypnotic. "In that case, my lady, you leave me no choice but to control your mind sooner rather than later."

"What?"

He doesn't bother to explain. Immediately I feel a sharp stab of energy. He moves closer and the energy that holds me suddenly changes, twists, piercing like a dagger straight into my mind. It is so intense it hurts, and takes all my concentration to stop it from penetrating my brain so deeply I feel sure it will cause permanent brain damage.

I try to break free, but all attempts prove useless. My legs give out on me, but the power of Rhauk's punishment holds me frozen. The energy grows and electricity jolts through my body in shuddering waves.

I know the moment I start to lose it. Control, the remaining trickle I cling to, finally disappears. I begin to plead, in my mind, through my mind. I don't know if he hears me, or whether it incites him more, but I understand that if he doesn't release me now, my mind will never be the same, but altered, damaged. Forever.

I fall to the floor in a heap, the connection finally severed. I don't know why he let go, except perhaps he doesn't want me that way—brain-dead. Whatever his reasons, I'm too drained to think at this moment.

I do hear him though, as I start to lose my grip on consciousness. "You will never escape me, Lady Katherine. That was just a sample of what is to come for you. After I'm done with your lover, and after I've delivered the gift of wine to my traitorous brother, I will attend to your training. And you will be mine—*completely*."

I think he is going to leave, but at the door he pauses. "It was something I wanted for Eloise, but her mind wasn't as strong as yours." He turns back for one last look. "By the time I've finished with you, my lady, you will appreciate the beauty of Blacklands, and enjoy being my queen."

Jarrod

I'm aware of the exact moment my time runs out. Rhauk does something to Kate. Power, a surge of energy so strong I feel it in my own head, like someone is twisting a corkscrew into my skull. I wonder, fleetingly, if she will live through it. Her pulse is slow, so slow. But she lives. For now, that's all I have.

So I am forced out of training and into a challenge. Tomorrow, at dawn, I will meet Rhauk in battle.

"Jarrod, what's wrong?"

Richard's voice is concerned. He breaks through my image of Kate near death. I explain what I feel. "It is time, my lord."

His eyes grow in alarm. I hear his mind thoughts, reading his doubts. We both know I've trained hard, and with his and Malcolm's help and that of the other knights, and of course the maid, Morgana, I can do incredible things now. Things I never thought possible. But still, Richard wonders if I'm strong enough to match Rhauk. Strong enough to *better* Rhauk.

I throw my arm around his shoulder. "I had better be, my uncle," I say, surprising him that I accurately read his thoughts. "Rhauk will not give me a second chance."

Kate

I come to while still on the floor. Slowly I drag myself to
the bed and sit, my head heavy in my hands, as if it's
filled with lead. I try to recall what happened and how I
ended up in this state, but I hear distant voices. The sound
is so unusual it has my instant attention. In all the time I've
spent at Blacklands, never once have I heard Rhauk in
conversation with anyone except his crow. But this is different. There are two distinct voices, both male, one definitely Rhauk's. The other . . . I can't place, yet it sounds
vaguely familiar.

I stumble to the door. It's not locked. There's no point,
no one can leave or enter Blacklands without an invitation.
It's magically enchanted. The gates operate at his command. Only the birds are free to fly in and out.

Thank God my head starts to clear. It gives me the
strength I need to find out who is Rhauk's visitor. Perhaps

it is someone who can help me escape. This thought triggers an adrenaline surge. I walk the corridors with bare feet, tracing the sounds of conversation.

I find them eventually in the Refectory, which used to be the room where the nuns did their learning. It still has several of the original chairs and desks. I stay just outside the slightly open door, my heart galloping so intensely, I'm sure I'm on the verge of swallowing it.

This close at least, I can make out their words. At first I think, At last, here's the help I need, if only to get a warning to Jarrod. The other voice is Malcolm's — Lord Richard's son.

It only occurs to me when I hear them laughing, that something is terribly wrong with this scene. They sound on too good of terms; and how did Malcolm get into Blacklands? By Rhauk's invitation? Or did Malcolm request this meeting? Knowing Rhauk, anything Malcolm requests will carry an expensive price tag.

I listen, cautious not to send out a mind probe as Rhauk would know instantly where I am.

"So," Rhauk's velvety voice echoes through the hollow rooms. "Your information is interesting in the least. Our mutual acquaintance has come far these past weeks. Of course, not nearly far enough to better me."

"Of course not."

There is an audible pause, then Rhauk again, "Do we have the same goal in mind?"

Unhesitatingly, Malcolm replies, "You know I treasure Thorntyne Keep as much as you do Blacklands."

Surely Malcolm isn't that naive. Rhauk wants Thorntyne Keep as well as Blacklands, if only to satisfy his need for revenge.

"Your information shall not go unrewarded," says Rhauk.

"I'm just glad I can be of service. The sooner this scoundrel is dispensed with, the better we'll all be. But . . ." There is a pregnant pause. I think my heart stops. "If you have a small reward in mind . . . Perhaps an evening with the sweet Lady? She still keeps you company I assume."

I fall back as if I've been physically pushed. My God! Malcolm means me! Rhauk laughs, his voice dripping with sarcasm. "Oh yes, she makes intriguing company. And, my friend, don't fear, for your reward shall be very sweet indeed."

I can guess what this means. As soon as this business with Jarrod is over, Rhauk will probably murder Malcolm, whom he no doubt sees as another threat to securing his inheritance. Can't Malcolm see this? Obviously his fear over Jarrod claiming his inheritance blocks his mind to other dangers. The man isn't only a traitor, feeding Rhauk inside information about Jarrod's emerging powers, no doubt informing Rhauk of Jarrod's strengths and weaknesses, but Malcolm is also a fool. He'll most likely die for his mistakes.

Well, it will be a just death.

The meeting breaks up, and I stumble in a mad panic to get out of sight. I don't go back to my room though. I can't. Somehow I just have to warn Jarrod that he has a traitor in his camp. A man that cannot be trusted. So I decide to give it one more try. Escape. I find my way to the stables. Ebony Prince neighs restlessly in his stall, several mares snicker as I pass their stalls. But I have to take this risk. The horses are the only things I haven't already tried. I've never had an opportunity like the one that's about to present itself. And Ebony Prince took me once to Thorntyne Keep, perhaps if I can convince him, he will again. I'm counting on a lot going my way. It all hinges on the gates. They won't open without Rhauk's request. But they're about to when Malcolm leaves.

I hear noises behind me and my body jerks. It's Malcolm. And he's on his own. I see the opportunity in my mind. Quickly I slide into Ebony Prince's stall, climb on to his bare back, crooning sweet calming words into his ear, probing his mind gently to keep his thoughts disorganized. I have never tried to mind probe an animal; it's a strange experience. At least he lets me climb on, shaking his head in an oddly bewildered way, and I sense my probe is working.

I hear the gates swing on their hinges. Without a second thought for the way I'm straddling the horse, or how my skirts have ridden halfway up my bare thighs, I dig my knees into Ebony Prince's thickly muscled stomach. He bolts through the outer stable doors, and with a little further probing, heads straight for the open gates.

Malcolm hears the pounding hooves and jumps out of the way. What I don't count on though is Malcolm's quick recovery. He is, I realize a short distance out of Blacklands, a trained knight. He jumps onto his own waiting horse and starts chasing me through the woods.

Low branches, sharp twigs, overgrown berry bushes catch at my clothing, my hair, my arms. I ride low to the horse's back, my arms tight around his thick neck, urging him to go faster and faster. The hooves pounding behind me grow too close for comfort. Malcolm is catching up fast.

Even though it is still daylight I find it more and more difficult to see where I'm going. I try to convince Ebony Prince to head in the direction of Thorntyne Keep, but the woods are thick around me, and I can't tell if my probe is working anymore.

Malcolm is so close now, I can feel his horse's grunts near my back.

I see the fallen tree only seconds before Ebony Prince leaps. Having nothing but the horse's neck to cling to, I'm not surprised to find myself flying through the air. I land on my back in a small patch of green meadow.

Momentarily stunned, all I can do is watch as Malcolm rides his horse right up to my face. "Well, well, such an interesting riding style you have, my lady."

Not ready to accept defeat, I struggle quickly onto all fours, with the intention of making a run for it. But Malcolm is with me in a flash, his superior knight's training undoubtedly the reason his reflexes are so sharp. He drags me back, tossing me to the grass. I land on my rear, looking up at him.

"He's going to kill you too!" I scream at him, hoping to make him see the reality here.

"Don't worry about me, Lady Katherine. I know what I'm doing."

"No, you don't know him like I do. He lies, he makes promises he has no intention of keeping. He's using you just as he used me. He tricked me into staying with him, and now he's tricking you. Only when he has complete control of Thorntyne Keep will his lust for revenge be satisfied." I lunge for breath. "He has no reward in mind for you, Malcolm, except your own death. And in a way that *would* be a reward. Far better dead than spend the rest of your life as Rhauk's mind slave. Believe me."

He stares at me, his green eyes narrow, thinking. An awkward silence stretches between us, then Malcolm glances quickly over his shoulders. With his attention back to me he reaches out a hand to help me up. I feel a fleeting moment of hope, and put my hand in his.

"You found her. Good work!"

Oh no. It's Rhauk, riding one of the mares from his stable. This one an elegant gray. He's even taken the time to saddle her. His arrogance has me seething.

Malcolm yanks me up harder than is warranted, twisting my hand behind my back. I force myself not to cry out. Just as suddenly he pushes me toward Rhauk. I fall against the gray mare who bucks in protest. "Irons, I think Rhauk, to keep this wench inside your castle walls."

Rhauk leans down and drags me up into the saddle in front of him. The feel of him at my back has bile jumping into my throat.

Rhauk nods at Malcolm, whistles to Ebony Prince, who trots faithfully, looking a bit disoriented, beside us. Then we are riding back to Blacklands. I swing my head around for one more look. Malcolm hasn't moved. He just stands there staring, the strangest expression on his face.

Strange, that is, for a traitor.

Kate

The challenge is delivered by a white dove just before sunset. I'm with Rhauk in the tower, my hands shackled together with irons as Malcolm suggested, watching with a sickening dread, as Rhauk finishes his cursed wine. He searched out the final ingredient, a winter-flowering herb, and in his laboratory extracted the oil he needed from the herb's own roots. As he blends this oil into the wine, his facial expression is one of complacency. It's as he glances across at me with a sickening, self-satisfied grin, that the white dove makes itself known.

It has Rhauk's attention straight away. "What is this?"

We both stare at it while it hovers over a window ledge, looking reluctant to land. The crow, which is sitting on his usual perch, squawks at it, attempting to chase it away, but Rhauk holds up his hand and the crow falls into a silent sulk.

Finally the dove lands on the window ledge. Rhauk picks it up in one hand and examines it. There's a message attached to one of its legs. Rhauk takes the tiny piece of parchment and drops the bird. It flaps its wings, losing a couple of feathers, regains its balance, and flies away.

I watch Rhauk's eyes as he reads the parchment. They widen with surprise, which he covers quickly with boyish excitement. Not once does he show fear. Why should he, now that he has Malcolm to watch his back? His eyes find mine. "The fool boy has dared to challenge me."

Dread and nausea hit me full on. Is this really happening? How can Jarrod possibly beat this maniac? Jarrod is just a gawky, clumsy kid, who can't see properly without his glasses. I wonder who helped him write the challenge. I doubt Jarrod's eyes would have managed the tiny script. And even if he has trained these past weeks, Rhauk's powers are as natural to him as breathing. What chance can Jarrod have? If only the odds were fairer . . . If only I could be there to help him . . . Maybe, our talents combined . . . Maybe, if we caught Rhauk in an unguarded moment . . .

Rhauk interrupts my thoughts. "He requests a duel."

"Duel?"

"By sword, on neutral ground."

This is terrible news. Swords are heavy; it takes years of training to be able to handle one with any form of skill.

"And since Jarrod named the weapon, I get to choose the ground." He glances outside thoughtfully. "Minneret Cliffs, I think."

My eyes bulge at this. Minneret Cliffs is a dangerous stretch of coastline, almost the exact center between the two peaks—Blacklands and Thorntyne. There are no tumbling sand dunes, only incredible sheer white cliffs.

"Tomorrow's dawn."

"No!" I exclaim. "This can't happen."

"Ah, but it is, my pretty."

Pleading, I decide, is the one thing I haven't already tried. "Please, Rhauk, think this through. You have the things you want. Let Jarrod go unharmed."

His lips twitch, watching me. "Yes, I do have you, and the curse. But it's not my fault that boy-man has no foresight. Obviously he can't see his own death looming in the coming dawn. I shall make it a vivid reality."

"I want to be there."

"Of course you do. I wouldn't have it any other way." His eyes narrow, assessing me. "But, I will have to do something to stop you from interfering."

"Noooo!" God, he's one step ahead of me every time. How can anyone beat this logic?

I watch, sickeningly, as Rhauk excitedly starts gathering bits and pieces from around his lab. An herb, a vial of blue liquid, a mix of powders.

My head swivels from side to side. Grinning, he comes at me with a frothing liquid mixture. It's a drug, of that I'm sure.

"Something to drain your energies, it won't taste too bad."

"No, I won't—"

"You only need a few drops." He grabs my chin with his free hand, gripping it with the force of a steel vice, his grin disappearing.

"No!" I scream, my hands useless and heavy in the chains. Quickly, I shut my mouth, adamant that not one drop of the drugged mixture will so much as touch my lips.

But I'm not prepared for Rhauk's tactics. He removes his hand from my chin, forms a fist, and punches me just below my ribs. My mouth flies open in exclamation as I struggle for air—shock and pain startling me. He throws the vile mixture into my mouth. It chokes me, burns all the way. I lurch forward at the blow to my stomach, doubling over with pain, and spit as much of the liquid out as I can.

Rhauk moves away, satisfied, and begins stirring the cursed wine. "After the challenge, I will begin bottling. A few more days, and Richard will have the King's precious gift."

I drag in several deep breaths, straightening carefully, trying to recover from the blow to my stomach. I wipe my mouth against my shoulder. The effect of the drug is immediate. The room swings away from me, becoming distorted. I sway, falling against a bench.

This distracts Rhauk. "You, my pretty lady, had better get to bed, for tonight Death will be your bedfellow. Do not be alarmed, he will not claim you, but simply take your strength." Carrying me down the long twisting staircase, Rhauk laughs, wrapped in a blanket of his own self-confidence.

He drops me on the bed, where I curl into a ball. Rhauk moves back, tilts his head so that he can peer into my face. "Yes," his velvety voice purrs. "You will be useless to the fool boy, drained of all your magic. Drained almost of life itself," he adds as an afterthought.

As he steps farther from the bed, my eyes close, heavy, like lead weights are dragging on them. I feel myself sink down, down, spiralling down. It's dark, black, it frightens me, but still I descend. I smell Death in this despair, grinning and sharpening his teeth, luring me even deeper.

Rhauk's voice drifts, blurred now, distant. But even in the depths of this dark pit I can still make out his parting words. "And Jarrod will be satisfactorily distracted, when he sees his lover so completely under my control."

And then I understand why he drugged me. Not only to stop me from helping Jarrod perform tricks, but to form a distraction, so Jarrod will lose his concentration during the battle. Rhauk is using me as a tool to help him beat Jarrod. It strikes me as ironic that my attempts to save Jarrod are now being used to murder him.

Moisture fills my eyes but I don't care that Rhauk or the devil himself sees my tears. I'm too drained to stop them.

Rhauk leaves me with the bitter taste of hatred in my mouth, and Death for company.

Kate

He dresses me like a queen, all royal red and gold silk, my hair twisted into a coil about my head. Around my throat he hangs a heavy gold chain of miniature twisting snakes. He wears his usual black, the serpent gold buckle fixed at his waist. He looks compelling, all-powerful. I am nothing more than a rag doll, my limbs unnaturally heavy, memories of last night's drugged nightmare-filled sleep slowly but thankfully receding.

It's not quite dawn when we arrive on Ebony Prince's back. Minneret Cliffs span alarmingly before us, the gray-pink streaks of early dawn shedding enough light to reveal stark white rockface. Rhauk drags me to the jutting point of a cliff edge, so close the breath of a seagull could tip me over. Earth and small chalklike rocks break free, collapsing under my fingers. I struggle to inch slowly away from the loose edge.

As well as my hands, Rhauk also chained my feet. I wonder why? In my drugged state I'm hardly a threat. Just concentrating is difficult. I haven't the strength to move, let alone work magic. I half sit, half lie, aware of the salt spray rising up from the dark lonely ocean far below, its heart pulsing to its own eternal beat.

We wait. But it isn't a long wait. Hooves pound the road descending from Thorntyne Keep as the sun cracks the horizon, spreading gray-gold fingers of light into this inevitable morning. Soon Jarrod rides into view.

He looks formidable and my heart, struggling to increase its pace, beats a little harder at the sight of him. He's dressed all in gold, the Thorntyne crest with two white doves hovering over a purple rose, blazes on his tunic front. A gold chain looks heavy at his slim waist. He wears no armor, and more alarming, he has no sword. He is accompanied by Richard, Isabel, Morgana the maid, Thomas leading a half-dozen of Richard's knights, Emmeline, and Malcolm the traitor, standing somewhat on his own, his head hanging low as if it weighs heavily with guilt. He glances up and I see his eyes are streaked blood red. I wonder why and look for signs of remorse, anything that tells me he has come to his senses.

In the end though, it makes no difference. No one here today will be able to help Jarrod, no matter how strong, or armed, or prepared. This duel is between

Jarrod and Rhauk. Except Rhauk has the advantage, thanks to Malcolm's inside information. Even Richard's most able knights will be useless in this duel of magic.

Jarrod sits on the white and speckled gray stallion as if he were born on the creature's broad back. He appears calm and confident. There's no hint of the gawky clumsy kid I once knew. Red tints in his blond hair gleam brilliantly in the rising sun. Gracefully, he dismounts. His eyes travel over me thoroughly, searching for signs of mistreatment I guess. They narrow and harden when he finds my bruised and swollen jaw.

He stares at me a moment longer, trying I think, to send some strength, but my drugged mind can't respond or absorb any of it. He senses this, it makes him angrier still. I plead with his mind to forget me, sitting here. *I'm just bait*, I try to tell him.

"My nephew arrives," Rhauk remarks casually, smugly. "A foolish challenge that will result in your death. Look at the sun, Jarrod. A beautiful dawn. It will be your last."

"Brave words," Jarrod replies with a calm confidence that takes me by surprise. Even in my numbed brain state, it makes me dare to hope. "From a man who sees the need to use a woman's distraction to win a battle."

The insult stings. Rhauk's black eyes darken impossibly further. Everyone stills, not a sound from Richard or Isabel or the others, as if everyone is holding their breath.

Rhauk visibly regathers his concentration. "Distraction is but a tool, my boy. Take this, for example . . ."

The hand at his belt lifts, palm up, fingers unfolding. Everyone waits. What trickery is Rhauk up to? Then it begins. At first I see only a glimpse of movement. I stare at Jarrod, hard. Surely, it can't be . . . God, no. I blink, yet the vision only grows stronger. The moving shapes become more distinct. I gasp, attempting to draw a hand over my mouth, but the iron chains and my weary muscles make it too difficult. I give up to watch in horror.

Snakes. Scores of them are circling, weaving and hissing over the entire top half of Jarrod's body. Some find their way around his throat, into his hair, lifting it. They're everywhere, slithering down his arms, completely covering his torso.

I recall Jillian's frightful vision. So this is what she foresaw. I wonder if I'll ever be able to tell her. I also remember Jarrod's repulsion. His fear of snakes.

I guess I expect him to run screaming insanely, and in that panic possibly run himself clear off the cliff edge into the cold, treacherous ocean. It might have been Rhauk's intention. But this new Jarrod is calm, though I can see his green eyes deepen, the navy circles vivid and intense.

I almost panic myself, have to struggle not to scream out at him to do something. Morgana starts screaming, but Isabel hisses at her while Richard raises a threatening arm.

She falls silent. But horror is written on all their faces. Even Emmeline, who stares with fixed wide eyes. Clearly, this is Jarrod's battle.

But he can't just stand there. A bite from even one of the foul evil creatures would probably kill him; Rhauk's snakes would be full of lethal venom.

He begins to perspire. Beads of sweat form on his brow, run down the sides of his face, and still the snakes hiss and weave around him. One arches outward, shifting its long diamond-shaped head to look Jarrod straight in the eyes, its venomous fangs exposed in threat.

Only seconds remain before this vile creature will strike. I focus so hard on that one snake that at first I don't see what the others are doing. Jarrod's face turns a dark, dull red, and sweat pours out of him. The snakes begin to slide down his legs, their movements all hurried, like they can't get off him fast enough. Even the one staring at him threateningly, suddenly turns away and slides down Jarrod's leg to the ground, and into surrounding dry scrub.

I taste relief, almost pass out with it, and curse Rhauk's lethargy drug. Jarrod, now free entirely of the wretched snakes, shrugs his shoulders as if he's just resettling his clothes after a minor disturbance. Even his red face starts returning to normal.

He won the first round, I realize, but this is nothing to jump and shout about. He may have outsmarted Rhauk by raising his own body temperature to a point that made the snakes want to get off, fast, but now Rhauk is incensed. Jarrod made him look the fool.

"Do you intend to play games the entire morning?" Jarrod teases.

Rhauk's eyes visibly narrow, his lips draw into a straight line. "So eager to die, Jarrod." He bows, formally. "I shall be only too pleased to oblige."

With this his shoulders lift, and though he too carries no sword, he reaches dramatically for a spot at his side, then straightens his arm, raising the other in a similar gesture, as if he's suddenly holding a heavy weight.

My eyes, as those of everyone else, are riveted to the sight. What next? I wonder in alarm. A silver flash suddenly charges out from his clasped fingers — an explosion of energy, light, and intense heat, like a blast from a hot furnace. It hits me full in the face and jolts me backward. Beneath my legs rocks tumble, the cliff edge giving way. Using any remaining fragments of strength I can find I scramble forward, enough at least, to stop from dropping with the crumbling cliff edge.

Rhauk has produced a sword of his own invention. It has a sharp, silvery look, yet moves in seductive waves with red tips. It's a sword of fire.

Jarrod, I realize sickeningly, is not looking at Rhauk's sword at all. His eyes, widened with real fear, bore into mine. I'm safe, he finally understands. His face visibly relaxes, and Jarrod turns his attention back to his adversary.

But Rhauk snatches the advantage. Jarrod's concern for me caused too long a hesitation. He did not produce his sword, and now Rhauk is charging at him with his eerie firesword.

"Jarrod!" a chorus of voices scream out. Richard, Isabel, Emmeline, and to a lesser extent, even Malcolm. Their concern is heartening.

Jarrod throws himself to the ground, rolling out of Rhauk's way just in time to avoid the lethal sword tip. Sparks fly as Rhauk spins around, shrieking angrily. Black fire swirls, an occasional glimpse of hot steel revealing itself beneath the dancing flames.

Jarrod too spins around.

"'Tis not a fair fight," someone calls.

"I don't play fair, my lady," Rhauk replies smugly. He's enjoying this.

"Don't worry, Lady Isabel," Jarrod replies. And with these words he raises his hands, puts them together, almost as if he were aiming a pistol. But a pistol, though it would certainly give him the advantage, is out of the question. He knows this. We can't introduce something that will not be invented for hundreds of years. It would change the course of history, something we would never intentionally do. Our presence here alone raises many questions, some of which we refuse to even think about. What effect will our time here have on the future? And if we die in this period, would we be reborn in our own time? No one knows for sure what might happen. We can only take what precautions seem obvious.

So I know Jarrod will not produce a pistol. He flashes me a quick warning; I prepare as best I can for the effect. He is creating his own sword. It erupts like a lightning strike, exploding, a mass of burning heat and energy. I bury my face in the dirt, hang on to the soil and bits of dry grass with my fingers, digging nails deeply into the earth.

A wave of intense heat washes over me. When it is gone I look up and see Jarrod holding a shining silver sword, blue-tipped flames dancing about it.

They meet in the center of the clearing. Swords clash, sparks fly. Some land beside me, one on my dress. I roll forward to put them out. As they continue to battle, sword against sword, fire against fire, sparks and flames ignite patches of the surrounding dry scrub. The gentle early morning breeze blows further life into the fires, which now crackle alarmingly, corroding like acid the frost-brittle grassy scrub.

As the flames grow stronger and find their way into the woody hillsides, the horses grow agitated. Richard orders their release. Malcolm, Thomas, and the other soldiers start working at putting out the runaway fires. They use anything they have, even their own tunics, not expecting something like this to happen.

Meanwhile Jarrod and Rhauk continue to duel, neither, it seems, aware of the fires they keep making with each clash of their swords.

All I can do is watch, helpless, pathetically frustrated. "Behind you!" I scream, draining my meager energy. Rhauk knocks Jarrod down, swinging quickly to attack from Jarrod's rear.

Jarrod spins, still on the ground, as Rhauk lunges, screaming.

In my mind I see it all in a form of slow motion. Jarrod on the ground, Rhauk, sensing, tasting victory, lunges forward, his sword outstretched. It would have pierced Jarrod's heart, Rhauk's aim dead-center of his chest, if Jarrod hadn't moved. But he wasn't fast enough to avoid Rhauk's sword completely. It pierces Jarrod's side. Deeply. Bright red blood stains Rhauk's sword as he jerks it out of Jarrod's flesh.

I don't have time to think about the depth of Jarrod's wound. Worse than that, Jarrod is now on fire. The right side of his tunic goes up in flames. The nauseous odor of burning flesh hits me.

"Nooooo!" I scream uselessly, feeling the flames as if they're attacking my own skin. "Someone help him!"

He rolls to the ground, putting out the flames. Richard runs straight over to comfort Jarrod, who is squirming in agony. I curse and curse the stupid chains at my feet and wrists.

He's lying still now, with Richard kneeling beside him. "Come here quickly, wench!" he cries out to Morgana.

Morgana's small body practically flies. She gently tugs the scorched fabric back. "The wound is deep. Worse than the burn. I'll need to stitch it." She shakes her head. "And even then, it will depend on blood loss."

"Get away from him!" Rhauk motions with his fiery sword. "I haven't finished yet."

"It's over, Rhauk, the boy is done," Richard snaps at his half-brother. "Get ye gone."

"This challenge is not over," Rhauk's powerful velvety voice booms, "until that fool boy is dead."

I try to get up, but fall flat to the dirt. It's a struggle to pull myself onto my elbows. "Leave him!" I plead, tears now uncontrollably pouring down my face. I can't accept that Jarrod might actually die here. It will all have been my fault. I brought him to this time and place to fight a battle with a sorcerer that no one can beat. Jarrod never had a chance.

"*No!*"

The voice is Jarrod's. He pushes Richard and Morgana aside as he staggers to his feet, in obviously excruciating pain. He clutches his wounded side. "I'm not done yet. We fight until death."

I stare at him. Where is the clumsy gutless boy I first met, who paled at the sight of blood, and ran when confronted with anything that didn't belong in his fanciful rule book?

Rhauk smiles slowly, sensing, smelling victory. He waves his sword at Richard and Morgana, who scurry back from the flames. "This won't take long, boy," he taunts mercilessly, and charges Jarrod with his sword.

Jarrod, his movements sluggish, still manages to sidestep the blow. And to my surprise, and moreso Rhauk's, manages a powerful retaliatory attack. Swords clash, more sparks and flames explode into the surrounding scrub, now well alight, and racing up both northern and southern peaks. Suddenly I realize both Blacklands and Thorntyne Keep lie in this fire's path. I think of all those thatched cottages inside the keep, the homes of servants, tradespeople, soldiers, the chapel, the stables. They will all be lost, the moat not wide enough to stop the energy generated by this destructive, raging fire.

Richard's soldiers, Isabel, Emmeline, and Malcolm with them, return from their exhausting battle with the runaway flames, their faces weary and flushed bright red from their attempts.

"'Tis hopeless!" Isabel cries. "Thorntyne Keep is lost."

"As is *Blacklands*!" I cry out in Rhauk's direction, remembering the shiny timber floors, thatched roofs of the once thriving convent, walls, benches, doors, and just about everything else that isn't stone. It will burn well.

Rhauk flicks a quick glance over his shoulder toward his beloved Blacklands and visibly pales. "My tower!"

"It will burn," I gloat, remembering the vast array of herbs and powders, oils and other liquids. I think of the curse. "And so will *everything* in it!"

Blood oozes freely from Jarrod's side, his strength rapidly weakening. He can't possibly hold up much longer. I don't know how he does it, catches Rhauk somehow off guard. Perhaps Rhauk's concern for his precious Blacklands causes a moment's lull in concentration. Jarrod senses it, and takes the advantage. In one skilled display of swordsmanship, Jarrod disarms Rhauk, whose sword flies off and explodes where it finally lands.

Now Rhauk's back is to the ground, while Jarrod's knee presses into his chest, his arms held high as he balances his flaming sword tip just above Rhauk's throat. All Jarrod has to do is lunge, and he has him. I wonder in this moment of truth if Jarrod can really do it. It will have to be a fatal lunge or there'll be no point in us having come this far. The ultimate test of courage.

Rhauk tries to fling Jarrod off, but Jarrod is finding an inner strength that goes far beyond mortality. With an almighty scream, Jarrod raises his sword, both hands tightly clasping the hilt, and lunges it straight and true.

Rhauk screams—confusion follows. Jarrod's sword explodes, sending him flying through the air. He hits the ground hard, lucky to escape the encroaching flames nearby, grabbing his side as more blood seeps out. I look for Rhauk but he isn't there anymore. In his place are the fluttering, wildly beating wings of a massive black crow. It flies at Jarrod and beats wildly at his injured side. It knocks Jarrod back to the ground, and covers him. Jarrod tries to crawl out from beneath, but the crow is too close. I remember the same crow hovering over me, and I realize what it is trying to do.

"No!" I scream, beating the air weakly with my fist. "It's trying to take you!"

Jarrod can't hear me with the flapping of wings at his ears. Emmeline's head shifts frantically from me to Jarrod, confused, while Malcolm's green eyes go wild. He grabs his sword, and I panic, wondering what this traitor is up to, but am unable to move. *"Jarrod!"* he bellows.

Jarrod's head swivels sideways to the sound of Malcolm's loud voice.

"Here!"

Malcolm tosses his sword. Jarrod seizes it with his outstretched hand, and in one lightning move, lunges it into the Rhauk-Crow's heaving chest.

The crow squawks a high-pitched sound as if unbelieving of what just happened. After a pathetic attempt to fly away it transforms back into its human form and drops, half on top of Jarrod, Malcolm's sword still wedged deeply in his heart.

"Eloise!" he calls in a ghostly squeal.

Jarrod crawls out from beneath a lifeless Rhauk. He is finally dead. As if he needs to assure himself, Lord Richard, his mouth hanging open in stunned awe, crosses himself against the obvious evil of his half-brother, then grabs a fistful of Rhauk's hair and yanks his head back. Rhauk's cold black eyes stare vacantly. Only then does Lord Richard nod his satisfaction.

Jarrod is exhausted. I'm frustrated that I'm so near, yet can't go to him. Suddenly someone screams, a soldier is on fire. Others run to his aid. I glance about, realizing we have formed a kind of close circle—the cliff at my back, Richard and the others now gathered right beside me. The fires have enclosed us completely.

Jarrod slowly moves and I see bloodstains on his tunic right down one side of his leg. "The fire surrounds us." His voice lacks life.

"But Rhauk is dead," I add.

Our eyes meet and he half crawls, staggering, until he is right in front of me. "What did he do to you?"

"He drugged me. My limbs are useless." I purposefully

look at Malcolm. "He sold you out, Jarrod. That man is a traitor."

"A traitor perhaps, but not mine," Jarrod replies softly.

"What's that supposed to mean?"

"He told me how you tried to escape."

"Did he also tell you he caught me and gave me back to Rhauk?"

Malcolm kneels in front of me, his face disturbed. "I wanted to help you, my Lady, but I knew Rhauk was watching your every move. I thought for a moment we could make it, but then he appeared. I had no choice but to give you back."

Jarrod's hand finds mine, our fingers lace. "Let me explain," he tells Malcolm, then to me he says, "At first Malcolm thought I wanted more than just Rhauk, but Thorntyne Keep as well. But somehow I managed to convince him of the truth. Then he started helping me train for this duel. He taught me all he could in the short time we had. He could see how worried I was for you, and came up with a plan: to feed Rhauk false information about my strengths and weaknesses, in exchange for a small reward. If he didn't ask a price for this information, Rhauk would only suspect ulterior motives." He peers up at Malcolm, who has one eyebrow raised, a smile tugging at one side of his mouth. "As I understand it, he played his part so well Rhauk didn't suspect a thing."

"Why didn't you tell me this in the woods yesterday?" I demand of Malcolm.

"With Rhauk's witchcraft he could have been listening to our conversation. I couldn't risk it. I had to keep Jarrod's plan alive."

"What plan?"

Jarrod interrupts, looking embarrassed, reminding me of the Jarrod I remember. "Let's finish this later."

"No!" I'm too intrigued to let this pass. "What else, Malcolm? What was this plan?"

Malcolm glances fleetingly at Jarrod, and smiles good-naturedly before answering. "I was to rescue you, if something happened to *him*. At least, under the guise of a reward, I had reason to return to Blacklands, securing myself a way to get in."

I nod at this, understanding it all now. Malcolm's treachery was a backup plan to rescue me if fate worked against Jarrod. "You risked your life."

"No more than Jarrod did for you and my homelands."

I'm so relieved Malcolm's not a traitor. I wonder how we would have coped if he had been. Malcolm will inherit Thorntyne Keep one day, then battle to keep it. I wish him well.

Jarrod takes my wrists in his hands, then, concentrating with eyes closed, focuses on the iron clasps. They fall open, releasing my hands. After doing the same with the iron clasps at my ankles, he pulls me into his arms, cradling me against his chest. "We're still in trouble, Kate."

"Put me down, Jarrod. Remember your wound."

He holds me tighter.

Morgana screams as the fire, buffeted by a subtle wind change, suddenly closes right in around us, pushing us frighteningly back to our only means of escape—the cliff. I peer briefly over Jarrod's shoulder and feel nauseous, no one can survive a jump that high. Let alone Jarrod, who is still bleeding openly from the stab wound in his side, nor me in my drugged lethargic state. Besides, there are also many jagged rocks directly below. "We're trapped."

"We're all going to die!" Morgana screams.

Isabel turns on her. "Shut up, child!"

"I can't swim," Richard mutters, peering over the loose edge.

"Nor can I," Emmeline adds.

"Is this how it's going to end, Jarrod?" I ask, as he's the only one among us who has the ability to do anything. "Is all your strength gone?"

He's better off forgetting me, forgetting us all, and saving himself, I balance in my thoughts. He alone right now has the gift. Of course he could use the amulets and take us both back to Jillian, but this would mean Jarrod would have to live with the fact that he fled his own ancestors, leaving them here to burn or jump to their deaths. And this is not how their lives are supposed to end.

He peers into my eyes as if he can read what I'm thinking. "I could never desert my family, Kate."

My mouth drops open in awe. *He did read my thoughts!* His gift must be immense! *Then use whatever powers you have, Jarrod,* my mind-thoughts say. "Save us."

A smile forms and he nods. "I can only try."

I don't know what he plans, but it had better be fast-working. His eyes close, and almost instantly a wind starts to blow. It builds rapidly in strength, twisting in a northerly direction, not only away from us but away from Thorntyne Keep as well. And better still, it's bringing with it dark, thunderous clouds. They roll toward us with lightning speed. Morgana whimpers, overwhelmed. But the raging fire is still too close. The heat is intense, scalding us, while smoke invades our lungs, making us choke. The knights have fallen to their knees, coughing and gasping and mouthing silent prayers.

"Hurry, Jarrod," I urge softly, curling into his chest, knowing a horrid death is only seconds away. "Bring that rain."

And suddenly it's falling in torrential sheets, driven by gusty winds. It becomes dark, almost as night, as the rain puts out the fires at our feet and all the way up the southern slope to Thorntyne Keep. Cheers erupt in the distance as servants and soldiers alike realize Thorntyne Keep is safe.

It's over, and we live. Relief makes me light-headed. Isabel, Emmeline, and Morgana openly weep. Even Richard's eyes are glassy, the moisture on his face not all caused by the sudden rain.

"Look!" Malcolm points toward the northern peak to Blacklands. There, it is not raining at all. The sky is still blue, and now the fire has Blacklands by its heart. The tower too, burns fiercely.

I look up at Jarrod, who's still holding me tightly. He has purposefully not let it rain over Blacklands. This way the curse too will die. "Brilliant," I say softly. He looks down at me, smiling. "I didn't really want to live with Rhauk, you know." Suddenly I have to explain.

He nods. "I know."

It's all he has to say. But it's enough. I return his smile and feel some of that drug-induced lethargy leave me. Strength starts returning slowly to my limbs. I fight back tears.

"It's another crow!" Morgana squeals, pointing to the tower of Blacklands.

It's not Rhauk, but his faithful trained companion.

We all look, and stare, mouths gaping in a mix of astonishment and horror. The crow is on fire.

"Oh!" I cover my mouth with my hand.

"It burns," Jarrod says softly.

The rain stops, the overhead clouds disappear. I only fleetingly notice. We're all watching, mesmerized, as the burning crow squawks in agony, spinning around in pain-induced insanity. Finally, it drops with a thud into surrounding burning scrub, its whole body quickly engulfed in flames.

"Oh no," I groan sadly. It was after all only a bird.

An explosion drags my focus back to Blacklands. The tower is erupting. Rhauk's laboratory, with the cursed wine inside, explodes. We watch entranced as broken stones and bits of timber, glass, precious tools, and anything else that hasn't already burned, shower the surrounding land-scape.

After a long time the explosions stop, and it falls silent.

Kate

Richard declares Thorntyne Keep should celebrate. Jugglers, jesters, poets, and musicians prepare to entertain us in the Great Hall. With Rhauk now dead, so too is his claim on Thorntyne Keep. And so the cause for a celebration.

Jarrod and I are keen to return home, to Jillian, to our time. But Jarrod's wounds need immediate attention. I watch over Morgana's treatment. She stitches him up well, working through layers of muscle skillfully, soothing his burns with an herbal balm with anesthetic qualities. Still, I'd like Jillian to have a look. A real doctor would be a very last resort. He would ask too many questions.

Emmeline follows us everywhere, not allowing us a minute of privacy. She's edgy, barely tolerating my presence, but is hanging all over Jarrod. If anything I begin to think she's particularly distressed that I've returned safely.

I don't like this feeling at all. Later I get a chance to quiz Jarrod, but he's totally unconcerned. "She was just born a thousand years too early," he explains. "She's bored and frustrated. Malcolm says he's trying to talk his father into sending her to Court."

Midafternoon, the feast begins. We sit with Richard and Isabel at the head table in the Great Hall, enjoying their company and entertainment for the last time. Emmeline is sitting beside Jarrod, looking sullen and sulky, and I start to see hopelessness in her eyes, as if all her dreams have recently been shattered. It's a strange thought as everyone else is really excited. I realize Malcolm is right, and the sooner Emmeline is sent to Court the better, for her own sake. As for Lord Richard, I think he is celebrating the hardest. His cheeks are rosy, his eyes glowing. He's deliriously happy, and I think his disgustingly harsh wine has helped him on his merry way.

"A toast," he suddenly declares, pushing back from the table. Rising unsteadily he moves to stand behind Jarrod and me. When he has the attention of everyone in the Hall he raises his goblet in one hand, and with the other thumps Jarrod's back affectionately. "To my nephew and Lady Katherine, may all their children be born here in my castle before I die, so that I may look upon their cheery faces and know they will be safe."

The Hall thunders with applause and riotous cheering. I don't share their enthusiasm. I'm having enough trouble stopping the heat from turning my face crimson at the thought of Richard's suggestion.

"A mighty thanks to Jarrod for annihilating our greatest enemy, a man who gave us more worry than the restless Scots on our border."

More thundering cheers erupt. Richard drinks heartily from his goblet like there's no tomorrow. Both Isabel and Richard look at us expectantly. Reluctantly I lift my wine-filled cup and sip.

For a second I think the world has tilted off its axis. Goose bumps skitter like lightning across my skin, making me shiver. I take another sip, just to be sure.

The wine is sweet, smooth, robust. Nothing like Richard's usual rough, dry red. Everything like . . . No . . . !

Richard sits, his head tilting forward politely. He's trying to hear the words my mouth is having trouble spitting out. Finally, "Wh-where did you get this wine?"

His face beams proudly. "From the cellar, my dear. Isn't it spectacular? We use it only on auspicious occasions like this one, or weddings, or other important feasts." He shrugs.

I choke in a strangled breath. It can't be . . . "Who gave it to you?"

"Why, the King of course, for services well performed. Our victories over the Scots are legendary. Only the King's talented servants can brew such fine wine. And it's strictly for family members, by order of the King."

I stare at him, speechless, my mouth gaping.

He thinks I don't understand. "It's a gift from the King," he emphasizes every word.

"How-how-how long?" I stutter badly.

"Oh, for about twenty years or so." He seems to consider this, glancing at Isabel for confirmation.

She says, "The first crate arrived not long after Jarrod's father left us. I remember it well as it brought life back into our family. We had reason to celebrate once more."

I glance at Jarrod. He has his cup of wine in his raised hand, my conversation with Richard having momentarily drawn his attention. Now, he glances at his cup as if seeing it for the first time. "Sweet, you say," he mutters mostly to himself, and puts the cup to his lips.

I panic and whack the cup straight out of his hands. Emmeline screams as sweet red wine saturates and spoils her pretty blue dress. She jumps out of her seat, her dismal mood exploding into frustrated bursts of idiot speech. Her anger seems a little overdone, and I think there must be more to it than Jarrod's explanation of her just being bored. I remember how she barely tolerated my return. I'm thinking about this when, out of the corner of my eye, I see her pick up a shiny platter of salted meats.

Luckily, Malcolm sees her too. Both of us are too late

though to stop her throwing the platter directly at my head. Shoving me out of the way, Malcolm physically restrains his cousin, and Isabel goes into a rage. Lord Richard turns brighter red, staggering to his feet. "What's wrong with this wench? To Court I think, Malcolm, just as you suggested. Make the arrangements immediately."

I have no time, nor wish, to think about Emmeline's problems now, but will remember to ask Jarrod again later. I have enough concerns of my own.

Jarrod's head swings from me to Emmeline, then back to me again, stunned. This distraction is what I need to quietly slip away.

"I'm sorry for spilling the wine," I mumble quickly, and drag Jarrod away by his elbow. I don't let go until we're clear of the smoke-filled Hall and into the cold twilight air of the bailey.

There are two knights on sentry duty on the wall nearby, and by their merry cackling, it's obvious they aren't doing much guarding, but I need a quiet, isolated place, so I drag Jarrod into the courtyard that houses Isabel's private gardens.

"What's going on? Why did you spill my wine?"

Breathing deeply to try to restore order to my jangled nerves, I find the nearest stone bench and sit, yanking Jarrod down beside me. But I'm too hyped up to sit and start pacing the short length in front of him.

"Kate, will you calm down. Can you explain what this is all about?"

"It's the wine."

His face is blank. He doesn't understand, so I backtrack. "Remember when we dined at Blacklands and Rhauk told us how he was brewing his curse in the tower?"

He nods and I try sitting again. I explain about the curse being in the wine, and how Rhauk tricked his half-brother by making him think the wine, of a far superior quality than his own, was a gift from the King.

"You've got to be kidding."

"Am I laughing?"

He finally catches on. If there's anything funny in all this, then the joke is on us. Jarrod's head falls back, considering. His gaze explores the darkening sky, seemingly enthralled in the pattern of emerging stars. Eventually they drift to mine. "Jillian was out by twenty years."

I shrug. "No one's perfect."

"But why did Rhauk tell us he was still brewing the curse when he'd finished it twenty years ago?"

I think about this for a long moment, and then it comes to me. "He was always playing games. And he lied to get what he wanted."

"He wanted you."

"Yes, to replace Eloise. And he wanted revenge. The

curse was his revenge, but as long as we thought it wasn't complete yet, he could manipulate us to suit his plan."

'To have you," Jarrod confirms.

"He promised he wouldn't produce the curse as long as I stayed with him. That was the arrangement."

"So what was that wine in the tower?"

Finally I understand. "That was the curse, all right. Just more of it. He probably gave Lord Richard a fresh supply every year, under the guise, of course, that it was from the King."

Jarrod straightens and moans. "So what does this all mean, Kate? Was it all for nothing?"

I have to think. "No, I won't believe that." And then I remember the words from the ancient scripts. *"The only way to stop the curse is to end the sorcerer's life."*

"What?"

I start pacing the short plot of grass in front of him again, this time with excitement. "Let's stop and think a minute. The ancient text said you had to end the sorcerer's life. Jarrod, that's exactly what you did. You killed Rhauk — the sorcerer."

"Which means, exactly . . . ?"

Suddenly everything fits into place. "The curse is ended, Jarrod. For you at least. From this moment on."

He stares at me, a glimmer of hope in his eyes.

"I don't mean this moment in medieval times. Nothing

will change for your ancestors, the curse will still run its course. After all, your ancestors have been drinking the wine for twenty years. I mean when we get back to our time."

"I hope you're right, Kate."

I smile, actually I beam. Smugly. *I have been so far,* I can't help thinking.

He stands over me, peers down into my face, both eyebrows lifting halfway into his forehead. Belatedly, I remember he can read my private thoughts!

Heat burns my face, and I wish it was even darker. I wonder, how am I going to cope with someone who knows what I'm thinking? I could try to block him but my powers haven't returned yet. I hope my gift hasn't been permanently damaged. I couldn't stand that.

Suddenly a shout erupts from the battlements. *"Scots!"*

The single word reverberates as word is passed on. Chaos erupts. But it's a chaos with a certain order to it. These people have done this drill before—and they're ready to do it again—to defend their lands and livelihoods. As the villagers are rushed into the bailey Isabel takes control, arranging suitable locations and jobs for them. Lord Richard is putting on his chain mail and ordering his knights to action.

It's an amazing scene, something I consider myself

privileged to witness. And as much as I'd love to stay and be a part of this battle, nowhere in these grounds is going to be safe.

Jarrod has the same thought. "Let's get out of here."

I nod and look for a quiet place in the organized chaos.

Part Three
RETURN

Jarrod

She makes me promise *never* to read her thoughts, no matter the circumstances. I don't want to anyway, so the promise is easy to keep. Without it, there would be a problem with privacy. This agreement makes things easier between us.

We arrive back at the same place we left, by the creek in the forest. Jillian's still standing where we left her, keeping a silent vigil in the rain forest, keeping the circle blazing and protected. It turns out we were only away a few hours, even though it was over a month at Thorntyne Keep. She hands me my watch and glasses. I thank her, glad to have them back.

It darkens quickly with the candles extinguished, but I hardly notice. We're both exhausted, the return journey has taken a lot out of us both, but especially Kate, who hasn't recovered completely from Rhauk's drugs. Jillian and I have to help her walk.

At the house, Jillian sits us down at the kitchen table and brews Kate a hot herbal drink that smells vaguely familiar. When she's made sure Kate's drunk more than half of it, Jillian starts pounding us with questions. Hours later we're still talking. Jillian wants to know it all. We tell her as much as possible without revealing everything, especially the sharing the bedroom part. Her eyes never leave us. She hangs on every word, and laughs when Kate tells her about Emmeline's "crush" on me and how she almost came back with us, startling us both with her presence just as we were saying the Latin chant.

"Luckily I was able to stun her thoughts, long enough for us to escape," I explain.

Jillian agrees it would have been disastrous if Emmeline had forced her way back with us. "Your father's heritage book is very clear on Emmeline's future," Jillian informs us. "She is sent to live at the Palace, where she meets and becomes the Earl of Drysdon's mistress, bearing him three illegitimate sons. She is never happy though, as the Earl's wife makes her life miserable."

Jillian astonishes us with this information, and suddenly I feel sorry for my ancestral "cousin."

Kate starts telling Jillian about the battle with Rhauk. Immediately she gets up to take a look at my wounds. "The stitches look fine, I'll dress them again in the morning."

It's not long before Kate starts falling asleep at the

table and Jillian sends her to bed. When she's gone, I try to thank Jillian, and I mean for everything she's done. But I know simple words are not enough. She collects my clothes, making a huge fuss over them. They're not the original ones she stitched for us, but, as these are truly originals, she will treasure them more.

I doze eventually on a mattress laid out for me on the floor, and it turns out Kate and I sleep for two whole days. We wake on Friday morning, having missed a couple of days of school. We're not particularly worried about this as Jillian covered for us at school and with my mother. I do worry about Mom and Dad though; it's time I phone.

I use the phone at the front of Jillian's shop. Mom's voice is unbelievable. She actually sounds happy, something I don't hear very often. She tells me Dad's improvement in the last forty-eight hours has been remarkable, both mentally and physically. His leg is almost pain-free and he's walking now with just a cane. "It's a miracle, Jarrod," Mom says, crying. "I wish you were here. When are you coming home?"

"Soon, Mom," I assure her. She goes on to tell me Dad's mental state of mind has also improved, probably due to his having to cope with less physical pain. Apparently the psychiatric doctors are amazed. There's even talk of releasing him soon. I hang up with a lump in my throat the size of a watermelon, fighting back tears.

These things are signs, our first, that our luck is changing.

"Good news, huh?"

I nod at Kate, unable to speak at this moment without disgracing myself. I pull her into my arms, burying my head in her shoulders. After a couple of minutes she moves back, noticing Jillian standing patiently in the doorway. I fill them both in on Dad's improved health.

"That's wonderful, Jarrod," Jillian says, her voice husky, wiping away a tear. She gives me a hug and I thank her.

"Oh, no," she says, waving a hand at me. "You did it all yourself."

She goes into the kitchen to make herself some tea and Kate comes back into my arms. "I'm so happy for you," she says. But her voice has a deflated edge to it.

"What's wrong?" I ask.

She shrugs. "Nothing, really. Just my magic. It hasn't returned yet."

"It probably just needs a push to break it free of Rhauk's lingering hold."

Her eyes narrow. "And how do I do that if I don't have any magic to do it with?"

"Hmm, good point. But don't worry, Kate, I have enough magic for the both of us."

"That's great for you, and no offense, but it's hard living with the idea that you'll always be stronger than me.

I want my own powers back so we can be equal. Jarrod, I lived with these things all my life. I feel like I've lost an arm, or worse, part of my soul."

I know the second the thought hits her. "Of course, your powers are so extensive now, fueled with *Old Magic*, there must be something you can do. You beat Rhauk once, maybe you can do it again 'cause it's his drug that did this to me."

"D'you think I can help you get your magic back?"

"Why not? It's worth a try."

We go outside and walk around for a few minutes while we think about how to do this.

"What about a spell?" she asks.

"My magic doesn't work that way."

"Oh."

Suddenly it hits me and I spin her around so that we're standing face-to-face. "How much power do you want, Kate? What would make you happy?"

She starts thinking, and this one time I ignore her request never to read her mind-thoughts. She's thinking about the weather and how she's always wanted to be strong enough to manipulate it. But she doesn't tell me this, she just shrugs.

It starts to rain, sprinkles, icy cold. I shiver, not used to this mountain weather yet, then realize it's colder than rain ought to be, even for this time of year. Kate lifts her hands, palms up. "Jarrod, it's sleeting." She shivers all over. "We're going to freeze out here. Let's go back inside."

She goes to move but I stop her. "Just a minute."

"What? What is it?"

"Close your eyes and think warm."

She gives a little laugh, like she's humoring me.

"Concentrate," I tell her and start working my thoughts into her head, searching for remnants of Rhauk's magic.

"What are you doing?" she squirms. "It's ticklish."

"Keep your eyes closed and concentrate on something you really want. Go with your heart, Kate," I say softly.

She stops squirming and thinks about being warm.

"More, reach deeper."

Suddenly it stops snowing and the air grows warmer. So warm, in fact, I'm thinking of taking off my sweater.

Kate looks around us, her mouth open, her eyes staring widely. "What's going on?"

I follow her stunned gaze. Everywhere is still snowing except here, directly over the two of us, like we're standing inside a protective dome. "Thanks, Kate. This is great."

"Don't thank me."

I smile at her without saying a word.

"What?"

"I didn't do this," I say.

"Don't be annoying, Jarrod." Her eyes suddenly squint, then I feel her—probing inside my head. I tell her with my thoughts that she's the one who made the snow stop, and warmed the air around us.

With a sudden burst of comprehension she pulls out of my head with a loud gasp. "Oh, God!" she whispers hoarsely. "I was in your head," she says in a rush. "You did things to me. You gave me powers."

I shrug one shoulder. "I didn't give you anything that wasn't already there. I just put you in touch with the gifts you were born with."

She grins and laughs and spins around. "Wow! This is fantastic. I made it warm."

The crunch of tyres coming up the winding mountain road puts Kate into a spin. "The circle of warmth?" she asks quickly.

"You made it," I tell her. "You get rid of it."

She nods and closes her eyes. In a second sleet starts driving through us again. Quickly we dive inside, finding warmth in Jillian's shop.

It's not long before the chimes sound customers. And of all people it has to be Tasha Daniels and Jessica Palmer. This time Ryan and Pecs are with them.

"Hey, bro." Pecs sickeningly slaps my back. "How's your pop? Heard he was in hospital."

"Better, thanks."

Tasha slips her long fingers into the crook of my elbow. Jillian is nowhere to be seen and Kate starts disappearing into the background, instinctively searching for a quiet unnoticeable corner. I try to catch her eye, but she's avoiding me. And even though I don't invade her head I know exactly what she's thinking. We're back, quickly slipping into our usual routines. Everything we shared in that other time will be forgotten, as if it was only a dream. Tasha and her pals will come first in my life, over her, again.

"You weren't at school for two days," Tasha purrs. "I was starting to worry."

"Er, well, I'm fine, thanks."

"So, what are you doing here again?" She throws a fleeting glance at Kate, but returns it quickly, dismissing Kate from her thoughts. "Are you picking out a costume?"

For a second she throws me. What is she talking about? Then I remember, Ryan's fancy dress party—the event of the year, always held on the first day of winter. And that's tomorrow. "Actually, I have my costume ready."

Kate slinks farther away as not one of these four snobs acknowledges she's even in the room, yet they must have seen her when they came in.

"What time will you be picking me up?" Tasha commands.

I unhook myself from her solid grip, lunge right back and link fingers with Kate, tugging hard. Awkwardly, reluctantly, Kate lands in the middle of our circle. "I won't be picking you up, Tasha."

Tasha flicks a brief look at Kate, then stares at me with hard, wide-open eyes. "What? And why not?"

I position Kate right in front of me and slide my arms around her waist.

Possessively.

"Well, that's easy. You see, I'm going to be taking Kate."

Marianne Curley

lives in Australia with her family. She has experimented
with different genres, but finds writing for young adults
to be the most challenging and satisfying.

From the #1 *New York Times* bestseller
Not all vampires are out for blood. . . .

dark visions
by L.J. Smith

You don't invite the local witch to parties. No matter how beautiful she is. That was the basic problem.

I don't care, Kaitlyn thought. *I don't need anyone.*

She was sitting in history class, listening to Marcy Huang and Pam Sasseen plan a party for that weekend. She couldn't help but hear them: Mr. Flynn's gentle, apologetic voice was no competition for their excited whispers. Kait was listening, pretending not to listen, and fiercely wishing she could get away. She couldn't, so she doodled on the blue-lined page of her history notebook.

She was full of contradictory feelings. She hated Pam and Marcy, and wanted them to die, or at least to have some gory accident that left them utterly broken and defeated and miserable. At the same time there was a terrible longing inside her. If they would only let her *in*—it wasn't as if she insisted on being the most popular, the most admired, girl at school. She'd settle for a place in the group that was securely her own. They could shake their heads and say, "Oh, that Kaitlyn—she's odd, but what would we do without her?" And that would be fine, as long as she was a *part*.

But it wouldn't happen, ever. Marcy would never think of inviting Kaitlyn to her party because she wouldn't think of doing something that had never been done before. No one ever invited the witch; no one thought that Kaitlyn, the lovely, spooky girl with the strange eyes, would *want* to go.

And I don't care, Kaitlyn thought, her reflections coming around full circle. This is my last year. One semester to go. After that, I'm out of high school and I hope I never see anyone from this place again.

But that was the other problem, of course. In a little town like Thoroughfare she was bound to see them, and their parents, every day for the next year. And the year after that, and the year after that. . . .

There was no escape. If she could have gone away to college, it might have been different. But she'd screwed up her art scholarship . . . and anyway, there was her father. He needed her—and there wasn't any money. Dad needed her. It was junior college or nothing.

The years stretched out in front of Kaitlyn, bleak as the Ohio winter outside the window, filled with endless cold classrooms. Endless sitting and listening to girls planning parties that she wasn't invited to. Endless exclusion. Endless aching and wishing that she *were* a witch so she could put the most hideous, painful, debilitating curse on all of them.

All the while she was thinking, she was doodling. Or rather her hand was doodling—her brain didn't seem to be involved at all. Now she looked down and for the first time saw what she'd drawn.

A spiderweb.

But what was strange was what was *underneath* the web, so close it was almost touching. A pair of eyes.

Wide, round, heavy-lashed eyes. Bambi eyes. The eyes of a child.

As Kaitlyn stared at it, she suddenly felt dizzy, as if she were falling. As if the picture were opening to let her in. It was a horrible sensation—and a familiar one. It happened every time she drew one of *those* pictures, the kind they called her a witch for.

The kind that came true.

Secrets don't always stay buried....

Dark Secrets 1

by Elizabeth Chandler

Author of the *New York Times* bestseller

Kissed by an Angel

LAST NIGHT I visited the house again. It looked as it did ten years ago, when I dreamed about it often. I've never seen the house in real life, at least not that I can remember. It is tall, three stories of paned windows, all brick with a shingle roof. The part I remember most clearly is the covered porch. No wider than the front steps, it has facing benches that I like to sit on. I guess I was never shy, not even at six; in the dream I always opened the door, walked inside, and played with the toys.

Last night the door was locked. That's how I awoke, trying with all my strength to open it, desperate to get inside. Something was wrong, but now I can't say what. Was there something dangerous outside the house from which I was fleeing? Was there a person in the house who needed my help? It was as if the first part of my dream was missing. But one thing I knew for sure: Someone on the other side of the door was trying hard to keep me out.

"I'm not going," I had told my father back in June. "She's a mean old lady. She disowned Mom and won't speak to you. She has never had anything to do with Pete, Dave, or me. Why should I have anything to do with her?"

"For your mother's sake," he'd said.

Several months later I was on a flight from Arizona to Maryland, still resisting my grandmother's royal command to visit. I took out her invitation, the first message I'd received from her in my life, and reread it—two sentences, sounding as stiff as a textbook exercise.

Dear Megan,
This summer I will see you at Scarborough House.
I have enclosed a check to cover airfare.

Regards,
Helen Scarborough Barnes

Well, I hadn't expected "love and kisses" from a woman who cut off her only daughter when she had decided to marry someone of a different race. My mother, coming from a deep-rooted Eastern Shore family, has more English blood in her than Prince Charles. My father, also from an old Maryland family, is African-American. After trying to have children of their own, they adopted me, then my two brothers. It would be naive to expect warmth from a person who refused to consider adopted kids her grandchildren.

Now that I thought about it, the meaning of my dream the night before was pretty obvious, even the feeling that something was wrong. The door to my mother's family had always been closed to me; when a door kept locked for sixteen years suddenly, without explanation, opens, you can't help but wonder what you're walking into.

"Megan? You made it!" the woman said, crumpling up the sign with my name on it, then giving me a big hug. "I'm Ginny Lloyd, your mother's best old friend." She laughed. "I guess you figured that out."

When Ginny heard I was coming, she'd insisted on meeting me at the airport close to Baltimore. That October day we loaded my luggage into the back of her ancient green station wagon, pushing aside bags of old sweaters, skirts, shoes, and purses—items she had picked up to sell in her vintage clothes shop.

"I hope you don't mind the smell of mothballs," Ginny said.

"No problem," I replied.

"How about the smell of a car burning oil?"

"That's okay, too."

"We can open the windows," she told me. "Of course, the muffler's near gone."

I laughed. Blond and freckled, she had the same southernish accent as my mother. I felt comfortable with her right away.

When I was buckled in, Ginny handed me a map so I could follow our progress toward Wisteria, which is on the Eastern Shore of the Chesapeake Bay.

"It's about a two-hour drive," she said. "I told Mrs. Barnes I'd have you at Scarborough House well before dark."

"I'm getting curious," I told her. "When Mom left Maryland, she didn't bring any pictures with her. I've seen a few photos that my uncle Paul sent, showing him and Mom playing when they were little, but you can't see the house in them. What's it like?"

"What has your mother told you about it?" Ginny asked.

"Not much. There's a main house with a back wing. It's old."

"That's about it," Ginny said.

It was a short answer from a person who had spent a lot of time there as a child and teenager—nearly as short as my mother's answers about the place.

"Oh, and it's haunted," I added.

"People say that," Ginny replied.

I looked at her, surprised. I had been joking.

"Of course, every old house on the Shore has its ghost

stories," she added quickly. "Just keep the lights on if it feels spooky."

This trip might turn out to be more interesting than I thought.

Ginny turned on the radio, punching in a country station. I opened the map she had given me and studied it. The Sycamore River cut into the Eastern Shore at an angle. If you were traveling up the Chesapeake Bay, you'd enter the wide river mouth of the Sycamore and head in a northeasterly direction. On the right, close to the mouth, you'd see a large creek named Wist. The next creek up is Oyster. The town of Wisteria sits between them, nearly surrounded by water, the Sycamore River on one side and the creeks on the other two. As for my grandmother's property, it was the large point of land below the town, washed on one side by Wist Creek and on the other side by the Sycamore.

We crossed two sets of railroad tracks. I watched the scenery change from outlet stores to fields of corn and soy and low horizons of trees. The sky was half the world on the Eastern Shore. Ginny asked a lot of questions and seemed more interested in talking about life in Tucson than life in Wisteria.

"What's my grandmother like?" I asked at last.

For a full minute the only response was the roar of the car engine.

"She's, uh, different," Ginny said. "We're coming up on Oyster Creek. Wisteria's just on the other side."

"Different how?" I persisted.

"She has her own way of seeing things. She can be fierce at times."

"Do people like her?"

Ginny hesitated. "Have you spent much time in a small town?" she asked.

"No."

"Small-town folks are like a big family living in one house. They can be real friendly and helpful, but they can also say nasty things about each other and squabble a lot."

She hadn't answered my question about how others saw my grandmother, but I could figure it out. She wasn't the town favorite.

We rumbled over the metal grating of the drawbridge. I hung my head out the window for a moment. In Tucson, creeks were often just trickles. This one was the width of a river.

"We're on Scarborough Street now," Ginny said. "The streets off to our right lead down to the commercial docks, where the oyster and crab boats are. The streets to the left border the college. In a few blocks we'll be crossing over High Street, which is Main Street for us. Want to drive down it?"

"Sure."

We passed a school, went a block farther, then took a right onto High. The street had a mix of houses, churches, and small shops, all of the buildings made of brick or wood. Some of the houses edged right up to the sidewalk; a few had tiny plots of grass in front of them. Pots of bright chrysanthemums perched on windowsills and steps. The sidewalks on both sides of High Street were brick and ripply, especially around the roots of the sycamore trees that lined the street. But even where there weren't roots, the brick looked softened, as if the footprints of two and a half centuries had been worn into it.

"It's pretty," I said. "Are there a lot of wisteria vines around here?"

"People grow it," she said, "but actually, the parcel of land that became the town was won in a card game called whist. That was the town's original name. Some upright folks in the 1800s, who didn't approve of gambling, added to it. I guess we're lucky they weren't playing Crazy Eights."

I laughed.

"There's my shop, Yesterdaze." Ginny slowed down and pointed to a storefront with a large, paned window that bowed out over the sidewalk. "Next door is Tea Leaves. Jamie, the owner, makes pastries to die for.

"The town harbor is ahead of us," she went on. "Only

pleasure boats dock there now. I'm going to swing around to Bayview Avenue and show you where I live. You know you're welcome to stay with me if things get difficult."

"Difficult how?" I asked.

She shrugged. "I find it isolated out there on the other side of the Wist. And Scarborough House seems awfully big without a family to fill it up."

"Is that why my grandmother invited me? She can't get anybody else to come?"

"I doubt *that's* the reason. Mrs. Barnes has never liked company—whoa!" Ginny exclaimed, hitting her brakes hard, sending shoe boxes tumbling over the seat from the back of the station wagon.

A guy in an open-topped Jeep, impatient to get around a car making a turn, had suddenly cut in front of us. The backseat passengers of the red Jeep, two girls and a guy, held on to one another and hooted. The girl in the front seat turned briefly to look at us, laughing and tossing her long hair. The driver didn't acknowledge his near miss.

"Jerk," I said aloud.

Ginny looked amused. "That was your cousin."

"My cousin?" I twisted in my seat, to look down the side street where the Jeep had made another sudden turn.

"Matt Barnes," she replied.

"I thought he was in Chicago."

"Your uncle moved there, and Matt's mother is somewhere in the North, I believe."

"Boston," I told her. It had been an ugly divorce, I knew that much.

"Matt has spent nearly every summer in Wisteria. He transferred to the high school here last winter and is living full-time with your grandmother. You didn't know that?"

I shook my head.

"She bought him the Jeep this past summer. Rumor has it he's getting his own boat. Matt's usually carting around jocks or girls."

Spoiled and wild, I thought. But things were looking up. No matter what he was like, spending two weeks with a guy my own age was better than being alone with a fierce seventy-six-year-old. I'd just fasten my seat belt and go along for the ride.

"Does my grandmother drive?" I asked.

"Pretty much like Matt," Ginny replied, laughing.

When we got to Bayview, she pointed out her house, a soft yellow cottage with gray shutters, then returned to Scarborough Road.

We crossed the Wist, rumbling over an old bridge, drove about a quarter mile more, then turned right between two brick pillars. The private road that led to my grandmother's

started out paved, but crumbled into gravel and dirt. Tall, coni-
cal cedar trees lined both sides. They did not bend gracefully
over the drive, as trees do in pictures of southern mansions, but
stood upright, like giant green game pieces. At the end of the
double row of trees I saw sections of sloping gray roof and brick
chimneys, four of them.

"We're coming up behind the house," Ginny said. "The
driveway loops around to the front. You're seeing the back wing.
That picket fence runs along the herb garden by the kitchen."

"The house is huge."

"Remember that you are welcome to stay with me," she said.

"Thanks, but I'll be fine."

Now that I was here, I was looking forward to the next two
weeks. I mean, how much of a terror could one little old woman
be? It'd be fun to explore the old house and its land, especially
with a cousin my age. Four hundred acres of fields and woods
and waterfront—it seemed unbelievable that I didn't have to
share them with other hikers in a state park. A wave of excitement and confidence washed over me. Then Ginny circled the
house and parked in front.

"Megan," she said, after a moment of silence, "Megan, are
you all right?"

I nodded.

"I'll help you with your luggage."

"Thanks."

I climbed out of the car slowly, staring up at Grandmother's house. Three stories of paned windows, brick with a shingled roof, a small covered porch with facing benches—it was the house in my dreams.

I took my luggage from Ginny, feeling a little shaky. For the second time in twenty-four hours, I walked up the steps of the house. This time the door swung open.

Sarah Mussi   Sarah Beth Durst   Nick Lake   Jessica Bendinger

Get a taste of
our best-kept secrets.

Lit Up.

New authors.

New stories.

New buzz.

A teen online sampler
from Simon & Schuster.

Available at
TEEN.SimonandSchuster.com

twitter.com/SimonTEEN

Margaret K. McElderry Books | Simon & Schuster Books for Young Readers | Simon Pulse
Published by Simon & Schuster

Amy Reed   Jessica Verday   Lauren Strasnick   Rhonda Stapleton

  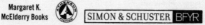

SiMONTEEN

Simon & Schuster's **Simon Teen**
e-newsletter delivers current updates on
the hottest titles, exciting sweepstakes, and
exclusive content from your favorite authors.

Visit **TEEN.SimonandSchuster.com** to
sign up, post your thoughts, and find out what
every avid reader is talking about!

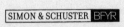